# Unfinished Business
## Book Two
## Part 1
## The McKinnon Legends
## A Time Travel Series

Ranay James

**Ranay James**
**1209 South Main Street**
**#126**
**Lindale, Texas 75771**
www.ranayjames.com

Publishers Note: This is a work of fiction. Names, characters, places, and incidents are a product of the author's imagination. Locales and public names are sometimes used for atmospheric purposes. Any resemblance to actual people, living or dead, or to businesses, companies, events, institutions, or locales is completely coincidental.

**Unfinished Business: Book Two Part 1 of The McKinnon Legends A Time Travel Series — 1st ed.**
ISBN 978-0-9967862-6-3

# Other Series By Ranay James

Series by Ranay James available in e-book format at all major retailers through the following website:

## WWW.booklaunch.io/ranayjames

*The McKinnon Legends* A Time Travel Series

*The McKinnon American Men* A Romantic Suspense Series

*Vampires Of Nirvana* is a ten part series that with each book will leave you begging for more. If you love the McKinnons, then you are going to love the royal family of Nirvana.

**Print Editions Available**:

Vampires of Nirvana:Book 1- Never Kiss Me Goodbye
Vampires of Nirvana: Book 2 - Point of No Return
The McKinnon The Beginning: Book One Part 1
The McKinnon The Beginning: Book One Part 2
Unfinished Business: Book Two Part 1
Unfinished Business: Book Two Part 2

**Large Print Editions:**
The McKinnon The Beginning: Book One Part 1
Vampires of Nirvana Book 1 - Never Kiss Me Goodbye

# Print Coming 2016

**Vampires of Nirvana:**
Vampires of Nirvana Book 2 - Point of No Return (Large Print Edition)

**The McKinnon Legends-A Time Travel Series:**
Shades of Grace: Book Three Part 1
Shades of Grace: Book Three Part 2
Of Purest Blood: Book Four Part 1
Of Purest Blood: Book Four Part 2
The Missing One: Book Five Part 1
The Missing One: Book Five Part 2

# Audiobook Editions:

**Audiobook Bundles available at Audiobooks.com and Audible.com**
The McKinnon The Beginning: Book 1 Parts 1 and 2
Unfinished Business: Book Two Parts 1 and 2
The McKinnon Legends Books One and Two: Parts 1 and 2

**Individual Audiobooks:**
The McKinnon The Beginning Book One Part 1
The McKinnon The Beginning Book One Part 2
Unfinished Business Book Two Part 1
Unfinished Business Book Two Part 2

To my husband—thank you for being my partner through life and supporting my dreams.

*I have been impressed with the urgency of doing. Knowing is not enough; we must apply. Being willing is not enough; we must do.*

## —LEONARDO DA VINCI

# Part One

# Chapter 1
## Failure Is Not An Option

West Coast of England
April 13, 1494

The sound of clashing weapons was carried away on the wild, ripping wind. All other sound lost any relevance as the angry, deafening thirty-foot waves crashed white on the boulders hundreds of feet below. If one were to believe in the existence of titans, then the mighty Poseidon had awakened from the watery depths, showing his might as a force that no human dare reckon.

Morgan Pembridge, Seventh Duchess of Seabridge, stood unmoving on the jagged cliffs of her ancestral home with her gaze fixed on her husband and uncle as they danced the deadly dance so close to the razor's edge. Swords arched and clashed, calling the very lightning from the sky just as if Thor's hammer brought the crashing thunder.

The right to her freedom hung in the balance with the outcome of this battle. It would seal her fate and that of every successive generation to follow. Her husband and uncle were engaged in a fight that would be to the death, and the gods of old knew they would be appeased here this day, demanding nothing less than a blood sacrifice.

Morgan didn't see the man creeping from behind her, intent on taking her life.

Cullen did, and the young knight dove toward her, placing himself between a woman he loved and her assassin.

1

After the first strike, he tumbled to the ground, pushed her aside, and deflected the second blow while using his body again as a shield to protect her from the strike designed to end her life.

Rolling just as the man was raising his sword to strike a third time, Morgan saw Cullen's sword still clutched in his hand, and she placed her hands around his hand to help him thrust upward, piercing the assassin's heart.

The man was dead before he hit the ground.

Nic McKinnon, Seventh Duke of Seabridge, pushed Lord Brentwood ever closer to the rocks. Brentwood was faltering and was no match for Nic's superior skill and driving need to end this threat to his wife and three small children.

Nic smelled Brentwood's fear and sensed victory; he instinctively knew the end was near.

"You're mine, Brentwood, and I shall gladly kill you and kill you slowly for the seven years of hell you put my woman through. You shall never again threaten me and mine."

"I won't give you the satisfaction." Knowing Nic would make good on his threat, Brentwood jumped from the cliff, falling hundreds of feet below to his death where the mighty Poseidon received his offering, sucking down the gift into the watery depths of the gray, foamy sea.

Nic sighed. It was over. The nightmare was finally over. Morgan was free from the clutches of the madman, who, for years, had been set on stealing Morgan's birthright through treachery and deceit.

Turning away from the edge, Nic watched Reagan, who was a healer and a friend, kneel on the ground next to his beloved younger brother. Morgan was clutching Cullen's hand, holding it to the side of her face.

Connor Holden, his friend and blood brother, along with two other men-at-arms stood back, ready to defend them in the event they hadn't killed all Brentwood's men in the bloody battle for the right to claim Seabridge and the riches it represented.

The scene took a moment to register in Nic's mind. Finally, he understood Reagan was frantically working to save Cullen. Nic ran to the small group as he heard his wife anxiously pleading for Reagan to help. Nic knew his brother's life was slipping away.

"Reagan, you are a healer. You must save him. Please, you must," Morgan sobbed.

She had grown to love her brother-in-law. He was a good and honorable young man, as well as a good friend. Giving her support and encouragement, he had helped her through the long, terrible months when Nic had been imprisoned. Cullen had never let her give up hope that Nic would come home alive.

Nevertheless, more important than her selfish feelings, Nic loved him and he was family. He couldn't die so young.

"Please, please," Morgan begged again.

"I am doing the best I can," Reagan said, never looking up from her effort to stem the blood flow, pressing his wounds with long strips from her underskirt that she had ripped off to use as packing.

The young knight was bleeding out from the internal damage he had sustained. Now, it was only a matter of time before he, too, became a casualty of this senseless battle that had been driven by Lord Brentwood's insanity and greed.

"How bad is it, Rea?" Nic was on his knees beside his brother. He knew Cullen's injuries were grave. Far too long a soldier, Nic didn't need her to tell him what he recognized to be a fatal wound. He had lost many good men. Now, it looked as if fate was going to take Cullen as well.

"His condition isn't good, Nic," Reagan said, shaking her head. "He's losing blood very fast."

Cullen was dying, and for all Reagan's skill, she could never hope to save him here.

Morgan was crying, sorrow and guilt stabbing her, as she looked over Cullen's body at her husband.

"Oh, God, Nic, this is my fault!" Morgan sobbed. "If I had gone to York instead of disobeying you, he would be all right. He wouldn't have taken the blade for me. This is entirely my fault."

"Don't, Morgan… beg you… not your fault," Cullen pleaded with great effort as blood streamed from the edge of his mouth.

Morgan took the hem of her dress and gently wiped the blood away, placing tender fingers across his lips.

"Shh, now, don't try to speak. Save your strength. Reagan will save you. I know she can." Morgan looked into Reagan's eyes. "You can. I feel it. You have a way. I pray you, from whatever direction the help may come, just do it before it's too late."

Reagan looked at Nic, Connor, and then Morgan. "Yes. There may be a way."

Reagan's voice was steady. Still, Connor saw the doubt reflected in the Irishwoman's eyes as she looked back at him. He had come to know her, and her expression told him she was unsure. Connor found her trepidation unsettling. In all the time he had watched her, fought with her, and dealt with her, he had never seen her waver… until this moment.

Reagan looked to Connor again, and she had no idea why but in some way his towering presence reassured her.

"Nic, my idea is beyond risky in Cullen's current condition, but it's the only way to save him."

"Then do it," Nic said. "You're the only one who can save him."

She looked at Connor a third time.

Connor believed she had just looked to him for reassurance. He gave her a nod and a tight-lipped smile of

4

resolve. If she needed his strength and his belief in her abilities in this time of crisis, then, by God, he would give it to her, regardless of their past differences.

He saw the moment she made up her mind as all misgiving fled, leaving only the firebrand he recognized and had grown to admire.

Reagan turned to Morgan. "Is there a hallowed place anywhere close? Think, Morgan, and do so quickly. Men bleed to death at the same rate no matter the century." She was startled with her last comment. She was so adept at keeping her secret that she was surprised it had slipped out, even under pressure.

Morgan did not have to think except for a split second. "My mother worshipped the old gods. My father had a shrine built for her. I do not know if it still exists," she said as she sprang to her feet.

Reagan pushed all her medicines back into her bag and pulled the black leather strap over her shoulder. "Then take me to it. It isn't the altar so much as it's the place itself. Connor, you and Nic carry Cullen. Try to be as careful as possible. We must hurry. We're running out of time."

Morgan led the way. The shrine was just over a small rise, not far from their present location, and Reagan recognized the place instantly as it sent her to her knees.

"Ahhh," Reagan cried as she sensed a power more potent than anything she had ever felt before. The ancient power flowed through her like a raging river bent on consuming anything in its path. This was an intersection where space and time forcefully collided, thinning the veil separating the dimensions of the past, present, and future.

"What is this place?" Connor shivered, helping her to her feet as he felt the hair stand on the back of his arms and the pulsating sensation racing along Reagan's skin.

"It's an ancient place of energy. Those who have the ability to call and harness its power can use it."

5

"Use it for what?" Connor asked as he raised one dark brow in question.

"It depends on the gifts," Reagan answered, keeping her attention on Cullen and placing pressure on his wounds.

Connor grabbed her wrist, stopping her movements, and pulled her attention to him.

She was not a small woman, but it was no matter to Connor. He was an extraordinarily tall man and any woman felt small to him. Reagan was no maiden at twenty-eight. Neither was he so young at thirty, but her wisdom and knowledge were as attractive to him as nectar to bees. Her clear skin was fresh and translucent in the early-afternoon light, and her hair was like spun fire as the rays caught its shine. He shook his head in wonder as to why, in all this madness, he was just beginning to see how truly beautiful she was.

"And your gifts would be?" Connor demanded, looking into her warm cinnamon-brown eyes.

"Healing…" Reagan said, then looked away.

Connor knew she wasn't telling him everything. "And what else, Reagan? Do not withhold from me. I want the truth." He held her chin, forcing her to gaze into his eyes. "What else, Rea? I will have the whole of it from you."

"Time travel." She felt the barely discernible movement of his fingers slightly tightening on her chin. "My gifts are healing and time travel. Put them together, and I have training in modern medicine, Connor, really, really modern medicine, as in twentieth-century modern medicine."

"You are from the future?" Connor asked, not showing his surprise.

"No. I was born in 1466. I have been to the future on countless occasions to increase my learning. I am what one in the twentieth century would call a doctor of internal medicine."

Connor was finally getting the answers he had been seeking for months, and he did not like the answers at all. The thought of her powers made him uncomfortable, and he stepped back from her.

Reagan felt the sting of his withdrawal, but she also felt the power of the shrine calling to her. She knew time was growing critical. Turning away from Connor and back to Cullen, she placed her right hand on his face.

She had to know.

"Cullen, I must be sure you agree to this. If I take you forward, you will never be able to return. Once you cross over, you will be gone to them, and they will instantly be dead hundreds of years to you."

"I am dead to them either way. Am I wrong?" Cullen's voice was now barely above a whisper.

Reagan studied Cullen's skin. He was turning gray and taking on the mask of death. He would be dead in minutes.

"I can't save you here. I'm sorry," Reagan answered him honestly. He deserved as much.

"Cullen, oh, Cullen, I am so sorry." Morgan softly cried over him. "You are my friend, and I love you. You know that, do you not?"

Cullen nodded, taking her hand. "I will always love you, and not just as a friend. It has been my greatest joy to serve you."

It was the confession of a dying man. Cullen looked at his brother. He knew he would do it all again for Morgan's sake and for Nic's. Only their happiness mattered, and he hoped fate would reward his selflessness. Morgan was Nic's one true love, and Cullen loved his brother as much as he loved Morgan. "Nic, take care of our lady. I have always thought you were a lucky man."

Morgan leaned down and kissed Cullen softly on the forehead as Nic took Cullen's hand. Death was closing in rapidly.

"Goodbye, brother. Remember us. Reagan said to me one time none of us were truly dead until the last person with a memory of us is also gone."

Reagan pulled Connor to the side while Cullen, Nic, and Morgan were saying their final goodbyes.

"All right, Connor, here is the deal. I know this is a shock, but if we are to save him, this is what I will need waiting for me."

Quickly, she wrote out what she would need, explaining what each item represented. "It's instantaneous for us. You have five hundred years to get it right, keeping in mind there's a lot of time for things to go wrong as well. If one generation forgets, he will be lost. I could be lost, as well, if this place isn't preserved."

Connor took her hands in his, needing contact with her. "I shall see to it you have what you need, Reagan. When will you return?" he asked. Their time was drawing short.

Reagan looked into Connor's eyes and felt her chest tighten. He could make her angrier than anyone on the face of the earth, but she knew, even with the differences they had shared, she would miss him.

She slipped her hands from his, turning away. "I won't be coming back, Connor."

Connor grabbed her shoulders and turned her to face him. Then he took her chin in his hand, forcing her look at him. "Nay, Reagan. I will not accept this. You must return for Nic and Morgan's sake. They will need the closure," he demanded softly.

"It doesn't work that way, English. God, how I wished time travel did work that way, but it doesn't."

There were only so many times she could cross. Six years earlier, she had made the crossover and felt her powers drain considerably on the return trip back. This was to be the last as her power was weakening to the point of being nearly spent. Without an adequate amount of power, she couldn't risk trying to come back. She could get lost in between. Such was the way of the gift.

Reagan felt time slipping away. The proverbial train was leaving the station, and as it was, she knew she would have to run to catch it.

"Then I will go with you, so I can bring word back to them." Connor was resolved to follow her. Nic and Morgan would need the news of the outcome of Cullen's situation.

"That can't happen. A man without the gift can only cross over once, and once they do they can never return. Otherwise, I would send Cullen back once he heals and is out of danger."

Reagan placed her palm on the side of his face. Her tender gesture surprised Connor. "I'm sorry, English, but this is a voyage where none can follow and none will ever return." A silky tear slipped down her cheek as she closed her eyes against the pain of leaving.

Connor did not understand the sudden anger that overpowered him. She was leaving, and it was not acceptable to him.

"You owe me for helping you get Nic to go to Morgan last night. He did go to her, and they have begun to mend the rift between them. You gave me your word that I could name my price. Well, this is my price, Reagan O'Riley. You *will* come back, and when you return, you will spend one year and a day with me at Featherstone."

She looked at him with surprise. "Oh, and is that all you want?" Reagan didn't have any time to wait for his answer. With the final moments on them, she was frantic. Her heart hurt, her chest was exploding, and there was no time to figure out exactly why.

Fate had not been kind. She had no time to prepare mentally for the pain that she knew would follow this separation by time and space. She was not being given the chance to say a proper goodbye to the people she had grown to love and think of as family. Neither would she have any closure because the likelihood of her ever returning did not exist.

"Nay, that's not all I want." Connor grabbed her and crushed her to him, kissing her with everything in him. He poured into that single kiss all the intense emotions he could not convey with words. He had no idea those emotions even existed until she had said she would never return. He pulled back from her lips, reluctant to let her go, but did not release her completely.

"Time is short. Now, go. Save him. Do not make this parting be for naught, and know I await your return. One year and a day, Reagan. That is my price."

She stepped away from him. "Then it looks like you have five hundred years to find the way back for me. That's if I choose to come back," she said, brushing a lock of shoulder-length auburn hair away from her face.

"Oh, you'll come back, Reagan. Remember, m'lady, we have unfinished business."

She stepped away. "Goodbye, English."

Suddenly, a shimmery cloud like a veil appeared, and she and Cullen were gone.

~*****~

Connor stood looking out over the rugged cliffs of Seabridge as the unrelenting wind whipped his dark, unbound hair. The mighty waves crashed against the jagged boulders below while the lingering power of the ancient place swept over and through him.

Nothing had changed, yet everything was no longer the same.

His piercing blue eyes focused on some far-off, unknown point, and those who knew him would have recognized the stance. He stood with his fists balled on narrow hips with his claymore, still bloody from the mortal battle he had fought and won not a half-hour past, by his side.

The price of victory had come at an enormously high cost. It was a cost none could have fathomed at the onset of this journey.

Connor was now engaged in a new battle.

He felt as if his heart had been pulled whole from his chest and thrown into the crashing sea.

"Reagan," he softly spoke her name with a longing born of regret.

She had become woven into the fabric of his life. Those delicate threads of her healing touch, her laughter, her caring tenderly for those entrusted to her care—all had wound tightly around his heart.

He hadn't realized until he had kissed her how important she had become to him. That one kiss before she stepped through the veil of time had forced him to see what a fool he had been and what she could have been to him.

Only he had seen it too late, and the thought of all the time they had wasted in a fruitless battle of wills, which in the end had accomplished nothing, set him reeling.

He knew once his lips had met hers, a kiss would never have been enough between them. She had tasted like honey, sweet and satisfying, and had set him on fire in a way he had never felt before, leaving him longing for more.

"So just like that, she is gone?" Connor said to the wind.

It was hard to believe, but he had seen it with his own eyes. Reagan had called the power to her, punching a hole through the veil where time and space collided, and like a slingshot, it catapulted her and Cullen far into the future to the year 1994.

In doing so, she was forever beyond his reach, and he was dead to her the moment she emerged on the other side. How he could ever accept this, he didn't know.

His heart began beating wildly in his chest as he thought of what she had asked of him. What if he failed her?

"Nay, failure is not an option," he said, realizing the enormity of the situation. "I have never failed, and I'm not about to start now," he vowed as he looked down at the paper she had shoved into his hands.

She had faith in him and entrusted him with her very life. He felt the weight of that life as if he held it in the palms of his hands instead of a scrap of paper. If he could not hold the woman, then he would hold her memory, devoting the whole of his life to fulfilling what she needed from him. So, he vowed that he would give her all she had asked as long as he lived. She was now his call to arms, and he would never let her down so long as he drew breath, praying someday fate would bring her home again.

# Chapter 2

Five Hundred Years Later
Seabridge Castle
McKinnon Memorial Hospital
April 13, 1994

"We're losing him!" Reagan shouted to the group gathered for the express purpose of saving this very life, which was quickly ebbing away.

"Quickly, the paddles! Everybody, CLEAR!" Rafe demanded of the trauma team, hitting Cullen with a jolt of electricity in an attempt to restart his still, silent heart.

"Nothing, damn it! Let's hit him again! CLEAR!" Rafe said as he looked at the monitor. "You will not die, Cullen. Not today and, by God, not on my watch," Rafe McKinnon, MD, and native Texan, said with enough conviction that all who heard him believed. Rafe was going to will this young man back to life. He had to for the sake of his Texas pride and in no small part, for the sake of this lovely Irishwoman standing beside him, who was working just as frantically to stem the flow of blood.

"Hit him again! Clear!" Rafe wasn't about to give up. Suddenly the beeping sound of the monitor sprung to life. The heartbeat was weak but there. It was a start and the odds weren't good. Everyone knew it, but none were prepared to give up.

Rafe and the others had been standing by. The legends had been specific. Therefore, they knew the exact day and time of this arrival to the Seabridge hospital. The team knew everything except the outcome that history had yet to reveal. However, today the story would begin again. Rafe just prayed the ending would be a happy one.

This hospital had seen its share of critical patients through the years, and all were important, but none were as important as this young man. The hospital complex had been erected just for this event. Nic had commissioned the hospital to be built in 1500 and demanded its maintenance through the generations for the sole purpose of saving his brother.

Rafe knew the twenty-three-year-old knight had been transported through a time portal by the efforts of Dr. Reagan O'Riley from the year 1494.

This odd but awesome event was unfolding just as the legends foretold.

Sworn to secrecy, the staff knew Reagan was unusual. Reagan, trained as a doctor in the late 1980s, freely moved back and forth through the veil of time, gaining the knowledge of modern science. They knew from the legend that she had inherited this gift from her mother and grandmother.

Alice, Reagan's grandmother, was born a decade before the turn of the twentieth century, and disappeared at the age of twenty-eight, while working as a nurse during the World War I. Fate pushed Alice through a thin spot in the veil and took her to Ireland in the year 1440 where she fell in love with a fine Irishman, and she never saw fit to return or so the legend went.

Rafe McKinnon, on the other hand, was totally grounded in the twentieth century, and the only transporting he ever did was by plane, train, or automobile.

This was an event most men of science would have never believed possible, but he had been raised on the McKinnon legends. That background was possibly the reason the McKinnon Foundation had selected him for this momentous occasion in McKinnon family history. Today was the most important day of his surgical career. He had only one shot to get it right.

If he didn't, it would cost Cullen his life.

14

For better or worse, Reagan and Cullen were here in 1994, and he had to be sure every effort was made to save Cullen's life.

According to the legends handed down from one McKinnon generation to the next, there would be no going back for either.

~*****~

Standing helplessly by, Reagan watched as they rolled Cullen through the double doors and into the operating room. She knew Cullen's life was in the hands of a higher power, and she had done everything humanly possible for him. If he was meant to live, he would. She prayed bringing him here would not cause some irreparable damage to the timeline.

He was never meant to be here, but here he was and so was she.

"Reagan?"

She spun around. "What? Oh, I'm sorry. I didn't hear you approach." She had been so lost in thought that she had not heard the nurse. Reagan looked into deeply intelligent eyes still sharp in spite of advancing age.

"Come, child. Cullen is in good hands, and you have done your part in getting him here."

When Reagan thought of the accomplishment this hospital represented, she was amazed. It had been a long shot; she knew it. However, she also knew she had no other options to try to save him. With so much time passing, so many things could have gone wrong, but miraculously they hadn't.

Connor had been true to his word, and deep down she knew if what she requested from him could be done, he would see to it. He was a man of honor, even if they hadn't always seen eye to eye.

A deep sadness swept over her. In the McKinnon victory, there was also defeat. Everyone was now gone, long dead.

"Child, are you all right?" The old nurse broke into her thoughts.

Reagan continued to stare out the plate-glass window overlooking the landscape. It was strange to see the castle off in the distance and to know that no one was there she loved. "I will be. Thank you." She smiled, feeling a deep sadness roll over her.

The nurse placed a hand on Reagan's arm. "You're right, Reagan O'Riley. You will be fine. You have your grandmother's strength. Never, ever forget that."

Reagan nodded. Turning away from the window to face her future, she left her past behind. What other choice did she have?

# Chapter 3

So the old nurse had known her grandmother before she died. As strange as her life had been the last few months, Reagan did not find that at all surprising.

Standing under the spray of the scalding hot shower, Reagan couldn't help but think back over what had transpired since she first met Nic the previous fall in southeast Ireland. Her life had taken such a drastic turn that day, and now she could see no clear way out of the maze that had become her life.

At first blush, it had made sense for Arlen O'Brian to bring Nic to her. Who better to care for O'Brian's injured prisoner than the local healer? Nic had endured several hellish months as O'Brian's prisoner before Reagan had risked everything to help him leave Ireland and get back to Seabridge. Lester Brentwood, Morgan's nefarious uncle, had planned on returning Nic to Seabridge to lure Morgan back to the castle, for Brentwood wanted Seabridge for himself, and he had no qualms about killing them all to gain it.

She would have never let that happen. So she had left everything behind to aid Nic in escaping Ireland, and her life had never been the same for it.

Once Nic and Reagan made their way back to England, Nic had commanded his brother Cullen to take Reagan to Featherstone Castle and entrust her to his friend Connor to protect her from Brentwood and O'Brian for her part in Nic's escape.

Thinking back on those days spent at Featherstone Castle, she realized she had settled in comfortably behind the sturdy walls of Connor's estate, accepting his protection even though she knew she could never stay. The sick were everywhere, and once the cry went out that there was a

17

qualified healer in residence, people came to see her by the dozens. She had quickly come to love Featherstone's people. She also had come to regard their welfare as her responsibility. The people and the place had worked their way into her heart before she had realized it.

Standing there in the hospital shower, Reagan feared what she would have done had circumstances been different. If there was no need to bring Cullen forward, would she have stayed at Featherstone with Connor? Would she have been happy with him?

It was a moot point now. Certainly, had she failed to bring Cullen forward, he would have died from the mortal laceration he sustained while shielding Morgan's body.

Cullen had agreed to come forward in time only because he knew he was gone to them either way. Reagan thought perhaps he had agreed to come so that he would not have to continue living a life so close to Morgan, knowing his love for her would never be returned if he survived.

The young man was in love with his brother's bride, and in 1994, she would be well and truly out of his reach.

Reagan knew he had never acted on those feelings, for he was too honorable. She had known for months that Cullen was a young man in deep pain, his heart broken and bleeding. The young knight, just like her, had sacrificed everything on these rugged cliffs.

He had done it out of love.

She had done it because it was the right thing to do.

~*****~

Finished with her shower, Reagan left the private doctor's quarters. She pushed through the door and made her way back into the hallway. Wondering around in the maze of corridors, she came to a dead end almost as if she had been led there. She gazed at the mahogany double doors, and the

18

gold letters affixed to the polished wood left her without a doubt of the room's purpose as the founder's gallery and library. Trying one of the doors, she found it unlocked, easing it open with caution as she peeked inside.

What she saw within caused her to draw in a breath of excitement.

"Oh, my goodness," she said.

Finding the light switch, she entered. There, front and center, on the most prominent wall of the room was a life-size portrait of Nic McKinnon surrounded by his family.

It would seem Nic and Morgan had six children. She saw the adopted twin girls whom she had rescued when they were only a day old. Both had grown into beautiful young women.

There were four young men in the painting. All were fine looking, so handsome with the look of the McKinnons. There was a set of twin boys who looked like a darker version of Nic's father whom she had met upon coming back to Nic's home. One son looked like Morgan with his jet-black hair and beautiful green eyes. The carbon copy of Nic was undoubtedly William, the oldest son whom she had helped to deliver.

She wondered about the other children. Who were they? What had they become in life? From the look of the painting, they had lived long and full lives.

She felt this would bring some solace to Cullen. Looking around the room, she saw row upon row of McKinnon ancestors gracing the multipaneled walls, and each portrait had a bound volume below it. At random, she picked up one of the volumes and thumbed through it.

The volumes contained the entire life history of the McKinnon whose portrait was hanging above it.

She had outlined for Connor before they left why it would be important for Cullen to know what had become of them. The knowledge would facilitate his transition into his new life. The connection to his past would help bridge the gap to his present.

Connor had seen to this. It was beyond her wildest dreams, and she owed him a debt that she could never repay.

Turning to leave, she spotted the portrait of the man she was coming to better understand. She should not have been surprised to see it. He was as much family to Nic as any trueborn McKinnon. However, unlike Nic, he was seated alone. There was neither wife nor children to surround him.

"Oh, Connor," she said while softly brushing away the single tear slowly rolling down her cheek.

She wondered if he had ever married.

*It would be a crying shame*, she thought, *not to pass those extraordinary good looks and good genetics onto future generations.*

He was undoubtedly the most handsome man she had ever seen, whether in his time or any other, for that matter.

The painting was well done, capturing his essence: strong, proud, and intelligent. He was in his twilight years. Even so, he was striking, seated as he was in front of the fireplace. Moving closer to get a better look, she noticed the letter in Connor's hand resting purposely in his lap. The writing was just visible, having faded over time.

*One year and a day. Remember, we have unfinished business.*

"Oh, my God," she softly said with a sharp intake of breath, bringing her hand to her lips.

Those words were meant expressly for her.

"Remember, we have unfinished business." Those were the last words he said to her as she had been ripped through the portal.

She and Connor had started off on rocky footing when she first came to Featherstone, and theirs had been a barely civil relationship. A truce had developed in the months that she had spent in his home, simply by having no contact with each other.

They were in each other's company only when necessary, tolerating it when there was no other alternative. Therefore, the price for his help of getting Nic to talk to Morgan had come as a surprise to her.

The man was unbelievable.

He showed her not one ounce of attention for months except to irritate her. Then right before she left, he kissed her as if he never wanted to let her go. It was a kiss to be remembered for sure, full of passion and promise.

Thinking of that kiss, she unconsciously put her fingers to her lips. She had been waiting for that one kiss all her life.

She brought her attention back to the painting. It appeared he had waited all those years for her to return, too.

Quickly, she turned away from the painting, unable to look at his likeness any longer. His eyes were so real she felt as if they were drilling into her soul and searching her heart. She did not understand why she felt heavy with guilt. She hadn't asked him to wait. If he had waited, he had done so of his own free will.

She stepped out of the room, then quietly began to pull the door closed, yet she felt a powerful pull from the painting. Looking back over her shoulder at the portrait of Connor Holden, she felt it burn into her psyche. Then and there she knew, no matter where she went and no matter how many years passed, this man would haunt her for the rest of her days.

# Chapter 4

Rafe had looked for Reagan once the grueling surgery was over. He found her in the waiting area, feet pulled up under her, head resting on her fist. She was asleep with a *Ladies Home Journal* from December 1992 across her lap. Lightly touching her arm, he woke her. "Dr. O'Riley?"

Rafe looked into warm cinnamon eyes fringed by dark auburn lashes. No longer covered in blood, she was just as striking as he knew she would be.

"Hi, I'm Rafe McKinnon." He stretched out his hand even though he felt as if he already knew her. "We didn't have time for formal introductions earlier."

Reagan chuckled even though she was exhausted. More important things than social introductions were going on when she and Cullen appeared in his world—that was for certain.

"I'm pleased to meet you." She took his hand. "How is Cullen? Is he out of danger?" she asked, shifting positions on the sofa as Rafe seated himself in the chair across from her.

"He's critical, but stable." He paused, then continued. "He's young and in extraordinary physical condition. More importantly, he's a McKinnon. I'm confident he'll survive. I have to admit, it's a small wonder that we didn't lose him on the table. We'll just monitor his condition over the next twenty-four hours," he said.

"That's great news," she said, nodding her head, smiling at the hope she had just been given. "I'm so grateful for all you've done so far. I'll help where I can, once I feel stronger," she said in her soft Irish brogue.

Somewhat concerned for her well-being, Rafe looked at her through doctor's eyes and knew she needed food.

"Want to go grab something to eat down in the cafeteria? I'm starving and I doubt you've eaten."

"Come to think of it, I haven't eaten," she answered. There had been neither time nor desire.

Rafe held out his hand to help her up off the couch and she took it. As they passed through the doorway, he placed his hand at the small of her back so she could go ahead of him. Once out in the hallway, Reagan followed his lead to the deserted basement cafeteria.

They got their food, and Rafe chose a table by a window with a beautiful view overlooking the sea, if one was so inclined to look. Reagan was not inclined.

She was exhausted and felt disjointed. Having just experienced leaving Connor at these cliffs, she wasn't ready to look at them again. It was too painful considering the wounds her heart and soul had sustained, which felt just as gaping as the wounds to Cullen's body.

"I'm not sure I'd ever get used to this view," Rafe said, looking out over the wild crashing waves as they rolled in the distance visible in the full moonlight.

"May I call you Reagan?" he asked, turning his attention back to her.

"My friends call me Reagan or Rea. We're both doctors and family in a strange sort of way. So, aye, yes."

"All right, Reagan it is then, and call me Rafe. I'm dying of curiosity about you, but I'll satisfy your concerns first."

He didn't have to tell her Cullen was sporting massive internal injuries. As a doctor, she certainly knew this. He had removed Cullen's spleen, there was a laceration to his right kidney and liver, and a portion of the large intestine was severed. The blade had passed through his stomach as well.

"He's a very lucky young man. He would be dead had you not been there to give him immediate medical attention. He almost bled out. I'm sure you knew from looking at your clothes."

Listening to his evaluation, she agreed. "I had suspected he was close to bleeding to death. It took time to get him from the cliffs to the place of power; time, I feared, was vital."

"Well, he was hanging over the edge, but you nailed it." Rafe had not wasted valuable time searching for wounds to repair. Fortunately, the stomach was the only thing she hadn't mentioned and even that was no surprise when Rafe saw the angle of the blade's penetration. The blade had made a straight shot through with no deviation of the angle. "He is, as I said, very lucky. The next twenty-four hours will tell."

"And you will continue to be his primary care physician? He's in intensive care, I gather?" Reagan asked, then took a sip of her coffee, a habit she had developed in college and took full advantage of when possible.

"Yes, he's in the ICU, but I hope my work is complete." *God forbid*, Rafe thought, *if we find it necessary to go back in.*

"I have passed his care to another doctor named Jeff Preston. He's the world's leading doctor in internal infections and a leader in critical wound care. He will continue to look to Cullen's care as long as Cullen is here."

He had also lined up experts in physical therapy, psychiatry, and stress management as she had directed. His language and life skills lessons would begin soon. Rafe was certain Cullen wouldn't know the difference between a refrigerator and a lawn mower given neither were invented at the time he made the crossing.

"Man, I wouldn't wish on anyone the culture shock he'll face. I'm glad it's not me." Rafe smiled compassionately as he shook his head. "I feel sorry for Cullen being *dropped* into a strange place and time without the benefit of current modern language skills. It is going to be hard on the young man."

"Rafe, I'm so grateful to everyone for helping to pull this together. I know that so much could have gone wrong. This day has shown the true mettle of the McKinnon heart. It was important enough, even for those generations who knew they would never know Cullen, to keep the maintenance going on as planned." She had taken another sip of the black coffee, savoring the warmth.

"I think it had become a call to arms of sorts, and our family honor was at stake, if you will. None of us wanted to be the McKinnon who dropped the ball," he said, then shrugged his broad shoulders.

Nic and Connor had treated this as a military campaign, using the keen minds they possessed. Rafe explained how Nic and Connor had set up a network that involved certain family lines having certain responsibilities. Each family was to ensure their line continued to follow the given path, and if there was any problem like a family line dying out, a backup plan was in place. Redundancy was key.

His own family, for instance, had been assigned the task of ensuring Cullen had a place to live. Rafe's ranch was partly Cullen's now. It always had been. His great-grandfather had gone to America from England and had bought the ranch with funds provided by the foundation set aside for just such a purpose.

Other families were responsible for identification, a plausible story for his life history, a bank account with sizable funds, and paperwork allowing him to work in the twentieth century.

26

It was now Rafe's job to help Cullen begin building a life. That he was also a surgeon was just a bonus.

"I appreciate your being here, Rafe. I know I wouldn't be much good to him at the moment with the shock my system has sustained. It's always hard on me when I make the crossovers. The trauma of Cullen's injuries, coupled with the fact that I can never go back, has heightened the effect, I think." Reagan paused. Rafe understood that she was collecting her thoughts. "It has left me feeling that I have left behind so much unfinished business." Reagan sighed, shaking her head at the thought of all she should have done but didn't, and all she could have given and hadn't.

"Do I need to take a look at you?" Rafe saw the signs of fatigue and stress lining her face. She was pale, but not alarmingly so.

"I'll be fine. I can tell you're not from around here, but I can't place the accent. I don't believe I have ever heard it before." Reagan accepted the coffee refill he offered, along with another scone.

"No, I'm definitely not from here," he said with a smile, as he replaced the coffeepot, and then with straight, white teeth he tore into a bag of chocolate-covered peanuts. "I'm from San Antonio, Texas, in the south central part of the United States. I work for the University of Texas Health and Medical School, and I'm chief of surgery at one of the hospitals there in town. The McKinnon Foundation Board of Directors called me in to do the honors, and I've been here about a month preparing for this moment. I decided to come over early and take some much-needed time off," Rafe said before dropping a handful of candies into his mouth.

"So, how do you like it so far? Most find it damp and dreary. I quite agree," Reagan said, looking again out the window into the inky night sky.

27

"This country is breathtaking and wild, and quite different from what I'm used to. I was in the service for a while but was never stationed here. This is a first for me. But you know something, Rea? From the moment I stepped foot onto Seabridge soil, I have had this almost overwhelming since of déjà vu. It's as if I have been here before. I knew where every room was, every crook and turn. It was bizarre."

"Yes, I know what you mean. This place has a strange effect on me as well."

Reagan and Rafe sat in silence for a moment as she studied the man seated across the laminated table from her. Although he was American, there was no doubt he was a McKinnon with his rich dark-brown hair, sprinkled lightly with gray, and eyes the color of rich milk chocolate. At six foot three, his height alone told of his McKinnon ancestry.

*Genetics is a funny thing*, she thought. The ability of traits to appear, disappear, or even skip generations at a time before resurfacing fascinated her. Rafe could have been Nic's older brother, the likeness was that uncanny.

"It's amazing how much you look like Nic," she said. "You're a McKinnon." It was a statement not a question.

Rafe had seen the portrait of the McKinnon patriarch and conceded there was a strong resemblance. He was a McKinnon and proud of it.

"Oh, yes ma'am, true blue, through and through. I grew up on the stories. My great-grandpa went over to the United States as an immigrant and brought the stories with him. He kept them alive, just as every other McKinnon does. I grew up hearing about the explosion in the underground tunnels of the castle that forced you out onto these same cliffs," he said while inclining his head toward the glass-paned windows. "The conflict with Morgan's uncle was spelled out. How Nic and Cullen had faced him and his two armed men. How, in the final moments, Nic forced Brentwood over the edge, and how Cullen had

28

thrown himself in front of an assassin's blade to protect Morgan. However, let's not forget the fair Reagan who sacrificed much to bring the young knight forward to save his life."

Rafe grinned and Reagan had to catch her breath. He looked so much like Nic that her heart ached at the loss. "Reagan, I must confess, I think I had a crush on you growing up. You see, I have a thing for strong-willed women and heroines with supernatural abilities. You ranked right up there with Wonder Woman, Catwoman, and Florence Nightingale," Rafe good-naturedly poked fun at himself, but then he turned serious again. "Rea, you wouldn't believe how through time the stories have taken on a life of their own; still, the undercurrent was there all along, and the kernels of truth remained."

Reagan looked away, unable to meet his gaze. She was uncomfortable with the assessment because she didn't feel like a hero.

With the immediate danger past, she was beginning to feel the loss very acutely and wondered if she had done the right thing after all. She was second-guessing herself, which was something she didn't do under normal circumstances. It did no good to look back. What was done couldn't be undone; she believed that pining over things which could not be changed was useless, but tonight was different. She felt very much like crying, pining, and expending energy over the events.

"Now, I've embarrassed you. I apologize."

"I'm just a woman, Rafe. I'm nothing more and nothing less," she said, running the pad of her index finger around the rim of her cup.

Rafe found the slow circular motion almost hypnotic. Shaking off the effect, he reached across the table and took her free hand, covering it with his.

She noticed the clean, short-clipped nails, the light dusting of dark hair on his hand, and the absence of a wedding ring on his finger. She looked up to meet his warm brown eyes as they gazed into hers.

"Well, Reagan, that remains to be seen, now doesn't it? I think you're not just another woman, Rea. You're an extraordinary woman, not only for your abilities as a doctor, but for your big heart. I can see the stories are accurate on that point," he said as he gently squeezed her hand, showing the sincerity of his opinion of her.

"Well, when I feel like I can keep my eyes open, I'll get you to recite some of the tales of my daring heroism." She laughed softly at the thought. "It should be good for a laugh, but not tonight. Definitely not tonight."

"I understand." He smiled sympathetically.

"Thank you for being here for Cullen. I'm so grateful. He's in good hands, but for now, I'll say good night, Rafe."

Rafe stood up as she did, and they walked out together to the elevators.

"Are you staying in the doctor's quarters? I can walk you back," Rafe asked as the elevator door opened on the basement level.

"Thank you for the offer, but I think I would like to take a walk. I feel like I need to clear my head," she said as she hit the lobby button on the elevator control panel.

"Do you want company?" Rafe was puzzled at where the question had even come from, yet he felt compelled to ask. He wasn't usually one to intrude on a person's private time. Having so few of those moments himself, he comprehended how important these times were to someone like them. So much of their lives were devoted to others that time for self was rare and usually jealously guarded.

"Nay, but thank you." The elevator doors had opened and she stepped out. Rafe held the door, keeping it from closing as he dispensed his medical advice.

"Try to get some rest, Reagan. That's doctor's orders. Call me on my cell if you need something to help you sleep. Here is my number," he said, handing her his business card.

After taking his card, she raised her hand to wave goodbye. "Good night, Rafe. I'll see you later this morning." Her smile was a weak one as the doors closed on Rafe's handsome face.

Yet, as handsome as he was, he could never match Connor.

# Chapter 5

Turning to the main entrance doors, she walked past the receptionist and into the night. Since she had no real destination in mind, she allowed her feet to lead her, giving her time to think.

How long would she stay with Cullen? How long would he need her? Once he didn't need her any longer, where would she go? Where would her new life take her?

How would she function without identification and records? Could Rafe maybe help her? They knew that she was coming and would never be able to return. Perhaps they had made arrangements for her too. She made a mental note to ask. The world was a wide-open space for her, and the prospects were almost overwhelming. She found herself in a garden, startled to realize she had walked so far. It was nothing compared to where she had been.

For the first time in her life, her future was unclear. Her neatly mapped out life was now a series of uncharted roads with no signs for guidance. She sat on a bench next to the quiet place.

Up had been down, and back had been forward since Nic had come into her life. Nothing had felt right except being in Connor's arms.

Looking down and to the left of the bench, she noticed there was a tiny memory marker.

Mary Catherine Holden
I Loved You
Even Though I Never Knew You
May 23, 1500-May 23, 1500

"Oh no," she said with a sigh and realized she was in a sacred place.

Connor must have lost a child, and her heart constricted painfully in her chest at seeing the tiny marker. The pain was almost personal for her. She couldn't imagine the pain of holding her child and losing her.

The place affected her strongly, and she recognized it immediately. She was in the place of power, and it called to her, whispering ancient prose and promises on the damp night air. The old holy place was full of ancient forces. It was rich with possibilities for those who could call and harness those forces. Places like this were rare and used by those with the gifts throughout the eons. Those gifts and this power were the very things that had pulled Cullen through the veil of time.

The power this place wielded made her spine tingle, her pulse race. The energy passed over her skin, making the fine hairs on her arms stand on end. She felt the whispering breath and caress of the power as it danced the ancient dance.

She could feel how different it was compared to all the other times it had called to her. It was only a light touch, not the gut-wrenching pull she normally had when she entered such a hallowed place. It was more like an echo. It was distant, faint, the barest brush of a lover's kiss.

She knew her gift was used up; the power of it was spent. She had crossed over for the final time to bring Cullen here to be saved.

Despite the pain she felt, she would do it all again if it meant saving his life. It would have never crossed her mind not to. She was a doctor and had taken an oath, which she believed should be upheld, no matter the personal cost.

*Right now, the cost seems extremely high*, she thought as a mist settled around her.

In this garden Nic had built, alone and feeling so isolated, she hung her head and did something she hadn't done for years. She cried tears not meant for others, but selfish tears just for herself.

34

She grieved deeply for the loss of the life she had known and the loss of loved ones left behind. Now, they were long dead and hundreds of years had passed. She would never see them again.

She would never see the babies grow up to be the fine adults the portrait showed them to be. She would never again spar with Connor, and she would never see her fair Ireland again, at least not as she had left it, pure and wild.

She had given up much to bring Cullen over, but she would do it all again.

~*****~

Rafe could tell Reagan was adrift, and he would have followed even if the old nurse hadn't encouraged him to do so. He was worried and kept telling himself he wanted to be sure she did not need medical attention. He had no idea how traumatic time travel might be on the human body, and if what she said was true, this time had been the worst for her.

For hours, she had been sitting on the garden bench in this hallowed place. He had quickly discovered after his arrival that he didn't like coming here, and he wouldn't have except her safety was in question.

The place affected him.

Nonetheless, he would endure as long as he felt she might need him. So, silent as a specter, he sat on the wall west of her and waited in case she needed something. Rafe stayed and watched until the moon set low in the western sky and the dew rested heavy on the garden flowers.

Dawn was just moments away.

He slipped off the wall as he saw her lean over at the waist, bury her face in her hands, and let out several heartfelt sobs.

It racked him to his core.

He hated to see any woman cry, but he really hated to see a strong woman cry, and in some strange way, he felt connected to her.

*Perhaps the stories are true after all,* he thought. Perhaps she did leave Connor behind and in doing so, sacrificed her heart to save Cullen. He could see such a thing from this woman.

Going to her was the last thing he had planned, but his feet had a mind all their own.

"Come here, darlin'."

Pulling her into his arms, he held her head close to his heart. Reagan did not have the heart or energy to pull away. She welcomed the human touch.

Connor's portrait sprang to mind as she slipped into Rafe's embrace. Sobbing, she spoke her thoughts aloud, feeling the deep gut-wrenching guilt that Connor had spent a lifetime alone because of a promise she could never keep.

"Oh, Connor, I'm so sorry, please forgive me. Please," she sobbed into Rafe's chest.

"Shhh, Reagan." Rafe rocked her in his arms, giving her the comfort he sensed she needed. "It's going to be all right."

Squeezing her tighter in his arms, Rafe kissed the top of her head in a protective gesture. Whispering to the night, he added, "God, if you're listening, I could use a little help here, please."

Neither saw the specter appear in the garden. He gazed jealously on the embracing couple, his long legs spread wide, fists anchored to his hips, and claymore at his side.

"You made a promise to me."

Reagan heard Connor's voice ring clear as a bell through the predawn mist.

"Connor?" She snapped her head up as she called his name in surprise. Looking around, at first she saw nothing.

"Reagan, is there something wrong?" Rafe asked, looking around to see what had spooked her.

"I don't know. Maybe. I could have sworn I just heard… never mind. You won't believe me anyway. I don't even believe it myself."

"Do you remember?" Connor repeated, coming ever closer.

"Is that you? How did you get here?" Reagan asked as the shadows played tricks on her. She thought she was seeing a man who looked like the Connor in the painting, aged, yet still very handsome.

"Rea, who are you talking to?" Rafe asked her as he held her by the shoulders.

"Don't you see him?" Reagan asked Rafe, feeling the chill of uncertainty slide over her skin.

"See who?" Rafe asked.

He tightened his hold on her after he felt her body tensing. Rafe knew she was frightened. She realized he wasn't seeing the same thing she was.

"Reagan? What do you see?" Rafe asked, looking around for any sign that they were not alone. His keen hearing and sharp senses picked up nothing. He was certain no other living person was there in the garden with them.

"He cannot see me, Reagan. Only you can see me, love. Only you can hear me, but do not be afraid. I have spent my lifetime and ten more to protect you on your journey through time. You are safe, at least from me. Your promise to me, I ask again, do you remember?" Connor asked softly, tenderly.

Connor was standing right beside her now.

Longing swept through her, drawing a gasp from her lips from the pain in her chest. She could hardly breathe. He represented home. He represented family. He represented her past and everything she would never have again.

As she reached out to stroke him, her hand passed through him. He was the consistency of mist, and she could feel him but not touch him. She couldn't hold him. Rafe saw her eyes widen in surprise as a second soft cry of despair escaped her lips.

Finally, she softly answered the question. "I remember, Connor, but there's nothing I can do."

Surely, she was dreaming, asleep on the bench, she reasoned. The exhaustion and trauma of the day had finally gotten to her. *It has to be the only explanation*, she thought. Ghosts do not really exist, and if they did exist and Connor really was standing here, then he truly was dead.

He was dead.

The truth struck home, the grief welling up, overflowing. She couldn't keep the strong feelings inside, and she was no longer in denial. She couldn't go back. Cullen could still die, in which case her sacrifice would be all for nothing.

She had no home, no job, and no family, but worst of all, her loved ones were all lost to her. They were all truly dead. At that moment she felt as if her world would never be right again.

"I can't go home," she admitted, sobbing harder in agony as exhaustion and the reality of the day was sinking in. "I can't ever go home," she whispered in defeat, leaning her forehead on Rafe's rock-solid chest, all her tears nearly spent now.

Rafe held her so she could release the grief. It was better that way, and he knew from experience keeping it inside only hindered the healing process. He also knew from his same experience with death that time helped to heal, even if it was a cliché.

Reagan opened her eyes. Connor was still there, patiently waiting for her to look at him. "Reagan, love, you must ask. I cannot do it for you," the ghostly apparition spoke again, and Reagan wondered what it would have been like to hear him speak this tenderly to her in life as he just did in death.

"What can you not do for me, Connor?" Reagan was confused.

Rafe was really worried now. "Reagan, come on. I'm taking you back inside. You're exhausted."

Rafe turned to go back the way they had come. He thought the sooner he got her inside, the better. Mentally, he made a note to order a sedative for her, and he would get her in a bed if he had to tie her there himself.

Connor stepped into her path, stopping her, pulling Rafe up short. "Do you want to come home, Reagan?" Connor asked her. She could clearly hear the sincerity in his voice.

"How can you even ask such a question? Of course, I want to come home. But I can't. Not on my own."

"Ask!" Connor demanded sharply, taking her by surprise. Now, that was the Connor she remembered.

"What do you want from me! I'm a doctor, not a damn psychic, so stop jerking me around and just tell me what you want or go away and leave me alone!" she snapped back.

"You hold the key in your hands." Connor's cryptic words faded as he disappeared into the predawn mist.

"Connor? No! Come back, please. Don't leave me. Wait, please! Connor? I'm sorry," she yelled into the night. "Please, come back. I didn't mean it. Please!"

Turning away from the empty night, she looked back at Rafe and balled her fists into the front of his scrubs, burying her face in his chest as he encircled her in his arms.

"Rafe, help me, please. I don't belong here. I just don't belong here."

She needed him to take her back inside the hospital so she could try to regain some sanity. She needed to get out of this garden and away from whatever forces were at work on her psyche, making her feel out of control.

*Ghosts just do not exist, much less talk to the living,* she thought.

"Rafe, perhaps I'm dead, too and just don't realize it? Am I dead? Is that how I get back?"

Extremely concerned, Rafe pulled back enough to look at her but still held her arms. Her expression tore him apart. At that moment he would do almost anything if it would help ease her discomfort.

"Reagan, you're not dead, so don't even talk like that. You may feel like you're dying inside, but you're a fighter and you're very much alive. Don't think death is the pathway home. I'll not let you harm yourself, not today or any other. Just give me a little time and let me work on it, all right? I have connections all over the world. I can ask discreetly. Surely there are others like you somewhere in the world, and we will find them. Just give me time. I'll get you back one way or another. If that's what you want, Reagan, I will move heaven and earth to get you home again. I'll get you home."

Why had she not thought about another traveler? It was a possibility, she supposed. If she could bring Cullen here, maybe a traveler could take her home.

"You would do that for me?" Reagan asked softly, deeply touched that he would care enough to help her.

"Yes, I'll get you home. I would do that for you and so much more." Rafe smiled down at this pretty Irishwoman who had given her all for another. It was the least he could do for her.

"Promise?"

"Reagan, as a McKinnon, I promise," he whispered to her, and compelled beyond his own volition, he leaned in, cupped her face, and sealed that promise with a kiss.

The combination was perfect: the tumblers fell, the lock sprang open, and the power surged as never before.

# Chapter 6

Seabridge Castle
Dawn
April 14, 1499

"Wow! Now that's what I call a kiss." Rafe felt dizzy and light-headed. "I think I saw fireworks."

He leaned on Reagan for support. The bench was no longer there for him to sit on.

"Oh, God in heaven, Rafe, this can't be happening. Come over here and let me help you sit down before you pass out. The effects will soon pass." Reagan wiped the remaining tears from her face as she put her arms around him for support.

Reagan helped Rafe to the altar.

"What just happened and where are we?" Rafe asked.

"The question, Rafe, isn't *where are we*. We are at Seabridge. Don't you recognize the crash of the sea? The question is *when are we*. We punched through the veil."

"Holy crap," Rafe said softly, feeling like he needed to throw up.

"Yeah, and the passage felt very different."

"So, what do you think happened?" Rafe asked, wondering how they had been standing in the garden one minute, and then—BAM—they were still standing in the garden but only God knew in what century.

"I'm not really sure. Time has passed differently. We should have only been gone a single day. At least that's how it's supposed to work."

"How are you so sure things are different?"

"Well, for starters, here's the altar and there's no blood on it. Yesterday, it was covered with Cullen's blood and

41

was still housed in a small building, not out in the open like this. Look at this place. The garden is already started."

This could only mean one thing: they had missed the mark. Reagan turned in a slow circle, assessing their surroundings.

Turning back to him and shaking her head, she said, "This feels very wrong, Rafe. Very wrong. You should have told me you had the gift. I would have stayed away from you had I known. Being there in the place of power at the same time could have proved disastrous and may still prove disastrous."

"Rea, honestly, I had no idea. The place has always felt uncomfortable to me, but I had no idea why."

"Well, now you do know, and you will have to learn to call and control it. Without control, you're a danger to yourself and anyone else you touch in places like this." She reasoned her gift was so spent that it was no great threat but could have been the catalyst to elicit his.

Reagan thought perhaps it was the echo of her gift and the longing to come home that was the trigger. She had read in the meager writings she had managed to get her hands on that traumatic events were often the catalyst, springing the lock open on the gift.

Hers had come at age twelve after being struck by lightning while caught in a fierce storm. After that day, she had felt the power call and had asked her mother why she felt different. Once her gift revealed itself, her mother had taken her forward to a world full of wonder and excitement. It was a frightening world, but a world she eventually grew to understand.

Yet, for all its modern conveniences, she never really wanted to stay in the twentieth century. She belonged in her own time. Fate, it would seem, agreed with her.

The question was what century were they in if not the twentieth.

"So, Toto, we're not in Kansas any more?" Rafe was beginning to see what Reagan was talking about. The disorientation and dizziness were extreme.

"Oh, Rafe, I'm sorry, but no, I'm afraid not. Can you stand now?" she asked. Going back over to him, she helped him stand.

"Yeah, I think so," he said as he stumbled to his feet.

"Good, then let us go. I know a hidden path we can take. It will be light soon, so the going shouldn't be too treacherous."

Reagan led the way down the path to the castle. They got into the inner walls by a hidden gate that Morgan had told her about while she was at Featherstone, and they made their way towards the stronghold as the last of the night was fading.

"We should hide out in here for now," she said as they came to the stables. "I should be able to assess what is going on once daylight comes. At the first opportunity, we need to find some clothes. These scrubs won't allow us to blend."

*That's an understatement,* she thought as she looked at Rafe's turquoise surgical garb. If her smock covered in cartoon dancing mice wasn't screaming—*we're out of place*—nothing ever would.

"With the garden already under way, we couldn't have gone back further in time than 1494?" Rafe asked, pinching the bridge of his nose. It helped with the pounding headache.

"Nay, it has to be into the future or back to the current time. We cannot be in the same place at the same time with ourselves. Since I was born in 1466 and was here until April 13, 1494, I couldn't be here now if it's during that time frame. Does that make sense?"

"Strangely, yes it does. So that's why we knew exactly when you would appear yesterday."

"Right. For me the jump has always been exactly five hundred years forward or back. That's the way it always has been with any portal as far as I know. If there's a difference in this gateway, it could prove deadly for a person who doesn't have the mastery to control the gift. They could be thrown hundreds, even thousands, of years into the past or the future, or even into a different dimension altogether for that matter."

Reagan knew there was a different dimension where a completely dissimilar set of laws of physics and nature ruled. It was a place where the supernatural was natural and an alien people dwelled. Having heard of them all her life, she thought of the Fae people as merely fables or bedtime stories, yet she had seen the proof of their existence.

While looking for a book on herbal remedies of the late Iron Age for a class on toxic plants, she had stumbled upon an ancient text in the university library. The title on the card catalog had read *Book of the Healer*, and it had given a brief description as a book of home remedies in the Iron Age. She thought it looked perfect for her needs.

She chased the book down into the bowels of the library, but she was disappointed to find the text hadn't been there when she finally found the place where it was to be shelved. Knowing how careless people could be when placing books back on the shelf, Reagan had begun first to search in the immediate area around the vacant slot.

Not finding it, she moved her search outward, running her finger across the bindings, quickly scanning titles as she went.

Then she touched it.

*The Book of Light and Darkness.*

The binding had looked innocent enough. Reaching out, she touched it again, and she had sworn it had hummed in her hand. Pulling the book down from the top shelf, she skimmed the pages and knew immediately this book had no business being available to the public because in the wrong hands, it could prove dangerous.

Slipping it into the lining of her backpack, she checked out a dozen other books. When she set off the security alarm, the student at the front desk had waved her on, feeling certain he had just failed to deactivate the metal security strip in one of the twelve she had piled up in her arms.

After spending the weekend poring through the book, she knew she had knowledge very few of the dead, much less the living, had possessed.

It was a book of binding spells, spells of death, life, and truth. There were spells of enchantment and layering, giving the mortal person or Fae, whichever the case might be, the ability to pass undetected through the masses.

It gave in great detail the weaknesses, the history, and the location of the hiding places of the Faerie people.

Nevertheless, most frightening to her were the descriptions of and how to find all the Fae people's sacred relics that granted great and almost unlimited powers to those mortals who possessed them. Those relics consisted of the Singing Sword, the Shield, the Cloak, the Challis, the Talisman, and the most powerful of all, *The Book of the Words*. If a picture could paint a thousand words, then this book could create a thousand worlds.

Personally, she never wanted to see or talk about the realm of the Faerie and steered clear, giving the topic a very wide berth. Better yet, she wished not to discuss it at all.

It smacked of the druid arts, and in her opinion, it had the wizards of Atlantis written all over it.

The druids and the wizards of Atlantis were two subjects she never wanted to broach in casual conversation and certainly did not want to interact with them up close and personal.

She had taken the book and stashed it in a very safe place. The world would be much better off if it never resurfaced. She hoped it never did, but secrets seldom remain buried.

"All this talk of time warp is giving me a headache," Rafe said, snapping her back to the present.

"Nay, it's the aftereffects." Reagan knew exactly what he was feeling. It was certainly not new to her.

"How long can I expect this to last? I hope not long."

"You're a first, Rafe. No man has ever passed backwards through the portal as far as I know. I've never read anything on it."

All past records showed it was a female gift, so she guessed somewhere along the line the ability had mutated. She wasn't sure what effect the time travel would have on him but did assure him it would be over soon.

They needed to find clothing. Day would be breaking soon, and she did not want to be caught in the stables in the scrubs they were wearing.

"Can you stand now without feeling dizzy?"

"I'm fine." He was not, but he trusted her words that soon it would be better.

Finding the laundry was more difficult than they thought it would be, but the effort paid off. They were able to find clothes that fit well enough.

"Thank goodness, Rafe, you're not as tall as Nic or Cullen, but even then, the fit is questionable." To Reagan it seemed as if McKinnon men were just big, no matter the century they were born.

Scrubs discarded, they ventured out into the bailey to see what they could find out.

She took a deep breath for resolve. "Here goes—and let us hope we don't run into the person who owns this dress," she said as an afterthought. The dress was hideous, but she wasn't going to be choosy at the moment.

Rafe laughed and agreed. "I've been known to discard saddle blankets that looked better."

~*****~

Stepping out into the early-morning light, Reagan addressed the first gentleman she saw.

"Good morning, sir," Reagan said, turning on the charm.

He smiled at her. "Morning to you, as well, m'lady."

"If you could be so kind as to help me? I was wondering the name of your liege lord, and is there any way we might be able to see him?"

"Well, Nic McKinnon is liege, but he's currently not in residence. David Hale is our steward. Would ye care to see him?"

"Aye, please. Tell him Reagan O'Riley is here and wishes to see him."

The gentleman sent a boy to run ahead with a message to David that there were guests wishing to see him. Reagan excitedly explained to Rafe how she knew David as they made their way toward the main keep.

He had been at Featherstone when she had first arrived there. However, Connor had transferred David to York shortly after they had become friends. They had continued to write to each other after his transfer, and she felt sure he would welcome her.

The door to the stronghold swung wide and David walked out. From a distance she could tell he had filled out considerably since she had seen him last. His hair was still the beautiful shade of blonde, reminding her of polished gold. His eyes were a beautiful azure blue.

All in all, he was a handsome man, and unless he had changed, he was a kind man as well.

"Reagan, it is you!" He had come up to her, holding her in a bear hug. "It's wonderful to see you. Look at you.

You don't look a day older than the last time I saw you. How many years has it been? Six years, I think, since the last time I heard from you."

"David, has it been that long?" Reagan looked over at Rafe and translated. The look they exchanged was one of understanding. It explained a lot. They had missed the mark by well over five years. It wasn't 1494. It was 1499. Reagan felt there was always a purpose for everything. She guessed she would eventually find the reason for this as well.

"It's so good to see you, Reagan. Connor said you had taken a trip to some far-off place. I never understood and only accepted it after your letters stopped coming," David said as he led the way.

"Thank you, David, for the hospitality. I need to get a message to Nic if possible. Can you help me, or better yet, can you tell me where he and Morgan are now? Perhaps you could lend me two mounts and some supplies."

"Oh, of course. All this is Nic's, and he would spare no expense to see you safely back. Please, eat while I send my men to get the mounts and supplies ready for you." Stopping, David turned to face her fully. His hands slid gently up her upper arms to rest on her shoulders. His thumbs gently caressed her collarbones.

"You are as beautiful as ever." David cupped her face, kissing her lightly on the mouth. "I have missed you through the years, Rea. Are you sure you will not stay awhile or stay forever if you wish?"

Reagan placed her right hand over David's forearm. "Oh, David, I would love to stay and visit with you, my friend, but I do need to make all haste. But you have my promise, I will return as soon as I'm able."

"Well, then I guess I will have to settle for that at the moment." David's response was polite, but Reagan could tell he didn't like her answer.

Rafe could only understand a few words as they were speaking Gaelic, and Reagan seemed to be more comfortable with that as opposed to English. Still, he could easily read their body language. David was attracted to her, no doubt about it. *That's about as obvious as it gets,* he thought. There was history between these two, which no one had captured in the storybooks.

*Interesting*, Rafe added mentally, wondering how this would all play out.

They settled in the morning room. David had food readied for them. Sitting there with the early-morning light spilling through windows of stained glass worthy of any cathedral, Rafe was in awe.

The castle didn't look much different now than when he saw it the first day he had arrived—five hundred years in the future. It looked as if the restoration efforts had been accurate in the most minute of details. Many of the furnishings were the same.

However, there were a lot of differences in 1994. The main castle and grounds had been turned into a resort and tourist attraction in 1973. So many of the finer, more delicate furnishings had been put in the private wings or the vault, replaced by modern reproductions, which would hold up to the hordes of tourists flocking to the castle every year.

The McKinnon Foundation had seen to it the paintings and portraits hanging in the highly secured private gallery had been reproduced and hung in the halls of the castle for the tourists to see. The original pieces were too valuable to be hung in public areas, but the foundation had believed it good for people to see the history, so they had spared no expense on the reproductions.

The items of great market value such as the Da Vinci drawings, weapons, jewelry, and gold coins were in a secured vault and far from the public eye.

Those treasures never came out.

Rafe was seated at the very table upon which he had breakfasted the morning before the events began to unfold. It was the same, right down to the gash marring the surface. Now, as then, he wondered how that gash had gotten there.

"David, this is Rafe McKinnon. He's a cousin of Nic's. He doesn't speak Welsh, Gaelic, or the same King's English. I will translate if necessary."

"It's a pleasure to meet you, Rafe."

Reagan translated for Rafe and he nodded in greeting.

"He looks like a McKinnon," David said as he turned back to Reagan.

"Family ties to be sure, but enough about us, tell me what has gone on. I'm dying for news," Reagan asked, pushing her plate to the side and leaning forward to hear any and all news she could pull out of him.

David explained that in the years she had been away, Seabridge had become a major trading outpost and was prospering. Nic had appointed him steward of the estate two years past. He was honored to hold the position. He also let her know he had become a rich man in the process, and he had Nic to thank for it.

Nic and Morgan were doing well and living at Hearthill Manor, the estate Morgan had inherited from her mother, most of the time. It was less than an easy day's journey from Featherstone and halfway to London.

"Reagan, just so you know, Morgan is expecting again. They are overjoyed at the upcoming event. However, it is unspoken but still common knowledge that they're anxious about this birth after the stillborn child she delivered several years ago."

"Oh, I'm so sorry to hear that. I should've been here." Reagan's mind flashed to the marker in the garden.

David was sure Morgan would be grateful to have Reagan there for her third delivery.

William and the twin girls were now five years old, healthy, and precocious.

50

"And Connor?" she asked.

Rafe saw the tightening around the corners of David's mouth.

Connor was affluent and doing well for himself. It was recent news, David said, that Connor was granted the title of Duke of Featherstone and was now the standing earl of Rockport until the rightful heir could be found. Both titles were awarded for his faithful service to King Henry VII. It didn't seem to matter to Henry that the title of duke would normally be reserved for royal bloodlines. Nic had married into that royal connection. The king had proclaimed that Connor was "like family" and decided to confer the title even though it was unprecedented. He was king and could. No one was going to argue.

"Did Connor ever marry?" Reagan asked. She was thinking about the tiny marker in the garden.

"No," David answered quickly. David knew Connor was still unmarried, claiming a promise that had yet to be fulfilled.

"He keeps begging indulgence from the king for patience, assuring His Majesty his match would be well received by the court. However, it would seem Henry is growing short on tolerance and is abiding no more delays. Henry had demanded Connor marry in spite of whatever prior agreements he may have made. Henry is king and his word is final. I expect the announcement any day. The lady has yet to be selected as far as I know, but there's a line very deep, I assure you."

Reagan wasn't sure what she felt about this piece of news. It would free her of her bargain if he married, and it would solve a big problem as far as she was concerned. Yet, it left her feeling unsettled as well.

~*****~

After breaking their fast, Reagan was eager to begin the journey away from the coastline. The sooner they left, the more headway they could make today. Now that she was back, she was eager to see Nic and Morgan.

They stood out in the bailey saying their goodbyes as children played and locals hawked and bartered their wares.

Seabridge was a far cry from what it was the last time she saw it. It was a happy, family-oriented holding, clean and indeed prosperous. David and Nic should be proud of what they had accomplished here. She turned and offered her observations and compliments to David.

"We are proud, m'lady. It has been my pleasure to serve Nic."

Reagan observed that David was trying to impress upon her how easily he, as a husband, could take care of her.

"David, thank you so much for the supplies and horses. It has been good to see you. Take care and we shall visit again. I promise." She kissed him on the cheek.

David gently took her hands in his and kissed her fingers. "Rea, I want to call on you." His eyes pleaded for her to yield.

Seeing him like this broke her heart. She loved him well enough, and he had matured into a very handsome man, but what she felt for him was reminiscent of what she had shared with her first husband, Dolan, before he died. Their marriage had been a good marriage, comfortable and easy. She felt she could have that with David. He was a wonderful man and would make a wonderful husband in any century, and by any standard. Nic's faith in his abilities proved to her how capable he was.

However, she wanted more than comfortable and easy. She wanted a love and devotion that made her feel completely whole. She would settle for nothing less than a soulmate—a perfect other half.

"David, believe me when I say, if it were possible, I would welcome your courtship. You are a good and honorable man. A woman would be lucky to have you as husband, but it's not possible for me. I made a promise to Connor that I must fulfill. I'm honor bound, so please don't ask me to choose. The choice would be too difficult."

"What has he asked of you, Reagan?" David was angry at Connor for blocking his way to her. He was no fool. He knew Connor had transferred him to York to keep Reagan out of his reach, and now that she was back, Connor was between them again.

"Please, don't ask me, David. Please." Reagan placed her palm against the side of his face, beseeching him not to press.

He looked at her long and hard before answering. He took her hand and kissed the tender center flesh of her palm. "All right, I'll not press you, at least not right now. However, you can rest assured, I will see you now that you have returned."

Surprising her, he pulled her to him and the kiss he gave her was anything other than chaste. Reagan unintentionally compared his kiss to Connor's and found it lacking; this bothered her on several levels that she didn't want to probe.

"I will see you again, Reagan. I am no longer Connor's man, so he will give me a good reason if he thinks to keep me from you."

David, not wanting to take any chances with her safety, provided ten well-armed men, each bearing the blue-and-gold flying dragon standard, the crest of the Duke of Seabridge.

# Chapter 7

Rafe was glad to be on their way.

After riding through the gates and turning east, Rafe spared conversation to get accustomed to the unfamiliar horse. Being raised in South Texas on a six thousand acre working ranch, he was no stranger to horses or the fundamentals of horsemanship, but the saddle was different from the western saddle he was used to. It was taking him a little longer to find a comfortable gait. Yet his horse was steady and strong, and once he found the feel, it was like any other day on his ranch.

Riding in silence for a time, Rafe thought about the conversation he had witnessed between David and his new friend before leaving. He could tell David was unhappy about whatever she had asked of him.

"Reagan, care to share with me what is between you and David?" Rafe ventured.

"David asked to be able to see me now that I have returned." Reagan gave Rafe a sidelong glance.

*He's very astute*, she thought. He had picked up on the undercurrent.

"Are you going to see him?" Rafe asked in his smooth southern drawl.

"No. I'm afraid that won't be possible. Now that I'm back, I have a promise I must keep. Unless Connor wishes to release me from it, I'm honor bound. But even so…"

"Well, let me share something from a man's perspective. David won't take no for an answer. It's obvious he cares a great deal for you." He watched her closely. "Are you prepared to pass up a relationship with him because of a promise you obviously don't want to keep? And do I dare ask what this promise to Connor Holden is?"

"I… Connor, he…" Reagan opened her mouth but closed it. "Well, did your legends not tell you?" she snapped back, not quite comfortable telling Rafe what had passed between Connor and herself that day on the cliffs. It was personal.

Rafe shook his head. "Actually, no. The stories never mentioned any promise between the two of you. I apologize. I shouldn't pry. It's rude of me to ask."

Rafe could tell she was uncomfortable. Changing the subject to a safer topic, Rafe asked a question just as pressing. "How long will the trip take? Rough estimate will work."

"David said Nic and Morgan are about a day's journey to the north from Featherstone. We're better off to go to Featherstone first. It's on the way. It should take us about four days to get there as long as the weather holds."

"Four days, huh? If the weather holds?" Rafe grimaced. He missed his old pickup truck already.

"Aye, but we're talking England in spring, Rafe, so don't hold out much hope for it."

As if on cue, the clouds covered the early-spring sun, and the first raindrops began to fall.

Pulling his hood up and over his head, Rafe thought it was going to be a long four days and his pickup truck was not even a distant memory.

# Chapter 8

Featherstone Castle
11:30 p.m.
April 20, 1499

"Ho, keeper?" the man-at-arms roused the night patrol.

"Who wishes entry?" the night watchman asked, his gravelly voice carrying on the chilly night air.

Reagan recognized the voice instantly. The familiar old voice excited her.

"Albert? Is that you? It's me, Reagan."

"Reagan? Good Lord in heaven, girl, we never thought to lay eyes on ye again. Let me get the gates up, and we will get ye out of the night air."

After verifying their identities, the gates began to rise slower than Reagan remembered them moving, and with every inch they rose, her anxiety climbed along with it. Connor and an uncertain life lay behind this gate. One year and a day she had pledged, and one year and a day she would stay.

"Welcome home, young lady. Sir Connor will be happy to see ye return after all this time. I will see he gets the message ye have returned."

"Albert, it's good to be home," Reagan said, "but there's no need to rouse the household at this hour. I'll see Connor tomorrow. Time plenty to catch up then. Right now, I just want to get dry and warm."

"Then I bid ye good night. I'll tell my lovely bride ye are back."

Reagan had to smile at the fact he still called Martha his bride. They had been married fifty-two years.

"She'll be right glad to see ye. Ye can rest assured ye have been missed around here. Go seek your bed now."

"Good night, Albert. I'll sleep well knowing you're watching over me." She waved a friendly hand to him as she passed the man who had been looking out for the safety of the inhabitants of Featherstone through his nocturnal vigil for over fifty years.

# Chapter 9

Soaked to the skin, Reagan and Rafe were cold, hungry, and tired as they rode into the deserted bailey. It had taken them six wet, miserable, and decidedly uncomfortable days to get to Featherstone from Seabridge, and all she wanted to do was go to her quarters, which she hoped had been kept in her absence for five years. She wanted to take a hot bath, put on dry clothes, eat, and collapse in that order.

Rafe, on the other hand, was never more in want of a hot shower, a shower he knew he would not get for the rest of his natural life unless he somehow found the key to returning.

After the last six miserable days, he was going to do everything in his power to find that key and return to the twentieth century. He wanted his pickup truck with four-wheel drive, heat, and cushioned seats, and if he never rode another horse, it would be just fine with him.

"Rafe, if I still have my quarters, I did have an extra cot that you are welcome to use tonight. I would venture the household has all bedded down by this hour. If my quarters are still intact, we can heat water to get ourselves clean and dry."

Stopping in front of the small outbuilding that Reagan had used as her infirmary and living quarters, she found it encouraging, to see the shingle still hanging on the door, just as she had left it.

Reagan O'Riley
Physician / Herbalist
Welcome All Who Enter

Connor had given her the space as a peace offering after one of their many battles, and she had gladly taken it. It had been perfect for her needs.

She had also moved her belongings into the space after an even greater shouting match that had also included Nic.

Both men had tried, unsuccessfully, to convince her it was a bad idea to have her quarters away from the main house. Nic and Connor had lost this particular battle. However, through Morgan's negotiations, they managed to come to a compromise all could live with to one degree of comfort or another.

She was given a live-in assistant.

Pushing the door open, she saw a warm fire burning just as if someone were expecting her. It was a welcoming sight for the road-weary pair. The room smelled of the herbs and flowers that hung from the drying racks, the heat of the fire releasing the aromatic fragrances. Lavender-scented candles burned low on the workbench. Someone was working late.

"Hello?" she softly called. "Is anyone here? Marcus?" She called for the young man who had been her assistant and her *protector*. Could it be Marcus was still here after five years?

Then the storeroom door opened, and a much more grown up Marcus came through it. He had been thirteen when she had last seen him. He was a young man now.

"Lady Reagan? Welcome home, welcome home!"

"Just look at you, Marcus, you're huge!" Throwing her arms around his neck, she gave him a tight hug. "It's good to see you."

Turning him loose, she stepped back just enough to introduce Rafe. "Marcus, this is Rafe McKinnon. He's Nic's cousin. Right now we need a bath, food, and dry clothes. Are my things still here?"

"Yes, ma'am, I have made sure your things are fine, keeping all in good order. Sir Connor commanded a bath always be ready, just in case you came back unexpectedly. Tonight your food will be waiting when you finish your bathing."

"Marcus, Rafe is staying here for the night. I don't want the entire castle disturbed on our account. Tomorrow will be soon enough for the announcement that we have arrived. Can you see about a change of clothes for him?"

"I understand, m'lady. I'll begin his water while you bathe and dress."

"Marcus, thank you so much for keeping all my things together. You don't know how much this means to me." She gave him a kiss on the cheek.

"Do not thank me, m'lady." Marcus just smiled at her. "Connor insisted."

~*****~

Sinking into the warm water, she felt like she was in heaven. She had to remember to thank Connor for being so thoughtful with her things and her bath. The jasmine-scented soap was an unexpected luxury she couldn't resist.

She did not linger although the temptation was great.

Dressing as quickly as she could, she made her way back out into the main room. Rafe was patiently waiting to clean up and to get into some much-needed dry clothes.

While Rafe bathed, she took a quick inventory of the shelves, and aside from a few stronger pain-killing remedies, her inventory was in fairly good order. She was satisfied for the moment. It was spring. She could soon have her pharmacy stocked as well as it needed to be.

Rafe emerged from his bath and found that Marcus had managed to find him some clothes that fit well enough even if they were a bit big. They must have been some of Connor's.

They sat at the table, clean, dry, and full from the light supper Marcus had prepared, and she contemplated the recent events.

"Rafe, we have several decisions to make. The least is what you wish to do about being here."

"Now isn't the time, Reagan. After the last six days, I've no desire to stay here if this is the life I have to look forward to. I want my coffee with sugar, I want a nice, juicy steak, and I need chocolate-covered peanuts badly. I want to kick back with a good glass of wine, light my gas fireplace with the touch of a button, hit the remote on my stereo and listen to some light jazz, but only after I've had a hot shower. I have a headache, my back hurts, and my shoulders feel like they're on fire. In short: I want to get the hell out of Dodge."

"Just a little cranky, are we, Rafe? I thought we determined you weren't in Kansas any more." She grinned and knew she shouldn't tease him, but she couldn't help herself.

"Real funny," he said with a look that was anything but tolerant.

Although she wasn't unsympathetic, there was nothing she could do tonight, but tomorrow they would start looking for a solution.

"Well, I'll tell you this, I can't give you chocolate-covered peanuts or coffee, but I'll rub your shoulders." Walking around the table, she began to knead the muscles in his neck and shoulders.

"Oh yeah, that feels good." He dropped his chin into his chest. "Mmmm, yeah, right there," he said as she hit a tight spot.

"You're knotted up, but that's not unexpected, Rafe. You're not use to this. If you stay, you will find it will be easier in time. You might even find you like it. Here, there are no nuclear warheads threatening to destroy the world. Granted there's no television or chocolate. It will be years before sugar is available to anyone but the uber-rich, but there's also no smog and no pollution unless you go into London. Never look up while you're there, by the way," she said and gave him a playful pat. "That's unless you like the contents of a chamber pot tossed into your face."

"I'll keep that in mind," he said dryly.

"Life's slower here, Rafe, not necessarily less stressful, but it's a different stress. Certainly it isn't any less violent, but it's a different kind of life. The simple things bring so much pleasure here in this time," she explained. She examined her true feelings. "I'm not sorry that I'm back, but I am worried about Cullen. I won't be able to give Nic and Morgan total peace or answers to the questions they'll ask me."

Rafe had shifted to stand and pushed Reagan to sit in the chair he had just abandoned. Gently, he began to return the ministration, rubbing the knots out of her neck.

"Give them their peace. What harm will it do?" he offered. He began to speak after a short silence. "Listen, Rea, I usually don't hold to telling a family anything except the whole, unvarnished truth, but usually a family has a way of gaining closure. Nic and Morgan will have no opportunity to bury their dead if Cullen indeed does not make it. However, I think he will. His prognosis was good and he's a McKinnon. You know how stubborn we can be," he said with a half smile.

The silence hung between them for a moment as Reagan took in this information. "Perhaps you're right. History for them will never say otherwise. Mmm, that does feel good. Thank you, Rafe."

"You're very welcome."

He continued to rub her neck in silence for a time, each lost in their own thoughts.

~*****~

With Rafe standing behind her, it looked, from the vantage point of the man who silently entered the room, as if the man standing by the table was alone. Without a sound he drew his blade.

Rafe squeezed Reagan's shoulders. "Ahhhh, Rea? I have the distinct feeling I have a blade held to my back."

"Slowly turn around and keep your hands where I can see them," the intruder growled.

Reagan quickly spoke, knowing Rafe may or may not have any idea of the command he had just been given. "Rafe, he just told you to put your hands where he can see them and turn around."

The intruder heard Reagan's voice as she spoke a language he could only somewhat understand.

"Not a problem," Rafe said. Lacing his fingers together and placing them on top of his head, he slowly turned to face none other than Connor Holden.

Rafe was surprised at how large a man Connor was. The portrait and written descriptions of him didn't do him justice. He was every bit of six feet six, his dark-brown hair was long, and his ice-cold blue eyes pierced straight to a man's soul, making Rafe feel stripped bare.

Rafe stepped to the side just enough for Connor to see Reagan. She hadn't moved for fear it would prove fatal to Rafe. Instead, she was looking back over her shoulder and relief spread through her as she recognized the source of Rafe's discomfort.

"Oh, for heaven's sake, Connor, put that thing away before you hurt someone," she said, standing up and facing him.

"I am happy to see you, too!" Connor shot back. "You will tell me why you did not come to the keep straight away. Why have you forced me to seek you out like some beggar for an audience with *Her Royal Highness, the Princess Reagan*? And who is this man I have found you with? You will tell me, Rea, is he a spy?"

"Geez, Connor, some things never change. You're still a horse's arse, and no, he's not a spy. Will you just look at him?" she said as she pointed back at Rafe. "He's a McKinnon."

They were going toe-to-toe, and Rafe was beginning to think he had been wrong about these two. They were not two lovers reunited and happy to see each other. He would bet his medical license on that.

These two were about to go for a round, and he felt sure he was going to have to play referee. The dynamic would have been interesting except for a small fact— Connor had yet to sheathe his weapon.

Rafe, taking a chance, picked up a linen napkin off the table. Wrapping it around his palm, he slowly reached out. Using the padding of the napkin, he lowered Connor's blade.

"Easy, big fella, I'm not your enemy. Let's just all try to settle down here." Rafe spoke in that smooth southern drawl, trying not to spook Connor, but still gain his undivided attention.

"Connor," Reagan said and then crossed her arms over her breast, "he just asked you to be easy. He's right, English. Now, will you please put that thing away?" she said, pointing at his sword, which he was still holding at ready.

"What is going on here?" Connor punctuated his words by running his sword home into its sheath yet never took his eyes off Rafe.

She felt she owed him no explanation. What went on inside her rooms was none of his business. Reagan had no idea why she felt the need to prick him, but she did. She should have been elated. She should have felt the need to touch him.

Instead, he immediately placed her on the defensive, as if history were repeating itself where their relationship was concerned.

"Well, as you can see, he was giving me a neck rub, and I would like for him to finish. I would appreciate it if you would leave us."

Connor did not understand why it made him so jealous, and fast as lightning, he reached out and grabbed her by the arms. Rafe, being a southern gentleman, wasn't about to let Connor lay one finger on this woman in anger. He didn't care if the man outweighed him by sixty pounds of pure muscle. Rafe knew size didn't matter, but leverage did.

In the blink of an eye, Rafe put Connor facedown on the hard dirt floor of Reagan's quarters with he knee squarely in Connor's back. Having a black belt in tae kwon do and being a retired Navy SEAL did have its advantages at times.

"Translate this, Reagan, word for word." Rafe never took his eyes off Connor. "If you ever touch her again in anger, I'll rip your throat out and feed it to the dog. Tell him, Reagan. Now!" Rafe ordered.

After she told him what Rafe had said, Connor tried to turn his head to look at her. "You would like that, would you not? Have you become his woman, Rea? Would you whore with him while under my roof?"

"You bastard," Reagan said through gritted teeth. "Rafe, let him up. Get out, English, get out, and don't come back unless you have a medical need. I'll seek you out when I feel I can look at you without having the overpowering urge to surgically remove your privates and then cram them down your arrogant throat."

She was so angry that she was shaking, standing there with her fists balled at her sides.

Whatever Connor had said to her had angered her deeply, and Rafe didn't need to fully understand the language to know she was giving Connor an ass chewing. He had been on the receiving end enough in his life to get the gist.

Rafe placed a steady hand on her arm. "Rea, just leave it alone for now." Turning back to Connor, Rafe raised his hands in a gesture of surrender. "I know you don't understand, but you need to leave. I don't want to be on your shit list, and she needs time to cool off before you find she has made good on whatever threat she just delivered. Knowing her it's not pretty either."

Reagan translated, already much calmer and almost smiling.

Surprising them both, Connor threw his head back and laughed deeply as he dusted himself off. "Well, at least he has some respect for me, Reagan." Connor straightened up to full height. Turning his full attention to her, he stepped close enough to invade her personal space. She would be damned if she was going to back down. The challenge in him excited her somehow.

Connor's words were softly spoken, but the meaning was clear. "I will go for now, but we have unfinished business, Rea." Connor reached out and ran his index finger down the side of her face. She slapped his hand away.

His laugh was a warrior's amusement at the attempts of a lesser and already defeated opponent.

"We will talk in the morning at which time I will have the whole story from you. Do not, Reagan, think to avoid me." He smiled in a way that almost stole her breath. It was irreverent, it was knowing, and it held a hint of something she could not quite place. "In this, as in most things I desire, I will not be denied."

With that he softly pulled her to him, kissed her full on the mouth, let her go, and then left, leaving a shaken and troubled Reagan glowering after him.

Slamming the door, she mimicked his words. " 'I will not be denied.' Ahhhggg! It's always about him and what he wants! He's such an arrogant, pigheaded, frustrating man." She cursed in a combination of Gaelic and English as she threw the bolt home, locking the door behind him. What could she have been thinking? His arms may have felt good wrapped around her, but they were a disaster together.

"So"—Rafe paused—"that's Connor Holden. Not exactly the homecoming I expected you two to have." Rafe watched her leaning back against the door that she had not slammed but certainly had closed firmly.

"Why?" she asked, pushing herself off the door. "It's exactly what I would have expected from him. We have never gotten along. I don't see why now should be any different."

"Really? I thought you two were involved. You were in the stories."

That solicited a snort from her as she continued to tell Rafe exactly how the relationship was between them. She had come back to the table, taking the chair facing the fire, and Rafe sat in the seat facing the door.

He had learned his first lesson in Medieval Times 101: never leave your back to a door.

He had just gotten sloppy. Years of easy living had dulled the *soldier senses*. That would never happen twice. He was now in a very different world.

"He threatened to kill me the first day I came here," Reagan said as she began to unfold a square piece of linen cloth and sew small pockets and pouches into it. It would have to serve as her medical bag until she could get a new one.

"Well, we now have that in common as well," Rafe quipped, trying to lighten the mood, yet he wondered what Holden could have possibly been thinking to threaten her.

"Aye, it looks that way, doesn't it? Anyway, he told me the first day I arrived here if he found I had anything except honorable intentions for Morgan and her baby, he would save Nic the trouble and kill me himself."

Rafe whistled through his teeth. "Ohhh, bad move on his part, I'd have to say," Rafe said, seeing the scene in his mind, and the outcome wasn't pretty. "Mmmhh," he grunted, shaking his head.

68

"Needless to say, we're not exactly on good terms, as you have seen. We can't be in the same room without tempers flaring. He really is not a bad man. We just rub each other against the grain. It happens," she said with a shrug.

Reagan told Rafe about the fateful day she had first come to Featherstone. Morgan had just been through five days of pure hell at the hands of her uncle's lackey. She was six months pregnant with William, bleeding, and very close to losing the precious baby she and Nic had so desperately wanted.

Reagan had dared to come between Connor and Morgan in an effort to shield her friend from Connor's questioning of her lunatic uncle's capabilities.

Taking exception to her actions and to her lack of deference to him, he had pulled her aside and delivered his warning.

"What did you do?" Rafe asked as morbid curiosity got the better of him.

"I have only been driven to physical violence on a single occasion in my life. That was it." She would have slapped him a second time if she felt she could've gotten away with it, but even a man like Connor has his limits. "Besides, I see in retrospect he was just looking out for Nic." She shrugged her shoulders. "He can be charming and really is an honorable man when the mood suits him."

"So you really have agreed to something you don't want to do, and the reason you don't want to do it has absolutely nothing to do with your feelings for David, and everything to do with your relationship with Connor."

Reagan nodded. "You're right. I love David well enough. However, I won't settle this time for just being comfortable, Rafe. Don't get me wrong. I had a good marriage with my first husband. But if there's to be a next time, I want the whole package, and David isn't it. So, no, it's not about what I may or may not feel for David and everything to do with my feelings for Connor, the good, bad, and otherwise." She shrugged again, something Rafe saw she did a lot when talking about Connor.

"Tell me, Rea, what have you gotten into here?" Rafe was beginning to get an uneasy feeling. He had seen glimpses into something explosive between the two, and somehow he knew he was not going to like the answer Reagan was about to give him.

"I have promised I'll stay with him here at Featherstone for one year and a day."

"What were his stipulations, Reagan? Just how are you supposed to stay with him?"

"He didn't spell out specifics. As far as I'm concerned, as long as I'm here at Featherstone, it satisfies my part."

Rafe snorted at her naiveté. "Connor wants you, Reagan. I have no doubt he wants you, all of you. No man reacts this strongly unless there are potent feelings behind those actions. He'll never settle for the current arrangements any more than I'll let him use you."

She reached across the table and covered his forearm with her hand. "Rafe, please, don't put yourself in the middle of this mess. I appreciate the sentiment, really I do, but this is between me and Connor."

Rafe studied the Irishwoman for a moment. He could easily see Connor's obsession with her. By twentieth-century standards she would have been plump—there weren't nearly enough bones sticking out—but here in this time, she would be considered the ideal woman. She was beautiful in a lush and ripe sort of way. She was all womanly curves and soft flesh, clear, creamy skin, and thick, beautiful auburn hair.

There was also something deeper and just as lovely within her. Rafe's bet was her strong and independent spirit was the true attraction for Connor.

Sure the wrapping looked nice, but her strong spirit would most certainly call to a warrior like Holden. Even

Rafe felt her allure, but he knew she wasn't the woman for him, regardless of the fact he liked her immensely.

Rafe looked back at her. She was looking just a bit lost again, so he went without hesitation around the table and pulled her to him.

"Rea, I'm here if you need me. It looks like I have nowhere else to go for a while."

"Aye, McKinnon, it sure looks that way," she said as he kissed her on the top of her head.

# Chapter 10

Standing outside the door of Reagan's quarters, Connor was unable to make himself leave. She had come back. After all this time, she was home again.

His heart sung with uncustomary joy.

He had waited for her to come to the main keep, and when she had not, he made his way to the infirmary, fully expecting them to have at least a civil reunion. When he had seen the cozy little scene in her quarters, jealousy had sprung up, ugly and coarse.

He had no right to be jealous, but he was, and he had all but called her a whore.

"Poor form, Holden, very poor form," he said to himself as he softly tapped his head against the wall and closed his eyes tightly.

Feeling ashamed of his behavior, he had no idea how to correct such a grievous error. Deep down he knew she was a good woman, and the accusation of her behavior being anything other than pure had been most uncalled for. It seemed he was forever apologizing to her. He guessed she was right in that some things never seemed to change.

Just like her.

She did not look a day older. It had been five years, but she looked the same. She was just as beautiful as he remembered, perhaps even more so, for his wait had been long.

However, she had not come back alone. At least the man was a McKinnon, and surprisingly, he looked like an older version of Nic, which was some solace. He knew Reagan and Nic never had the slightest draw to each other sexually. Their relationship consisted of a mutually deep affection, but more like a brother and sister's affections for each other and not one bit romantic.

Connor continued to listen to the conversation going on behind the closed door. He wished he could understand all of what they were saying. He knew they were talking about him because from time to time he heard his name. He did understand a word here and there.

What did David have to do with her? Connor guessed Hale had seen her at Seabridge.

Knowing David had taken her leaving hard, Connor had no doubt the man would try to renew his relationship with her. That was not going to happen, not if he could help it. Reagan was still the heir of an earl. It was a secret Nic had sworn him to before William was born. Nevertheless, it was information that could not remain a secret forever. What was not a secret was David was the younger son of a lesser nobleman; therefore, he was well below her station. Besides, Reagan was his for one year and a day. Handfasting was no longer considered legal, but the agreement would stand. He had played a little dirty before with her and would do so again, no matter how bad it made him feel.

He was a man of great principles, but he would do whatever it took to keep her here with him. He had waited for her and would have waited for the rest of his life if it had been necessary. However, she was home, and so he would hold her to the bargain.

He had to have time to sort out what he was feeling for her, and her being here was the only way for that to happen.

Connor listened as silence greeted him from behind the closed door. His mind began going wild with the images of her soft and willing in the arms of this interloper.

Angry with himself for being angry with Reagan, he turned and went back to the main house before he did the McKinnon harm.

# Chapter 11

Connor's Solar
9:00 a.m.
April 21, 1499

Just as soon as he had heard the news of Reagan's return, Connor had sent out a messenger in the dead of the night to Nic and Morgan. No doubt by this evening he would have more houseguests. It had been several months since they last visited, and it would be good to see them.

Reagan would be pleased he'd sent word so quickly, and perhaps it would help smooth her hurt feelings. After what he'd said to her last night, a peace offering was probably also in order.

He would ask Morgan what he should get Reagan as a way to say he was sorry. He truly was contrite. He could tell he had hurt her simply from her reaction.

Connor had risen early after a fitful night's sleep and sent a message for Reagan to join him in his library. He had paced the floor, looked over the estate books, and paced some more.

Growing ever more impatient for Reagan and his other guest to make their appearance, he knew better than to seek her out. He was no fool. He was not going to invade her domain anytime soon. However, the longer he waited, the more ragged his emotions were becoming.

Unable to wait any longer, he turned from the window to seek her out. He stopped dead in his tracks. Standing in the doorway was the woman his heart had been waiting for all these years.

He had known he lusted for her. The kiss they had shared that day long ago on the cliffs still burned within him, but when had lust turned to love? In that instant he knew he was in love with this firebrand. He did not need a year and a day to figure out his feelings for her. He knew she was the woman for him.

*She is mine. She belongs with me.* The words seared inside his brain.

She excited and challenged him mentally and physically. Until this moment, Connor had not realized it was this woman he had been waiting for all his life. But how could he win her? He knew intuitively Reagan would not be won easily.

She was wearing the green dress she had worn at Morgan and Nic's wedding. Connor saw the color was perfect for her because it set off her creamy skin and beautiful deep-red hair. Her cinnamon-colored eyes were rich and warm. She was looking at him with an expression that was undeniable. She wanted him. Connor recognized it and reveled in it but too quickly the look was gone.

In its place was the cool, flat expression she had given him all those years ago. Connor had grown to hate that look. Today wasn't any different.

"Reagan, it is good to see you home again. Please, come, sit." He gestured to the leather chairs in front of the fireplace.

"Oh, you can do better than that, English. For goodness sake, you sound like you're giving orders to a dog. 'Come. Sit.' I'm surprised you didn't ask me to roll over and play dead as well," Reagan joked as she swept into the room.

"You do not need a weapon, Reagan. You have your shrew's sharp tongue to keep you safe," he said, and then he thought he saw a look of hurt in her eyes. Had she been jesting with him and he missed the intent? He thought so. "Forgive me. I believe I misconstrued your intent with that comment." Sighing, he continued. "Must we always bicker?" he asked with genuine concern.

Reagan quickly recovered. "It seems the safest course of action if being at the other end of the castle or in the twentieth century isn't an alternative," she quipped back with absolutely no sting in her words. She really did not want to fight with Connor. In spite of everything, she liked him and held him in high esteem. He could certainly be an ass, but he was still made of solid moral fiber.

Much to her surprise, Connor came to stand in front of her, taking her hand in his.

"Why is fighting the safest course of action?" His brow furrowed in question as he rubbed the pad of his thumb over the top of her hand. It sent warmth racing through her already heated blood.

The yelling, demanding, and overbearing Connor she could handle. This Connor threw her. This Connor made her want things that were forbidden. This Connor made her want him.

She sighed and looked straight at him. "Why? It's the safest course of action because Lord knows I wouldn't want to begin to like you." Then she winked at him.

She knew she already did. His efforts to save Cullen had shown her there was a fine man beneath the thorns and rough edges.

"You liking me would be a bad thing?" He brought her hand to his lips and lightly kissed her fingers.

"Disastrous and well you know it," she said, then slowly pulled her hand free. Walking to the set of chairs facing the fireplace, she sighed as she took a seat.

Its leather arms and seat were incredibly supple from years of use.

Connor looked at her as she sat there in his chair unconsciously caressing the arm with her long and supple fingers. Connor had noticed she did not have on a wimple, wearing her hair softly swept up with tendrils loose around her face and neckline. The style exposed her neck and upper shoulders, and Connor, standing behind her, could barely resist the urge to caress the back of her neck the way she was caressing his chair.

His fingers itched to feel her skin. Yet he did not dare. He knew he could not risk losing her, and right now any physical contact would send her fleeing to safety but only after she drew blood. His blood.

Through the years, he had figured out this woman's prickliness was her means of defense. He had tried not to take it personally, yet he was successful only part of the time. Nonetheless, he was determined to soften her shell and make what inroads he could.

Walking around to stand in front of her, Connor leaned his tall, well-muscled frame against the mantel. Reagan was having a hard time not seeing him as he had been in the painting hanging in the gallery of the hospital.

She was not unmoved by his good looks.

He was an Adonis, pure and simple. He was an incredibly good-looking man, and she was finding out she had desires no matter how hard she tried to deny them. Nevertheless, in her defense, she would have to be dead not to appreciate his physical attributes, and those attributes were plentiful.

When she had walked into the study, the sight of this warrior had stolen her breath. She had felt the same tightening in her stomach that she felt during those rare times when they were not at each other's throats, and being no maid, she recognized it for what it was.

Her body strongly reacted to him; the chemistry was undeniable. He had been standing with his back to her, and the view was sensational. With hands clasped behind his back and long, well-muscled legs tucked into riding boots, the view just got better from there.

He was just breathtaking.

"Reagan, you're not listening to me, are you?" Connor was grinning; her look had given her away.

"What? I'm sorry. I was… Never mind. You were saying?" she asked, bringing herself back to the conversation.

"I am asking if you feel that we can at least try to keep a civil tone with our discussion."

She began to feel uncomfortable with him standing over her, so she stood up and walked around to the back of the chair. Connor noticed the move and saw it for what it was. She had placed a barrier between them. He sighed heavily.

*This is going to be harder than I thought*, he confessed inwardly.

Resting her hands on the back of the chair, she looked at him squarely, brown eyes meeting blue. "Don't try to bait me. In return I'll try not to goad you. So, yes, I believe we can act like two adults. Talk, English. You seemed a bit impatient when I walked into your manly domain."

"Ah, your powers of observation do you credit, love. So, I shall get to the point. It seems too dangerous an endeavor to drag this out."

"Now whose powers of observations do you credit?" She teased him, and he was blown away at the way her smile totally changed her face from pretty to breathtakingly beautiful.

"Reagan, you look lovely, by the way. As I said the night of Nic and Morgan's wedding, that color does you justice."

She was so shocked by the unexpected compliment that all she could do was stare blankly at him.

"Well, at any rate, I do believe, now that you're back, we have arrangements to settle in regard to our agreement. May I assume you intend to uphold your end?" He had not moved.

Looking around, she noted his sanctuary. She had never been in there before with the exception of the first night she arrived at Featherstone. It had been dark that night, and all she did was open the door, never going through it. She had felt that had she done so she would have been tempting fate to sit and share a drink with the man who had threatened to kill her only hours before. The space fit his personality: orderly and tasteful, but not overdone.

Walking over to the bookshelves, she ran a finger past the very expensive and rare leather bindings yet did not pay attention to the titles. She was fighting the impulse to go to him.

*Oh, this isn't good*, she kept telling herself. *Move carefully. Just remember who you're dealing with here. One misstep and he'll have you*, she reminded herself.

She smiled at him again. "Things must have worked out between Nic and Morgan with another baby on the way. I won't leave, English, until the child is born—not after the stillborn birth. So, aye, I'll fulfill my end. I foolishly didn't ask for the terms before agreeing, but nonetheless, I will abide it. One year and a day here at Featherstone. Is that the payment?"

"Aye, those were my terms. You may move your things into the suite next to mine. It is ready for your arrival. You may continue to practice your craft out in the outbuilding, but you will no longer sleep there. You will be here at night."

"Nay," Reagan said flatly, then shook her head.

Her disappointment in Connor rose. Rafe was right about Connor's intentions. The idea that he would turn her into his mistress was beyond belief. Yet, she was angrier with herself.

Briefly, a feeling of excitement shot through her when he had said he wanted her close at night. The thought of Connor as a lover was almost sensory overload.

Her female intuition told her that Connor would be the kind of man who would totally dominate a woman in bed, and at the same time make her thank the Almighty he did.

He would leave no piece of flesh unbranded, demand total passion, give it tenfold in return, and be fearless about how and when he loved his woman. He was primal beneath that exterior of civility. If the trappings of polite society were stripped away, Connor would be pure unadulterated alpha male straight through to the molecular level.

"Nay," she said again.

"Aye, Reagan, you will. You understood what I was asking when you agreed. That was our agreement."

"Nay, it's not. You said, 'Stay with you here at Featherstone for one year and a day.' You never said to move into your quarters. If that's what you had in mind, you should have been more specific in your negotiations. I have every intention of fulfilling my end of this bargain, and I will stay for one year and a day, but you're too late to add or change the terms at this point."

His first instinct was to argue there had been no time to negotiate. He felt lucky to have gotten the time to seal the bargain at all. However, Connor was a seasoned soldier. He knew when to pick his battles, and he could tell this one was not going to be an easy victory. He had to concede this round to her and knew retreat was his only choice for the moment.

"Against my better judgment, you may stay in the infirmary, but the McKinnon man must not be there with you. It is not proper."

"Oh, please!" she said as she rolled her eyes. "You're such a hypocrite, Connor. You talk about me moving into your quarters so I can be convenient and then say it's not proper for Rafe to stay in the infirmary. Rafe stays with me. I stay in the infirmary. That's final, get used it."

Until Connor had said Rafe could not stay with her, she'd had plans on Rafe sleeping in the stronghold but not anymore. She would not give Connor that point in this game of wills.

"Reagan, do not push me," Connor warned, moving closer to her as he spoke. "I have waited for you to come home, and I am very glad you have, but I have come close to the king's wrath by refusing to marry the highborn ladies of his choice, all because we have an agreement. Now, you try to dictate to me what the terms are to be? And it is you, Reagan, who assume that my intentions are improper in having you move into the master wing. I would never think to compromise your reputation. I hope that you would already know that about me."

She could sense Connor's frustration.

They were at a stalemate and both knew it.

Softening, she placed a hand on his arm. "Would you just listen to us, English? How in God's name do you think we'll survive this week, much less a year, unless we are apart from each other's company? We are like gunpowder and flame." She drew in a deep breath and let out a long sigh. "I'll stay to honor my agreement with you, if for no other reason than Featherstone needs a physician, but let's not make this any harder than it has to be. And should you feel the need to accept one of the ladies offered up in marriage by your king, then feel free to accept. I shall not hold you to this bargain if you want to be free of it."

Connor was looking into the depths of her eyes, and for once she was unguarded. Somehow it hurt that she could so easily dismiss him. How could she be so unmoved when he was currently engaged in an internal battle that he was barely winning? He wanted to march over to the study door, throw the bolt, sweep the whole contents off his desk, grab her up, and place her across it, just to see how lush her body really was under that dress. Maybe his intentions weren't quite as moral as he would like to boast. Perhaps she knew him better than he knew himself.

Fearing that he just might prove her right, he leashed the animal by sheer willpower and stepped in front of her. Towering over her, he held her gently by the shoulders.

"Reagan, I hope I have to say this only once, so listen well. I shall not release you from this bargain, not today, not three hundred and sixty-five days from now or anything between, so do not ask. I shall not revoke this agreement, not for your sake, not for my sake, and certainly not for the sake of some father who has promised a duke for his spoiled twit of a daughter."

Connor was just barely resisting the urge to kiss her. She smelled like jasmine and felt like sunshine. Her mouth was full, and those moist, red lips beckoned him. It was going to be torture to be near her for a year and not be able to touch her, and he had no one to blame except himself. He had created a hell of his own making. Worst thing about it was she could still leave at the end of the year. Unless she agreed to marry him sooner. He would ask when the time felt right to do so.

"Do I make myself clear, lady?"

"Crystal clear. So, it would seem we're stuck for one year and what remains of this day, and we're at a stalemate. What shall we do about it, English? How shall we come to terms?"

Connor thought about it a moment before answering her, and she thought he was going to kiss her before he finally answered her question. Sliding his hands slowly down her arms, he clasped both her hands and brought them to his lips, kissing each in turn.

*She is mine. She belongs to me,* his inner voice demanded.

"Ever the negotiator," he said, dropping her hands after lingering over the kiss. Maybe an upfront approach was best. "Why not marry me, Reagan? It is inevitable, you know. You have but to say the word, and it will be done. I'm certain Henry would agree."

Reagan never missed a beat. "Aye, I'm sure it would be just that easy. I'm such a catch. And I see nothing to bar your way to having me as wife. But a girl really should have a little romance before diving off into such a commitment. Don't you agree? But in our case, we had best get right to it as I'm not getting any younger, and an heir is certainly desirable, aye?" she asked sweetly.

If Connor had not felt such a surge of happiness, he never would have missed the intended sarcasm.

"If it is romance the lady wishes, then romance she shall receive, but we need to have a few ground rules for this courtship."

"If that's how you choose to view it," Reagan said, feeling a slight bit of amusement as light laughter escaped her lips. *Courtship, indeed*, she thought.

He went to his desk and pulled out parchment and ink. He dated the document and then began to write. "Will you agree to dine with me each evening and share a game of chess or chance after?"

"Aye, I will dine with you, but never alone. And, in return, will you be willing to help me teach Rafe the rules of living in this time? It's the least we can do. He was the one who pulled me back. You knew that, right?"

Reagan watched as Connor wrote, assuming he was recording the terms of their "courtship" agreement. Seeing him there behind the desk, Reagan had to concede he cut a powerfully handsome figure. She drew in her breath when he unexpectedly looked up meeting her gaze.

Connor had felt her gaze boring into him. She was subconsciously sizing him up as a husband and as a man.

Could she trust him?

Did she dare let her guard down?

Was he friend or foe?

He knew what she was feeling and the inner turmoil she was experiencing. He had already gone through it himself with her. He knew where he stood and what he wanted from this relationship.

He wanted her, all of her.

*She is mine. She belongs to me,* his inner voice repeated. But, more importantly, she belonged with him, not just to him.

Connor nodded. "Aye, yes, I gathered it had to be so with your gift expended for Cullen's sake. For now, I will help Rafe, but you must, in turn, ride alone each morning with me. Also, will you be willing to translate for me? I would like to ask Rafe to teach me those maneuvers he did last night." Reagan looked at him suspiciously. Quickly, he held up his hands in a gesture of concession.

"I do not hold last night against him, love. In his mind he was protecting you from me. I must respect him for that as a man."

Reagan thought for a moment, carefully weighing his sincerity. "All right, I would be happy to translate, but in return you must allow him to teach me, too, and I want you to teach us both how to use a sword. He'll need to be able to defend himself."

The negotiations were going well in Reagan's mind. It was the first civil conversation they had had since her return. He did not answer her immediately. His hesitation did not bode well, but Reagan waited him out as he continued to write.

"Teach you weapons, huh? I must confess it goes against my better judgment to place a deadly weapon in your hands and turn my back to you." He smiled and Reagan felt her toes curl. His smile was a weapon all its own. No wonder Connor had women falling at his feet to do his bidding.

"All right," he said. "I will agree to let him train you in his warfare, and I shall train you both in mine, but you must do one more thing for me." Connor looked predatory and somehow smug.

Reagan didn't like the gleam in his eye. "And why, English, do I get the feeling I'm not going to like this?"

Had he cornered her, and she just did not see it coming?

"Oh, you might like it very much, if you only give me a chance." He knew *he* would enjoy it immensely.

*Oh, no*, she thought groaning internally.

He stood in front of her with only a few feet separating them. "I shall be discreet, but you will allow me to kiss you when and where I choose before I walk you back to your quarters each evening after we dine and have our game. I shall walk you back alone. That means no Rafe, no Marcus. I mean no one, and you will kiss me good night once we are there. I shall expect a real kiss, Reagan, not a chaste peck on the cheek from the woman with whom I am agreeing to give my name and to share all my worldly possessions. Those are my stipulations. Do you agree? Aye or nay."

He had trapped her. Rafe had to have the lessons or surely die. This was a time when no one could be left defenseless, but Connor was asking too much.

"Nay, Connor, I will not allow you to touch me after we dine or otherwise. You'll not walk me back alone, and I'll not kiss you, chaste peck or otherwise. It would not be proper and it would compromise my reputation. However, I will agree to everything up to that point."

"My stipulation is all or nothing. Therefore, if your answer is no, then we have nothing further to discuss in regard to Rafe's lessons. Good day, m'lady."

Bowing, he began to walk out of the room, leaving the document on his desk. He knew it was a gutsy move, walking away from the negotiation table. She could just as easily let him leave as concede. With her he never knew, but he had a feeling his odds were good. He felt sure she would concede.

"Wait, English. Wait," Reagan called after him before he could leave the study.

Connor stopped but did not turn around so he could hide his smile. He quickly removed it before turning to face her.

As she walked to the desk, she continued, "All right, English. You win this round." She had leaned over the desk and was signing the document Connor had been drawing up as they named the terms. "It's a small price to pay for his safety. But, Connor"—she walked toward him, her voice soft and dripping with honey—"you are oh... so... right... to hesitate to place a weapon in my hands." She walked up to him, framed his face with her hands and just before her lips touched his she veered to the right. She rested her lips lightly against his ear. "They say it is wise to keep your friends close and your enemies closer, English. I'm thinking ours will be a very close relationship," she whispered before walking out of the study door.

"I am to assume that you have read the document and you are satisfied with the terms, m'lady? I shall give you one final chance to rescind your agreement to my offer. Although I'm not sure why you would. It is a very generous one," he called after her as he picked up the document and smiled.

"Yes, English, we have a deal."

# Chapter 12

Just as Connor suspected, the carriages rolled up right after dark.

"Nic, Morgan, and the children by the sound of it," he said as the children's squeals and barking dogs disrupted a quiet but relaxed silence.

He, Rafe, and Reagan were in the main hall as it filled with children, dogs, and the Seventh Duke and Duchess of Seabridge.

The three stood in unison.

"Come! I'm so excited for you to meet them," Reagan said, quickly moving to the entry hall, dragging Rafe by the hand, and leaving Connor standing in the smaller private dining hall.

Morgan came first with arms open wide. "Oh, Reagan, thank the gods in heaven you have returned to me."

"It's so good to see you, all of you!" Reagan hugged her friend.

"You look wonderful, but look at me. I'm as big as an ox, and I'm not due for another two months. If it had been any other reason, Nic would never have let me come. It is fate you have returned at this point."

The women cried together. Even though it had only been a week since Reagan had seen her friends, the time seemed longer. The children were the most changed. Only babies the last time she had seen them, they were now five years old.

"Oh, my goodness, just look at the children. They're so big!" Reagan exclaimed.

Hanna was pulling at Morgan's sleeve. "Mamma, is this the lady who went to the future?"

"Aye, my sweet. She did, but she has come back home," Morgan patiently answered.

"Papa, did she bring you back, too?" Hanna asked Rafe, then looked back and forth between Rafe and Nic. It was apparent that she was confused at seeing two men who looked so much alike to her.

"Nic, Morgan, I would like for you to meet someone." Reagan pulled Rafe to her side. "Rafe McKinnon, meet Morgan and Nic, Duke and Duchess of Seabridge, your grandparents of who knows how many generations removed."

"Oh my, he does resemble Nic. It is *amazing*." Morgan's reply was not surprising.

"It is." Reagan nodded back at Morgan.

Patiently standing by as the women monopolized the conversation, Nic extended his hand to Rafe, and the two shook hands. Nic felt an instant connection to this man. Then he turned his attention back to the ladies.

"You two never met my older brother, Brandon. Rafe looks just like him. I'm pleased to meet you." Reagan translated this last for Rafe's benefit.

Rafe had slipped a little behind Reagan and had placed his arm around her back, resting his hand on her left shoulder. It was a gesture that did not go unnoticed by Nic. Looking past them, he saw Connor standing under the archway casually leaning against the wall.

Nic knew the stance of casual disregard was a farce. Nic understood his friend as thoroughly as he knew himself and could read between the lines. Connor wasn't happy to see this man touching his woman. It neither mattered that Rafe was a McKinnon, nor that Reagan had no idea she was Connor's woman.

Nic knew it was time to step in when Connor pushed himself off the wall and headed toward them.

"Connor, could we impose on you for a meal? We haven't eaten and the children have been driving me over the edge asking if we have arrived yet. I love my bairns. Still, I'm nay so sure I could have taken much more."

90

"Of course," Connor said as he stopped halfway. Then he turned to go back into the smaller dining hall, leading the way for everyone to follow. Nic caught up with him in two long strides, and Connor placed a welcoming arm around his shoulder.

"It is good to see you, Nic. Morgan looks wonderful. Motherhood agrees with her. And Reagan is correct. The children have grown a foot since last I saw them."

Hanna, managing to crawl onto Connor's back, gave him a tight hug and a kiss on his cheek.

"Hanna, love, you're choking me. Mind easing up just a wee bit there?" Connor asked patiently.

Morgan had taken Reagan's arm as they walked to the massive table. "Well, you must fill us in on everything that has taken place. I am near faint to hear about your trip, how Cullen is doing, and how Rafe has come to be with us."

"So am I," Connor's dry reply came under his breath as he plopped Hanna into a chair.

"I want the news of Cullen first." Nic was quick to request word of his brother.

Reagan looked to Rafe, interpreting the demand for news of Cullen.

"What shall I tell them, Rafe?" Reagan asked, pleading with him for guidance. She was still uncomfortable with not telling them the truth. Her arm was resting on the table, and Rafe placed a hand over hers and squeezed it gently.

"Tell them what makes you comfortable, Reagan. If you're not comfortable with what we discussed last night, then tell them the truth. However, keep in mind that reality will never give them closure."

"Well, they would never have had closure had we not returned," Reagan countered.

"Yes, you're right, but you have returned and to them five years have passed. They're waiting, Reagan. Tell them what you feel you need to, and I'll support your decision either way."

Reagan nodded before turning her attention back to the others at the table.

All were silently waiting.

Nic wondered what was between Reagan and this man from the future. He had the feeling Connor could possibly be in for some competition for Reagan's affections. *Not a good thing*, he thought, hoping it wasn't already too late for Connor.

Reagan took a deep breath and began. She told them what had transpired. "And thank you for everything," she said, looking back and forth between the two other men.

"You know we would have done everything possible, Reagan," Connor chimed in. "We wanted to keep you safe and save Cullen."

"Aye, Connor, and you were wildly successful," she said, giving him a soft and grateful look. She looked away, then turned to Nic. "Rafe did special surgery." Reagan was nodding her head as if to further affirm the statement. "With some of the best doctors in the world looking after him, we feel certain he'll survive. He's young and strong, and as Rafe said, most importantly, he's a McKinnon."

Reagan smiled, knowing that was going to be a decisive factor in his recovery. A lesser man wouldn't survive, but he was a McKinnon and they were not lesser men.

"It has been five years, Reagan. Is he not yet recovered?" Nic asked, confused about why it would take him so long to mend.

Reagan shook her head. "Nic, something went wrong when Rafe pulled us back. I was in the garden you're building at the site of the old shrine. I was disoriented, my power spent. I was so upset, grieving the loss of all of you and knowing I could never come home again. Rafe had followed me to be sure I would be all right. The crossing had been hard on me, and he wanted to be sure I didn't need medical attention."

She didn't want to tell how she had also seen Connor's ghost.

"While we were there, the portals unexpectedly opened and we were pulled back through. However, from my perspective, I only left a week ago. Five years have passed for you. I'm sorry, Nic, I can't tell you everything that has happened, but I do know Cullen was stable. It can be expected he will live."

Nic came around the table, knelt on one knee, and took her hand, brushing a kiss to her fingers.

"Reagan, thank you for everything you did to save him. We'll go on the guise he'll survive. Like Rafe said, he's a McKinnon." Giving her hand a little squeeze, he stood up and continued, "I'm well pleased with this news, and more so because you have been the one to deliver it. Welcome home, Reagan. You've been sorely missed the last five years, lass."

Nic pulled her to her feet and gave her a hug.

"Aye, welcome home," Connor added while raising his cup.

*So, I do have time on my side,* Connor thought. Reagan and Rafe had just recently met and did not have a long-standing relationship as he had first suspected. Placing his napkin down on the table, Connor continued, "So, when is Rafe leaving to go back?"

Nic shot Connor a look of warning. Miraculously, Reagan didn't rise to take the bait as Nic had expected. Both he and Morgan let out an audible sigh of relief.

Reagan did not notice, and she answered Connor's seemingly innocent question. "I do not have the answer to your question, English. It's so rare for anyone to have the gift and even more so a man. I don't know if anything has been written about it. He's the first man, as far as I know, to cross backwards. He may never be able to return, and I'll not push until he has had time to learn to control and harness the gift. His gift brought us back, Connor, not mine. So we're here until he masters the training and can call the gift correctly."

Connor looked into her beautiful brown eyes. The thought of her leaving again made him feel off center, and his reaction was honest and unvarnished.

"You belong in this time and with us. He can go back to the future or to hell for all I care, but you will not return to his time, Reagan. I forbid it."

Nic closed his eyes and knew there was no way to avoid the confrontation coming. It was imminent, as predictable as the winter storms.

Reagan slowly stood and laid her napkin on the table. Seductively, she walked to where Connor was sitting at the end of the table, completely unaware of the effect she was having on him.

Electricity filled the room, and she reminded Connor of a predator easing her way in for the kill. She was beautiful, and he thought she had never been more so.

Slowly, she moved behind him, and then she bent over his shoulder. Resting her hand on the table just to the side of his trencher and locking her arm, she leaned in, lightly pressing her breasts to his back.

She whispered the words into his right ear from behind. "You forbid it?"

Her voice was silky and seductive, sending shock waves through him.

To the others it looked as if she were delivering a message to a lover. As she moved to his left ear, she lightly blew on the back of his neck, raising the hair on his arms.

"My, my, my. You speak as if you actually have some say in any actions concerning me."

Standing back up, her tone changed completely. "Well, you had just better get it through your head, English, you don't own me. You're not my husband or my overlord. I owe you no fealty. I don't answer to you now, or ever, and if you think for one single moment I'll bow to your wishes just because you have spoken, you're very, very wrong. Your word, as far as my person, isn't law, not now and not one year from now. I'm here because I have this inexplicable drive to fulfill our bargain, but, mark my words, English, one year from today I will ride out of the front gates of this castle, and you'll not be able to stop me."

Turning to her friends with her carriage rigid, she said, "Nic, Morgan, it's so good to see you. We'll visit in the morning, but for now I wish you good night."

Reagan walked out with Rafe on her heels.

Connor stood to follow. Nic caught Connor's arm as he passed him on his way out the door.

"Nay, Connor. Let her go, my friend."

Nic's words were wise and Connor knew it, but, by God, she was magnificent. Her words should have angered him. Instead, the challenge she had issued excited him. She should think again if she thought he would let her walk away from him when the time came. If he could not stop her, then he would just see to it she never wanted to leave.

# Chapter 13

Reagan had stopped in the bailey. Rafe was not far behind. She waited for him to catch up.

"I'm sorry you had to see that, Rafe. You don't have to leave just because of me. Go, finish your supper."

"No," he said, shaking his head.

Rafe had felt the tension crackling between Connor and Reagan, and it was an uncomfortable feeling.

"Rea, I want you to think about leaving and going back to Hearthill Manor with Nic and Morgan. You need to get away before Connor hurts you."

Rafe was unsure if that hurt would be emotional or physical, but either way, it was on the horizon.

"I'll be fine. Besides, to leave just delays the day I'm free of the bargain. Better to stay and get it over with."

Reagan had mixed feelings about her decision as she looked back at the main keep. Leaving would be the smartest course of action, but her sense of duty and honor forbade it. If she were honest with herself, she would admit Connor excited her. He made her feel alive for the first time in years.

Rafe knew she wasn't exactly sure why she was staying. He thought perhaps it was because she felt obliged because she had given her word. Rafe understood the feeling, but he also knew there were times good intentions got a person killed.

"You don't have to honor this. What's at stake if you don't? It's not like anyone in this time would ever expect you to have honor." That, he remembered, was reserved for the men. "If I'm not mistaken, women were, or should I say are, just possessions. No one would think ill of you if you walked away, Reagan." *Especially those who understood these two*, he thought.

"I would think ill of me. I have my own code of honor, Rafe. Men aren't the only ones to possess it."

"As I'm beginning to see," Rafe said as he looked back at the castle with its warm light streaming through the expensive lead-glass windows.

"You may find it surprising the number of strong-willed and honorable women in this time. We have always been present throughout history and will continue to be. So, please, do not discount me."

The couple had reached the infirmary and were about to enter when she heard Connor calling her.

"Reagan, please, wait," Connor requested as he moved closer to the place where they stood.

Rafe gave her a questioning look as she stopped just outside the door. Reagan placed a hand on his arm. "Go on in, Rafe. It will be all right, really. I'll be in shortly."

"If you're sure about this, then fine, but call me if you need me. I'll be happy to lay him on his ass again."

Reagan laughed softly at the image until she saw Rafe's expression. He was deadly serious as he looked over her head at Connor.

"Really, it's fine, go on in." She slightly pushed him from behind, nudging him on.

Rafe gave Connor one last unmistakable look before reluctantly closing the door, leaving her outside with Connor. And, not to her surprise, her heart began to beat a little faster. He excited her, pure and simple. It was risky, she knew, to be alone with him. It was like feeding a lion by hand. Even though it can be done, it isn't safe to do nor is it wise. She knew their situation was dangerous, too.

"Reagan, please come back inside. Do not leave on my account. Nic and Morgan want to visit with you, and if it makes you more comfortable, I can go to my quarters."

That offer surprised her.

"Nay, Connor, I really do need to turn in for the evening. I'm still recovering from the trip from Seabridge."

She stood with her arms crossed, and Connor noticed the way they pushed her breasts up, rounding them above her bodice. His fingers itched to trace the rounded globes peaking over the top.

The silence hung between them. Taking the opportunity of the silence to decide his next move, Connor returned her look. Reagan studied him, trying to find some clue to what he was thinking. He had the best poker face she had ever seen.

"Very well then," he broke the silence. "I will collect my kiss before I leave you for the evening."

"Are you serious?" Her eyes grew wide with surprise that he would wish to kiss her after what had happened at dinner. Not exactly the kind of situation that inspires sensual overtures… Usually. But, Connor was an unusual man.

Connor would have heard the irony in her voice even if her eyes had not betrayed her. He realized that she found it amusing.

"Deadly," he spoke the single word, sending shivers of anticipation up her spine.

Reagan thought at least they agreed on that point. He was deadly to her sense of control where her carnal desires were concerned.

"I will kiss you goodnight, Reagan, as we agreed," Connor said, then stepped closer, expecting her to retreat. When she held her ground, he moved closer still.

Looking up at him, she felt the heat coming off his body in the crisp April air. He smelled of wine and leather, and like a pure unadulterated male in his prime.

*Ralph Lauren would make a mint if he could bottle that*, she thought.

Leaning in, he lightly traced his index finger from her temple to chin in the same way he had the previous night. However, tonight his touch felt different to her, less threatening somehow, more a lover's caress.

99

With his index finger curled under her chin, he lifted her face up slightly to receive his lips. It was the only physical contact between them. Tentatively, his lips touched hers. Their mouths joined briefly before he hesitantly pulled away.

She let her eyes flutter open and looked into his. She read his expression, and knew he was undecided about whether to go in for another taste. So was she. Reagan also knew she wanted to curl around him like a blanket, and fearing the way her body and mind were reacting, she stepped back.

"Good night, English."

"Good night, Reagan. I will see you in the morning for our ride," he said, giving her a polite nod of his head and kissing her fingers.

With a great deal of self-control, he turned, leaving her for the evening with the taste of her mouth still on his lips.

# Chapter 14

"Wake up m'lady. Come quickly!" Marcus called as he pounded loudly on her door.

Belting her robe, Reagan pulled open the door. "What is it, Marcus? What's happened?"

Her years as a doctor told her there was someone in need of medical attention. There was a level of stress that came across when another person was in a medical emergency. She felt it with Marcus.

"It's Connor. He's bleeding. Come quickly!"

She had not been asleep long when Marcus sounded the alarm. It would seem Connor's kiss affected her more than she cared to admit, and that caught her completely off guard. It was one small kiss, yet totally disarming. She tossed on her cot for hours after his leaving, and her yearning for more deeply concerned her.

After running to the keep, she was greeted by a sight that would have been comical had she taken the time to scrutinize the circumstances. However, Connor's well-being took precedence over humor.

Connor was sitting with Nic, Morgan, Hanna, and her dogs surrounding him. His hair was unbound around his shoulders, blood streaming down his forehead, and his once pristine white undershirt stained red. Reagan went immediately to Connor and applied pressure to his wound.

Looking around, she saw papers strewn everywhere, rugs bunched up, chairs overturned, and feathers still floated in the air, making his solar look like a hurricane had blown through. The guilty parties of this disaster were a wolfhound and a terrier. The terrier was lying over by the fireplace with his head on his outstretched paws. His little bushy eyebrows danced as he sheepishly cut his eyes this way and that. His cohort in this crime was sitting beside him acting innocent, completely unaware of how guilty he looked with a pillow, tattered and torn, still dangling from his massive jaws.

Hanna, trying desperately to run interference for her beloved animals, had her father by the hand, pleading their case.

"But, Papa, they didn't mean to. Goliath saw the mouse and had to protect me. David was just following him. I promise I will clean up Uncle Connor's solar chamber. I promise."

"Hanna, how many times have I told you not to let the dogs loose? If this continues, I'll make them sleep in the barn."

"Naaaaay! Please do not send them away from me. Please, Papa, please!"

"Hanna, I said if you didn't control them, I was going to send them out. I didn't say I was doing it this moment. It's Uncle Connor's decision whether they stay in his home after the awful way they have behaved. Look at this mess, Hanna," Nic said, looking around. He was frustrated but not angry, for many such disasters had already befallen the McKinnon household. It would seem no domicile was sacred to these two hellish hounds.

Hanna went to Connor. "Uncle Connor, I promise I'll keep them in my room, and I promise, I'll not let them get in the way, and I'll make your room look good as new. Please, don't send them out. Please."

Nic knew from experience Connor was doomed. Hanna had a way of getting under anyone's skin. She was his little darling, and he had never been able to say nay to her.

She wasn't a spoiled child, thank goodness, and hadn't used her ability to wind him around her finger intentionally to manipulate. If she had, he would not have allowed her behavior to continue, but she just had a way about her that sucked everyone in.

Still tending to Connor's cut, Reagan stood behind him observing.

Hanna walked to Connor, taking his hands in hers, pleading with a sad expression for forgiveness. The terrier's head was on his foot and the wolfhound's in his lap after leaving the fire place.

Connor pulled the little girl to him. Picking her up, he sat her in his lap.

Reagan was beginning to see Connor would probably make a wonderful father for some lucky lady's children. He was very tolerant of the youngsters.

"Hanna, sweetness, it's all right." He gave her a hug of reassurance and kissed the top of her head. "Do not worry. I know they did not intend to tear my solar apart." Lifting her out of his lap and setting her feet back on the floor, he gave her a gentle nudge toward the door. "Now, you go back to bed. It's late, but you will help me clean this mess up in the morning. Agreed?"

Hanna came back to him and threw her arms around his neck, giving him a wet kiss on the cheek. Cupping her hands around his ear, she whispered, "She's very pretty, Uncle."

Connor knew she was referring to Reagan. *The child is smart*, Connor thought as he looked into the face of this little angel.

"Aye, my little love, she is very," Connor agreed, winking as if it was their secret. "Now, go on back to bed."

Hanna turned to go, her beloved mongrels following. Rafe had been standing by the solar door where she came up to him and took his hand. Looking down into her eyes, Rafe envied Nic as a father. Yet he didn't.

Nic was rich for having such treasures in the form of his children. However, Rafe had seen the portrait. Knowing the beauty she was to become, he imagined Nic would have his hands full keeping the boys away.

Nic was going to give new definition to "beating the boys off." Forget the stick—Nic had a sword.

Rafe thought perhaps he should advise Nic to lock her away for the next twenty years. Life would be easier if he did.

Hanna pulled him out into the hall and proceeded to lead him farther into the castle and away from the study. On the way to the kitchen, which was to be her final destination, she looked up at Rafe. "Reagan is Connor's," she said.

He knew exactly what she meant.

# Chapter 15

Reagan got the cut to stop bleeding and was in the process of cleaning it. Nic and Morgan left the solar, returning to bed, after giving Connor reassurances the solar would be put to rights first thing the next morning.

Connor told them not to worry about it. He would have Hanna help him in the morning, agreeing with Nic that the little girl needed to take some responsibility for the fiasco.

Reagan wasted little time to move Connor closer to the fire for better light. He sat in one of the worn leather chairs.

The nights were still very cool even though it was April. The fire felt good to her, its warmth seeping into her robe and gown.

"I'm sorry that I don't have anything to dull the pain." She poured him a scotch and moved back to him. "I haven't had time to rebuild my stores of medicines. Drink this. It might help a little."

"Trust me, I don't need it. I'm drunk enough as it is. Just do what you need to do, and let me worry about the pain," he said, waiving away the cup.

"Have it your way then. But I still need to stitch you up. There's no way I'm leaving this cut open," she said. "It will scar as it stands. I guess that should humble you just a bit having a mar on your perfect face," Reagan teased him.

"So, you do find me perfect," he teased in response.

She retorted with a grunt. "A perfect pain in the... Well, never mind. How did you do this anyway?" she asked, leaving his request for validation of his perfection unanswered.

"I couldn't sleep. So, I came down here. I think the dogs must have followed. Although I'm not really sure how they got in. I do remember trying to get them out. That's when they got under my legs, which weren't very steady anyway."

"Ah," she said, finally seeing a clearer picture.

"I tripped and fell flat on my arse… I mean my back, just as a vase was falling from one of the pedestals over there. I think the vase is what hit me."

"Well, by the looks of all the pieces, the vase may have gotten the worst of the bargain."

"Are you insinuating that my head is the harder of the two?"

"I'm not *insinuating* anything. Your words, not mine."

"Just as I thought." He laughed again. "It's a good thing that my feelings aren't tender either."

"Well, tender feelings or not this has got to hurt. Fortunately, the wound isn't as bad as it looks. Head wounds bleed heavily." She continued to examine his scalp for any remaining shards of ceramic that might have gotten lodged there. "I think a half-dozen stitches or less should do the trick."

She worked quietly with only the crackling of the fire breaking the silence as she made final preparations to begin her stitching. Connor watched in fascination as she placed a small table next to her and laid out the things she needed.

"Where's your backpack?" Connor asked.

He was not too drunk to notice the pack she had never let get far from her was gone. She had replaced it with a piece of linen cut in a square with the ends brought together and tied in the middle with twine.

"Gone. I didn't have it with me when Rafe and I were pulled back. That's why I don't have any analgesic to deaden the pain."

"Oh," he said.

"Here goes," she warned. "You know, English, that was a nice thing you did for Hanna. She's really attached to the dogs."

She talked to distract him. She had found through the years this helped her patients during procedures that weren't necessarily critical, but were painful nonetheless.

"David and Goliath? Aye, she's attached," he said and nodded his head. "Ouch!"

"Sorry, but you have to keep still." She held his head on either side of his ears.

"All right, I got that one." He sat perfectly still even though the world was spinning.

"David and Goliath, huh? Now, that's an odd match to be sure. That's too funny when you think about it, but fitting. Please, tell me the terrier is David. I would hate to think the child has such a warped sense of humor at five."

"Actually, the terrier is Goliath."

"You jest!" She stopped stitching to look at him.

He looked up at her and saw her smile. "Nay, I may be drunk, but I do remember she said he has the heart of a giant. The mangy little cur has no idea he's as small as he is." Connor laughed softly, and the sexy sound shot through Reagan, caressing her deep in her core.

"Sometimes, such is the way of things," she said, still stitching. "If you don't believe you have limitations, then they do not exist. Hanna is a handful, is she not?"

"Aye, and growing more so by the year. I cannot help but love her. She is so full of life. I could fill your nights with stories of the things that little girl has gotten into, and I do not envy Nic. She will be an even bigger handful the older she gets. She will definitely need a man with a strong but loving hand, who will appreciate her for the wonder she is and will be."

"Well, she will be a beauty, and that alone will cause issues."

"It would seem that beautiful women are the bane of Nic's and my existence." He sighed dramatically, then placed his hands on her hips.

She wanted to tell him to remove them, but she didn't.

"Well, every man has his crosses to bear, I suppose. There. All done," she said and laid the needle aside.

He dropped his hands as she began putting on a salve.

"That was fast. Mind you, I'm not complaining. You're an angel of mercy, m'lady."

When she was finished with the ointment, he seized her hand and kissed it lightly.

"I guess for your sake you'd better be glad I'm not the angel of death, huh?"

Connor snorted a quick laugh.

She needed to complete her triage of her patient. "Are you feeling any dizziness, seeing double, light flashes, or headache?" she asked as she cleaned up and repacked her things.

"No."

"Any unusual feelings or sensations?"

Oh, aye, he was feeling sensations all right. With her this close, he was feeling a lot of sensation. She had been standing between his knees while stitching his head. He was sure she was unaware of her gaping robe. He had gotten a nice show of ample flesh silhouetted through her thin nightgown, back-lit by the fire, and he was having a hard time not reaching out and stroking her flesh. He indulged a little fantasy, and he could almost feel her in his hand as he brought her breast to his mouth to suck her pale pink nipple through the thin material.

"Hey, English, did you hear my question? Are you having any unusual sensations?"

Reagan's question snapped him back.

"Nay, I am fine. Just a little drunk is all. Reagan"—he paused—"I'm deeply sorry for what I said last night. Please, forgive me, love. I was out of line." He placed his hands on her hips.

She looked intently at his face. "Now, I *know* I'm not taking any chances. You took a blow to your head, and even as hard as that head may be, I'm very concerned. The

108

apology just confirms my suspicions. You have acute head trauma."

"You are a hard one, Irish." He grinned, knowing she was teasing him.

"Listen, Connor," she said while unconsciously tucking his hair behind his ears, "you know me well enough to know last night is water under the bridge. I don't have the temperament or the energy to waste on harboring ill will over a comment I know to be untrue. I have learned through the years that it doesn't matter what others think of me, but what does matter is what I think and know about myself. And you can safely bet that I'm harder on myself than any other human being could possibly ever be. Now, let me help you to your quarters, and then I'll see to it someone watches you through the night just to be on the safe side."

He dropped his hands to keep himself from pulling her into his lap.

"I'm fine, love. I'm sure the headache I'll have in the morning will have nothing to do with the dogs and everything to do with the empty decanter. Come morning, I might be hoping for the angel of death to swoop down and claim me."

He let her help him stand, knowing he could easily make his way by himself, but he was enjoying her pressing close to him in an effort to help him walk.

Making their way back up the stairs and to the room where he was sleeping, Reagan was struck by Connor's powerful build. He was still rock hard, even in his midthirties.

At six foot six he was a good ten inches taller, so she was little more than a minor stabilizing factor in helping him to his quarters. Once they reached the top of the stone staircase, Connor turned them down a hall and to the left.

"Here we are, m'lady. My bed awaits us." He made a grand sweeping gesture in the doorway.

Images of Connor's bed swept through her mind, and those images were anything but patient-doctor in nature. Irritated with herself, she shoved him into the room but left the door open.

"Come on, big guy, let's get you into bed. We need to make sure we keep your head elevated."

"Oh, I think as long as you're around, my head will remain erect. The good doctor will see to that."

"Connor, you're drunk; now behave, if that's at all possible." She was laughing with him and at him. At least he was not a nasty drunk, which was something to be grateful for to say the least. "Come on, work with me here, will you?"

Pushing him down onto the side of the bed, she began to try to undress him. He reached out, grabbing her by the hips, pulled her to him, and dragged her between his open legs. Her hands were forced to rest on his broad shoulders to steady herself and that allowed her to feel the iron-hard muscles as they worked to pull her to him.

"Mmm, you smell good. Can't place it," he said as he buried his face in her robe.

"It's called soap, English. Now, let me go. You're drunk and don't know what you're doing. Turn loose of me and give me your legs. I need to at least get your boots off."

"Oh, don't stop there." He wanted her to pull all his clothes off. He was hard and ready despite the liquor, and he wanted her. He wanted her naked and warm beneath him or on top of him. He didn't care which. He just wanted to be like his sword and sheathed to the hilt. He let her go reluctantly so she could pull his boots off, and with the task accomplished, she placed them on top of the footlocker at the end of the bed.

He was still sitting there on the side of the bed when she turned back around, and she just had to admit there most definitely had to be a God in heaven. Proof of that God sat there in the form of one of his best creations.

Connor had managed to pull off his shirt, and what it revealed was the mat of dark hair on his tan chest, dark nipples, and powerful pectoral and shoulder muscles. He was magnificent, and she was not unmoved by the sight.

What woman wouldn't be?

She would have to be dead and buried not to appreciate his physical appearance. However, it was unprofessional. She was a doctor, for Christ's sake, and he was her patient at the moment and drunk to boot. She didn't have the luxury of being a woman, no matter how delicious the prospect may be at the moment.

"Lie down, Connor," she said while pushing him over onto the pillows and pulling his long legs onto the bed. "You need to get some rest. It's getting very late."

He complied, much to her surprise.

"I will get Keegan to look in on you over the next couple of hours. He will need to wake you up each hour until I'm sure you aren't at risk of losing consciousness. Now, try to get some rest."

She fussed with getting the covers over him and looked one final time at his head before turning to leave.

Connor reached out and caught her wrist. "Will you stay and sleep beside me?" he asked.

As her eyes locked with his, she could almost swear he was sober enough to know what he was asking of her. She knew it was the liquor talking, and it hurt for some reason to know the request would never have come out of his mouth otherwise.

"Nay, English, that's out of the question." She knew it was just as well he was drunk and would not remember what he had asked for. She didn't want this to be another point of contention between them.

"Stay with me. Sleep next to me," he slurred, then drifted off into sleep. The hold on her slackened as he relaxed in slumber.

Reagan stood by the bed looking down on this man who aroused so many conflicting emotions within her. She leaned down and gave him a tender kiss on his forehead. "Good night, English."

She lingered a few more moments to be sure he was going to be fine before going to find his valet, Keegan.

She knew Connor was in good hands as she made her way back to her quarters. Through the very early morning mist, she heard the echo of his words.

*Stay with me. Sleep next to me.*

His request shook her. Her husband had been ill for several years before he passed away, and sex had been out of the question the last year of his disease. It had been two years since Dolan had died. So it had been longer than three years she had slept with a man. *Probably almost any man would do at this point*, she thought, trying hard to convince herself.

She saw Rafe was waiting up for her as she entered the infirmary. Instantly, she felt better with the familiar smells and surroundings soothing her wired nerves.

"Get him stitched up and settled in for the night?" Rafe asked in that easy way he had. He was sitting at the workbench identifying plants and learning their names. His thirst for knowledge almost matched her own.

"Yep, stitched up and tucked in. He took a pretty good blow to his head," she said, placing her linen bundle on the table. "He'll be fine, and I think his evaluation will be correct; his headache in the morning will be more from the drink than the blow. He was pretty wasted and is going to have a doozy of a hangover in the morning." She grinned.

Her reaction surprised Rafe. "I do believe you're gaining pleasure from the thought."

"Nay, but he sure has given me some good ammo to hurl back at him." She laughed even though she was tired.

"Ahh, I get it. All right then, I'll call it a night. I suggest you do the same. From the sound of what transpired, you have a major engagement to wage tomorrow with one unsuspecting knight."

"Good night, Rafe." Grinning at her friend, she closed the door to her room.

# Chapter 16

*Stay with me. Sleep next to me.*

Had he said that or did he dream it? Even if he did want her to stay, he was sure there was going to be hell to pay today if he had spoken the desire aloud.

Connor was thinking back over last night as he dressed. He wondered what Reagan's temperament would be like this morning. He was a bit foggy, but he did recall they had gone upstairs where she had put him to bed. They had parted on good terms. He was sure he'd passed out before he could do any real damage to his courtship prospects.

For now he would just follow her lead.

He entered the morning room to find it full of food, family, and two hounds from hell, who were behaving more like perfect angels than the demons from the night before.

Hanna sprang from her chair, bounding like a gazelle to him, excited with her news. Jumping into his arms, she had every faith he would catch her, which of course he did effortlessly, and was now holding her with one arm under her knobby little knees.

"Good morning, Uncle Connor," she said, kissing him on the cheek, arms thrown around his neck. "Aunt Reagan, Amanda, Mamma, and I have fixed your solar room just like new. I'm truly sorry about the jar. I couldn't fix that. I'll paint your picture instead. Mamma said I'll be a great painter someday."

"I am sure you will rival the greats one day, my little love. I thank you from the bottom of my heart, and I would lean over and kiss each of your fair hands for the effort, but I am afraid my head might explode if I do." Connor turned to his closest friend and then he put Hanna down. "Nic, would you please remind me of the way I am feeling right now the next time I try to drink a full jug by myself?"

"Are we feeling a bit rough this morning, brother?" Nic was grinning, completely unsympathetic to Connor's plight.

"Ahhh, you have no idea. God, now I remember why I stopped drinking like that years ago. It is definitely a young man's game." He rubbed his temples and squinted a bit at the bright early-morning light spilling through the large windows of the new wing he had built.

Rafe gave Connor a knowing look, remembering that hungover feeling from his college days. Not pleasant but not life threatening, either.

"It looks like we must forgo our ride this morning." Reagan was full of relief at the excuse fate had provided. She had a great "out" for the ride she had agreed to yesterday.

"Not so fast," Connor countered. He was not letting her off so easily. "I think the fresh air will do me good. I am not ill, just hungover."

"Let us come! Let us come! Please, Uncle Connor. Please, please, please!" Hanna had Connor by the hand and was not about to take nay for an answer. And how could he possibly deny her? She was just too adorable with her grin, which was currently missing two front teeth.

"How can I refuse? You may come if your mamma and papa say it is fine, but only if."

Connor had no intention of overstepping his boundaries with Morgan and Nic's oldest child. He knew she was, more times than not, in some trouble for her usual antics and unquestionably could be in the middle of a punishment, and most likely was.

Hanna looked at her mother.

"Mamma?"

"I think it would be fine, but do not dare let her out of your sight for even a second, Connor. I do not want her loose on a horse again, at least not any time soon." Morgan was very firm about this request.

"What happened?" Connor asked as he sat down in the vacant chair across from Reagan and Rafe. Filling his plate, he looked at Hanna. "Been on an adventure, I gather, young lady?"

"Oh, Uncle Connor, it was glorious, absolutely glorious! But I got into real trouble for it, so I guess I'm not supposed to say that, huh?"

Nic snorted, and Morgan let out an exasperated sigh, Reagan translated for Rafe's benefit, who was now grinning. William's eyes were wide, and Amanda was the one to answer Hanna's question.

"And when have you ever been silent?" she asked with a dramatic roll of her eyes.

Connor could not help laughing a deep belly laugh at the dynamic at the table. For the first time in his thirty-four years, he was wondering why he hadn't had a family before now. He had missed so much. He turned and looked at Reagan, who was unaware of his musings. Then in his mind he knew why he had not had that family. The right woman had just now come along.

# Chapter 17

After breakfast, Old Thomas, who was the groomsman, William, Amanda, Reagan, and Connor set out for the morning ride. Rafe had taken Hanna up in front of him at her insistence. The dogs were following, which no one was surprised to see.

They had left Nic and Morgan behind, and no sooner had the party left the bailey than Morgan was on Nic for answers.

"All right, Husband, spit it out. What is going on between our Reagan and Connor?"

"Leave it alone, Morgan. We are not getting into the middle of this one," Nic warned, knowing it was probably in vain.

"Into the middle of what, Nic? You know something. Now, out with it, McKinnon." Morgan was stood there with her arms folded over her rounding belly and with her eyes slightly narrowed.

Nic looked at his wife. He loved her madly, but he hated it when she called him McKinnon, knowing it was never a good sign. When she did, she was usually angry or so resolved he knew there was no fighting it.

"Niiiiiic?" Morgan drew his name out. "What has Connor done now? Reagan said something last night about having a desire to fulfill a bargain. What bargain?"

"One year and a day. He asked for one year and a day."

"A handfasting? What on earth for? When and why did she agree to that?"

"For us, that's why. She asked Connor for help in getting me to come to you the night before we came face-to-face with your uncle at Seabridge all those years ago."

"I'm listening." Morgan was remembering the morning after Nic had spent the night with her. She and Reagan had talked, and Morgan knew that Reagan had agreed to whatever Connor had wanted for his help. Nic did stay with Morgan through the night as was the agreement. Reagan had said she thought Connor was more jesting than not and the price would be minor. She was wrong.

"Well, his price was for her to stay at Featherstone for one year and a day," Nic said, leading her back into the morning room.

"Oh, my God! He does care! I knew it!" She was excited about the prospect of two people she loved dearly having feelings for each other. Then, sobering, she realized the ramifications of what that could possibly mean.

"Oh dear, they are like oil and water, Nic. Will they survive without killing each other?"

"I guess we'll have to see about that one. The night Connor came to me asking for my help, he knew she was leaving." Nic waved away the serving wench who was approaching the table. This was private.

"How could he have known that?" Morgan asked.

"He said it was just a feeling. He needed time to figure out what he felt for her. Knowing he could protect her but not command her, he was looking for a way to keep her close until he could sort out his feelings. It was a little sneaky when he did it, but he knew there was no other binding reason to have her stay."

Morgan wondered why he hadn't just asked Reagan to stay. "You know he might have been surprised."

Morgan's mind was working overtime. This had to be the promise that had kept King Henry at bay all these years. "Do you think Henry knows it's Reagan who Connor may have in mind for a bride?"

"Nay, I don't believe he does. But, aye, it would seem this is the promise keeping Henry wondering why Connor has not taken a wife."

120

"Would King Henry approve?" Morgan asked.

Nic did not see why not. She was the heir to the Earl of Rockport. Her uncle Evan died without issue, so she would be the sole heir even though her father had passed the title over to marry Reagan's mother. So, yes, he felt sure Henry would approve the match. She was of noble birth, so he saw no reason the king would not agree. Besides, Connor had asked Henry for the Rockport title and the earldom left vacant upon Evan Addison's death, and Connor had been conferred with it.

"Now, it's making sense to me." Morgan paused in thought. "Nic, Rea's sleeping out in the infirmary, and so is Rafe. What's between them, I wonder?"

"My guess by watching them is there's nothing more than friendship between them. I know Connor isn't happy about Rafe being here at Featherstone. He's even less happy about Rafe being in the infirmary, but he didn't win that argument with her. Connor knows he's on shaky ground with Reagan, so Rafe is an unknown element."

"What can we do, Nic?" Morgan asked, looking out the window at the party—now nothing more than a dot on the horizon.

"We do absolutely nothing. Nature will take its course, my love. We don't want to get caught in the crossfire, and you can rest assured there will be plenty of fire between those two. They'll either walk away, never looking back, or never let each other go."

Nic did not believe for one minute it would be halfway either direction.

Morgan knew he was right again, just as he always was.

# Chapter 18

Reagan and Rafe followed Connor, who was in the lead of the small group of riders with William, Amanda, and Thomas bringing up the rear. The dogs were dashing to and fro, flushing out a rabbit here and there and a grouse or two as they rode along. The beautiful and bright morning, so crisp and invigorating, was perfect for a ride.

Connor had a stable of which even the king was envious. All the mounts were excellent and well trained. Reagan was atop Gypsy, a red sorrel with a gleaming black mane and tail. Connor was on a massive black brute named Demon.

Demon once belonged to Morgan, and she had given Connor the horse as a gift for helping them destroy her uncle. It cost Nic six horses to reacquire Demon after he returned on the off chance he could buy him back. He was worth every one of those six horses too.

*The animal is absolutely magnificent and so is his rider*, Reagan thought.

As he rode ahead of her, she was able to see how well he controlled the massive horse. She watched his thighs gripping the side of the beast. His legs were well defined but not excessively so. He had let his hair grow since she had seen him last, and falling to the middle of his back, it was a lot longer than what was currently fashionable. She liked it and wished it weren't tied back with the leather thong. She had itched to run her fingers through his hair last night while she was stitching up his wound. She had not dared, which only served to whet her appetite.

Connor's hair was smooth, the kind most women would kill for, and it was still full even at his crown. The gray at his temples only enhanced his good looks, and she thought he was one of the most handsome men she had ever seen.

However, he was a duke, and the Lord in heaven only knew what other titles he possessed. She, on the other hand, was an Irish peasant. It did not matter that her father had been in line for an earldom. He had passed it over to his brother for the love of her mother. So, birth alone would preclude anything from happening between them. And that was only one of the reasons why she had not taken his proposal seriously.

King Henry would undoubtedly be growing impatient to have him marry, and it would never do for him to be involved with her, even if he had proposed, which was ludicrous even on the surface. She was surprised the king had not already insisted Connor marry for an increased power base or benefit to the crown. David had said that Henry was out of patience with Connor on the subject of his bachelorhood.

Marriage was used as a means of reward and to build or strengthen alliances, neither of which she could give Connor or his king. Besides, it was a rare occasion when they could be together and not have tempers flaring. They weren't meant to be anything other than exactly what they were, acquaintances.

He would see in time that she was right.

Her main reason for staying was to show him how wrong they were for each other and to deliver Morgan's baby. The quicker he realized that he needed to move on and take one of the highborn ladies the king had suggested, the better they all would be. It was foolish to look too closely or even encourage this feeling between them. The undercurrent was undeniable, and at times the sexual tension between them was strong. She was not naive and could recognize it for what it was. For her it was lust, pure and simple.

"There, I admit it," she said in a whisper. "I'm in lust with a capital *L*."

But, just like a riptide, that lust could quickly carry them way off course, and she needed to stay the course. She could still admire from a distance but never up close and never personal. The temptation would prove to be too much.

She knew getting closer would be deadly. Her body would betray her.

Turning her attention away from Connor and onto something safer, she looked at the children. Reagan marveled at how much they had changed since the last time she had seen them.

Hanna was a constant chatterbox, telling Rafe all about the area as if he understood every word she said. Rafe nodded just as if he did. He even answered back at times. Perhaps he did understand more than she realized.

William and Amanda, as always, were accommodating of their vivacious sister. Reagan watched them in fascination, studying the interplay between the three, who were growing up as triplets.

She remembered the day she delivered the girls. It had been a very cold day in late January, and it was not a joyous occasion. Sky Newton, their biological mother, was a widowed woman in one of the outlying villages of Featherstone.

Mrs. Newton had been malnourished and was grieving for the loss of her husband, who had died just before harvest the fall before the girls were born. The following day, Reagan had returned, suspecting the worst, and had indeed found her dead.

Bundling up the babies and heading back to the castle, Connor had intercepted her with the news that Morgan was in labor with William. She asked Connor to find a nurse while she went to oversee Morgan's delivery.

Unsuccessful in finding the wet nurse, Morgan realized the plight of the tiny little girls and insisted, in no uncertain terms, they be brought to her. The babies needed a mother to nurse them and a father to protect them. Morgan never once cared that they were of common stock.

So without qualms, Nic and Morgan adopted them, taking them as their own. They were bright and confident, having been brought up in a home so full of love and respect, and one that encouraged equality, regardless of the station one was born in life. That was a rare thing indeed.

~*****~

The trail widened, and Connor was glad when Reagan came abreast. He looked over at her, marveling at the way the morning sun gleamed off her hair. Reagan was looking at the way the sun shone off Connor's less than healthy pallor.

"Your color's a little off this morning, English. If you're not up to this, feel free to go back. Thomas and I can manage the children."

The offer was made in all sincerity. Connor knew she never joked where anyone's health was concerned.

"I have felt better, but it could be worse, I suppose."

"And I wonder why? Still wishing for the angel of death?" she teased, then smiled, giving him a sidelong glance.

"Hmm, yes, something like that," he agreed.

They continued to ride for a time in companionable silence, taking in the beauty of the morning.

"Can I assume," Connor asked, breaking their silence, "since you have not thrown daggers into me or threatened my person with the surgical removal of vital body parts that last night I managed to keep a civil tongue despite my inebriated state?"

126

"I just considered the source and went on," she said while glancing away with a shrug. She did not want him to see the color rising in her face. She felt flushed just thinking about the way his body looked and what he had said.

*Stay with me. Sleep next to me.*

Connor saw the flush under her skin and felt he knew the cause. So, he had said something to her last night. He had awakened naked, wondering if she had undressed him before putting him to bed. He felt sure she had not. It would have been hard to do it without his help. He remembered, after making it to the room, the blood loss and liquor had taken its toll. He knew he had been in no shape to help her although he did remember Reagan taking off his boots.

The second reason he felt she had not undressed him was the fact he would not have let her go. Drunk or not, he was a strong man with an ever-growing need to bed her. He knew she was not totally indifferent to him, so she too would have awakened naked this morning beside him. The thought was intriguingly erotic as his mind began to paint pictures of what he wanted to do with her. He was beginning to see the wisdom of her staying in the infirmary.

"Connor? Hello?" she said waving a hand at him. "My eyes are higher up. What were you just thinking about, or do I dare ask?" she asked with her eyes slightly widened.

She was wondering if his thoughts were heading down the same path as her own—a treacherous and rocky slope for sure.

"Do not ask," he commented dryly, then sighed heavily just before turning to her and giving her a smile that set her heart pounding. "That is unless you have plans on fulfilling those thoughts," he said as if the devil had returned in him. He knew better than to say something like that as he looked at her with one dark brow raised in silent question.

Her back was up instantly. "Just go find a willing wife, or whatever, and leave me out of this," she huffed, being much more exasperated with herself than Connor.

She was as prickly as a porcupine. He knew he was affecting her whether she liked it or not, and it warmed him to know she was not indifferent to him again. It lifted his spirits to see, as hard as she might try, he was getting under her skin.

"Cannot do that, I am afraid, love," he said while reaching over to tuck a dangling, wayward lock behind her ear. "I believe I have a bargain to fulfill, and as you once told me 'A promise is a promise.' Right?"

He was baiting her and he knew it.

"You know something, English?" she asked, narrowing her eyes.

"Hmm?" Connor felt her wrath coming and was having a hard time keeping a straight face. She was just so easy to stir up.

"I'm counting the days until I'm over and done with you and this bloody agreement," Reagan spat the words at him. Maybe it was not totally true but she wasn't about to let him know that.

He looked at her a moment, then raised a dark brow. "Would you care to place a wager on just how *over and done* you'll be come this time next year? You already belong here, Reagan. My money says you will not be able to leave." He threw the comment to her casually.

She knew he wasn't telling her anything she did not already know. The parting from Featherstone would be difficult even if she left today. She could just imagine the hardship it would cause her by staying another year. She had already come to love the people of Featherstone and was annoyed to know he was right. Admitting it to him, however, was not an option.

She shot him a look that would have withered a lesser man, but Connor was completely unaffected. He understood her. That understanding had finally come.

Then she smiled sweetly at him, batted her long auburn lashes, and he knew the challenge was on.

"Hey, English? Speaking of wagers, care to place one on who will still be breathing when we get back to the stables if we keep this up?"

"Ah, nothing like a fight to the death first thing in the morning to get a man's blood pumping. However, you are a woman, and it would not be a fair fight. So, in the interest of fair play and the fact I still possess some honor where you're concerned, I shall pass on that particular wager. However, care to place a wager on who beats whom back to the stables?" Connor was having just a little too much fun teasing her, and he knew he was stepping close to the line.

"I'll take that wager. I win, I leave," she said in triumph. He had opened the door, and she was damn sure going to capitalize by stepping through it.

Connor whipped around to look at her. How had he fallen for this? She was serious; he knew it, and he had to think fast. He knew her horse was swift. He had trained Gypsy himself, and Reagan was an excellent horsewoman. He was not feeling good and frankly, Demon never raced well against a filly, having a tendency to get distracted. He understood Demon's plight fully, but he could potentially lose this race if he didn't come up with something that would make her bow out.

"I will take that bet. And, Reagan, if I win, you sleep with me, in my bed, from tonight forward." Connor cocked his head, raising one eyebrow, confident she would back out. Such an arrangement would damage her reputation beyond repair. He was a cad to even suggest it, but it was just vulgar enough that she would have to back out.

"Nay, you win, I sleep with you for one night of my choosing, and I still leave once the babies are born."

"Nay, I win, you marry me in the chapel, today, and go nowhere, ever." *There, that should do it,* Connor thought.

"Well, that's no threat since you already proposed. Deal," she said with a wide smile.

She was off like a shot, leaving Connor behind to give instructions to Thomas. With a huge deficit now to recover, he was not sure how he was going to make up the gap. His heart pounded in time with the gallop, and with each bit of ground he was gaining, his heart was sinking, knowing Demon's speed would never be enough.

# Chapter 19

She was waiting for him at the stables. Leaning up against the corral, she had her slipper hooked to the bottom rung, arms resting on the top rail.

*Reagan is smug,* Connor thought as he came to a halt, *but she is so beautiful with her hair all windblown and wild.*

Reagan pushed off the railing. "All bargains, bets, and agreements are off, English. Now, I stay only for Morgan and her babies." She was smiling at him very pleasantly. "I'll let you know when I need your services." *And the way he looks that might be sooner than later,* she thought.

"All bets are off, you say? Then I am no longer honor bound to teach Rafe?" Connor asked, casually looking down on her from atop Demon, his arms crossed over the pummel.

Reagan's heart stopped in her chest and then dropped like a stone. She had not thought of Rafe's lessons. Connor was nonchalant in his demeanor but deadly serious. He would leave Rafe out in the cold if it suited his purposes.

She watched Connor dismount in one fluid movement.

"Nay, you're no longer bound, but it doesn't matter." She shrugged her shoulders to match his casual tone. "I will get Nic to do it. After all, Rafe is blood. You on the other hand are just—"

"Just what, Reagan?" Connor interrupted, his anger flaring. He was now standing in front of her, his arms pressed to either side of her on the railing. He had her trapped and was not about to let her escape until he had delivered his message. "Just Rafe's host, just allowing him to live in my home, eat my food, sleep with you."

"He's not sleeping with me, English. And even if he were, it shouldn't matter because I'm not sleeping with you either," she spat back.

Connor's anger was fueled by fear. He could lose her, and he was fighting back a feeling so intense it nearly choked him.

"I would be very careful were I you, Reagan," he said while narrowing his eyes. "You tread on shaky ground where Rafe is concerned. He is here by my good graces, and the only reason I tolerate him is the simple fact he brought you back to me. Do not make me change my mind about his being welcome in my home. I do not care if he's Nic's blood. I must look to my own first. And, keep in mind, as much as I love Nic, I owe Rafe nothing, not a damn thing, Reagan. Not a single, damn thing!"

For the first time, she was almost afraid of him. She could tell he was angrier than she had ever seen him. She had seen him frustrated, angry, and upset with her, but never like this. She had awakened something deadly in him.

"Now, princess, for your first lesson in combat. Never let your enemies see your fear." Connor felt her stiffen as he leaned in and placed his face into the crook of her neck, nibbling the tender flesh, and then he inhaled. "I can smell your fear, princess. I hate myself right now for making you feel this, but believe me when I say, you should never fear me. You are mine to protect, and I will do so with my very life. I promise no harm shall ever come to you from me, but that leads us to lesson number two."

Stepping back from her he continued. "Never let your enemies know your weakness. Rafe is a weakness for you. Now, princess, shall we renegotiate?"

"You bastard," she said, then drew back to strike him. Now, she was angrier than she had ever been barring the first day they had met.

Anticipating her move, he caught her wrist and drew it back behind her. He effortlessly pulled her into the full-length of his body. He pinned her there in an intimate embrace and was careful not to harm her. He could see the swiftly beating pulse at the base of her throat.

Coolly, he continued. "Hmm. What was it you said last night? I was drunk, but I still remember it. I believe it went something like this: you said that didn't care what others think of you. It was those things you know about yourself to be true that mattered?" Connor noted that Reagan was nodding her head in agreement.

"Aye, that's correct. So are you confirming or denying that you know you're a bastard?"

"Well, I have known for some time that I can be a cold bastard when it comes to protecting what is mine, so nothing new there, princess. However, what may be news to you, m'lady, is you are most certainly mine. Here are my terms: you will stay. You will uphold the terms previously agreed to with one minor adjustment. You will move into the suites next to my room and sleep there or Rafe is gone."

The gauntlet had been thrown down. Looking into the eyes of their foe, both knew it was a battle of wills. She realized he had won yesterday's battle after all, and she would be moving into the keep.

"There's a special hell for men like you, Englishman. It's called marriage. I pray you find a wife you adore, and she can't stand the sight of you. She'll leave you begging for her company and leave you wanting. You'll die a miserable old man with a portrait to hang in the memorial hospital, but nothing else to show for your life."

Connor had cooled considerably, regaining control. "You have made your feelings known. I shall take it under advisement. Move your things, Reagan. I will not ask a second time."

"You're such a royal ass, Connor! You didn't ask a first time, and if Rafe goes, I do, too." Struggling to get free, the threat fell on deaf ears.

"An idle threat and nothing more." Loosening his hold on her, he waved his hand in the air as if her comment was as insignificant as a buzzing fly. "You will have to do better than that. If you go, then someone else will have to deliver Morgan's precious baby. Who exactly would you trust to do that?"

The question hung between them as heavy as the silence.

"Ahh, see?" he asked, not expecting an answer. "Remember lesson number two, Reagan: weakness. And I know yours. Yet in your weakness lies your greatest strength."

Connor surprised her by leaning down and capturing her mouth with his, branding her, igniting her. Her body was treacherous and needy and opened to him. Without thinking, she kissed him back with as much abandon as he showed, matching his passion with her own. Pulling away, his voice was thick with desire. "Your heart is your fatal flaw, but I would have you no other way. Now, go move your things."

As Connor left, she was angry with herself for wanting more.

And when she deposited her belongings in the suite that Connor had made ready for her, she was surprised to find that Nic and Morgan had settled in next door into the room where Connor usually slept. Morgan had told her that Connor had taken other quarters so that she and Nic could have one of the better beds and Reagan would be close to her should the need arise.

"Now who's the royal ass?" Reagan asked softly, feeling exactly like one as she watched Morgan close the adjoining door.

# Chapter 20

June 19, 1499

Two months passed quickly, and with Morgan so close to term, it had taken very little persuasion to convince Nic to stay at Featherstone until she delivered the baby. It seemed logical to Nic and Morgan that they should stay rather than have Reagan come to them and risk her not making it in time for the birth. After the loss of their second biological child, they were taking no chances with the delivery of this baby.

Reagan remained silent even though she suspected they were having twins and the little boys would be healthy. After all, there could have been yet another stillborn child, or the other boy in the portrait could easily have been the next biological child born. However, she doubted a single birth simply from Morgan's size.

Reagan had been back nearly two months, and true to his word, Connor had begun teaching Rafe and her how to use a sword. Their lessons had gone well for the day, and they had moved on to the martial arts.

"Connor, you and Nic can pair up. Reagan, you and I will work together, so follow my lead," Rafe said. He then maneuvered her into position.

Nic joined in the training, wanting to learn this unique form of warfare, and Morgan was over her pouting at not being able to join in because of her pregnancy. An excellent swordswoman, she had been giving verbal instruction while Connor and Nic executed the physical maneuvers.

However, Nic was quick to forbid her any further action, and giving in with little fuss, Morgan knew he was right. Besides, in Reagan's mind, she was sluggish and awkward because she was due any day. Morgan satisfied herself with watching from the sidelines as the three big men practiced. At six foot three, Rafe did not meet Nic or Connor in size, but his quickness was miraculous.

Morgan had often dressed in men's clothes for training, so no one saw it as unusual for Reagan to be wearing a pair of Marcus's trousers. Her attire was distracting Connor. As a result, he was finding himself flat on the mats more times than he cared to count, and Nic took notice.

"Cullen gave me some good advice one time," Nic offered, extending his hand to Connor after he'd thrown him to the mat yet again. "He said, 'If you're going to train, then train. If you wish to daydream, go to the gardens.' I would think about that."

With everyone else speaking Gaelic more often than not, Rafe was coming along very smoothly in learning to speak it, almost as if he had been born to it. The training sessions turned into language lessons, enhancing his skill level. He no longer needed Reagan to translate.

Rafe turned to Connor. "Never give your opponent any advantage he can exploit. Never show him your weakness, Connor," Rafe said.

Reagan looked at Connor, who gave her a knowing little half smile. She turned away from him, but not before Rafe caught the exchange going on between them.

"Reagan is your weakness, Connor. Do not ever let your enemy see that, or you'll both be dead," he warned.

Rafe had revised his opinion of Connor over the last few weeks. Connor and Nic were good and honorable men. Connor had shown himself to be nothing except a gentleman in regard to Reagan, and Rafe, just like Nic and Morgan, was watching them closely.

Connor and Reagan were cordial to each other, except for the occasional skirmish, and usually after those times, there would be a peace offering waiting for her on the table in the infirmary.

The gifts had ranged from paints for her illustrated medical books to a new backpack, which was a fine piece of leather tooling, made specifically to carry her medicines. It had been delivered the day after Reagan had stitched him up and she had moved into the suites next to Nic and Morgan's.

Rafe believed those rooms had previously been Connor's, and he had taken other quarters for himself upon Nic and Morgan's arrival. Rafe was sure the only way Reagan would have moved into the main keep was for Morgan's sake. He could see no other reason she would have moved except to be closer to her. After all, her friend was in a high-risk pregnancy with two babies to carry and may need extra medical attention.

He had been assimilated into this group and felt genuine affection for everyone. The girls were a joy and William was exceptionally bright. Amanda had come out of her shell around him, and he found her to have a keen mind and a great sense of humor. She was just overshadowed by Hanna. That did not mean she was not an amazing child in her own right.

An easy camaraderie had developed between the three men, and Connor had warmed to him once he saw he was nothing more than a friend to Reagan. Connor had, on several occasions, invited him in for the game he and Reagan always played after dinner. Usually, it became a family night. On those occasions, he and Hanna would play a game or two of draughts. Rafe found he enjoyed this family time.

Reagan was right: simple things did bring great pleasure here. He would never have taken the time to have a leisurely game of chess to relax after a two-hour dinner, but then he was not expected to do 120 hours of rounds and surgery here either.

Over the last two months, his days had settled into a routine. He and Reagan would treat the sick coming to the infirmary, and then go out into the outlying areas for house calls. He was getting a taste of what it was like to have to stretch his knowledge. Without modern medical reference manuals, internet search engines, or tests to aid in diagnosis, he and Reagan would put their heads together to make the determination based solely on symptoms and information gleaned from interviews with the patients.

He held great respect for Reagan, and was beginning to see how brilliant a doctor and herbalist she really was, even by twentieth-century standards. Her ability with medicines was nothing short of miraculous, and he believed many of the medicines he used in the twentieth century had probably come directly from her research.

Rafe was feeling stronger than he had ever felt in his life. He had always been in good shape, but never had he had the training regimen Nic and Connor were putting him through on a daily basis. There were days when he wondered if they were intentionally trying to tear him apart by pushing him to almost superhuman limits.

The two men were incredible and confirmed just how huge a role good genetics played in developing the human body. He was starting to put on considerable mass while dropping the middle-age bulge he had developed over the last few years.

However, at thirty-nine, he knew he would never match the size of either of these two men. They had a lifetime of training behind them and carried themselves with an air of self-confidence and control Rafe had rarely seen.

Even Reagan was trimming up and developing a sleek athletic body he knew was driving Connor crazy. Rafe doubted it would be much longer before Connor snapped, no longer able to keep the tight leash of control with which he had managed to restrain himself. Self-discipline went only so far when it came to the affairs of the heart.

The tension between the two was intense, and he fully expected it would erupt any day. He just hoped he was nowhere around when it did.

# Chapter 21

10:30 p.m.
June 23, 1499

Connor sat across from Reagan at the game table. It was her move. He watched her as she carefully moved her chess piece, and he could not help but notice her lustrous hair and translucent skin.

Connor loved these times with her. He was able to be with her and not feel the usual tension and mistrust with which she often blanketed herself.

Their games were always very competitive, with neither giving an inch. Neither expected it, either.

"Ha! Check and mate! I got you tonight again." She stood up and did a little victory dance.

"So it would seem," he commented dryly before he set the board back up for another round. "Care for a rematch, and shall we make it interesting?"

He was looking at her with that half smile she had learned to be wary of when they played. She was beginning to know him well and had learned the hard way that this particular look always signaled a flank attack.

Her mood was upbeat, and with that being the case, she thought she would see where he was trying to go with this. Besides, she needed to practice her offensive. Sitting down, she leaned in, unaware the move had pushed the swell of her breasts up and over the top of the neckline of her gown.

"I'm listening, English, or shall I name the terms?"

Connor almost dropped the glass he was bringing to his lips. The look she gave him was one of pure sensuality. He felt the blood drain from one head and go straight to the other. In his opinion, she was playing with fire and she had no idea how close she was to driving him over the edge, which made it all the more alluring.

"Oh, by all means, let me hear your terms, princess. However, I must first place some boundaries on them. You may not change the terms of our original bargain. Those must never be touched. Agreed?" His voice was neutral, almost bored, belying the churning emotion he was feeling.

"Oh, of course. I wouldn't dream of it, English. Go on." Her voice was like silk running over his skin.

"And the wager cannot involve land, money, or any more of my horses," he added with an ironic smile and a definitive shake of his head.

Connor had fallen prey to her wagers on several occasions. He was now two minor estates, six purebred horses, and three thousand pounds a year for the next ten years lighter in the purse. At the rate she was increasing her skill coupled with her ability to distract him, she would soon be able to start her own stables, courtesy of the wealth she gained from their bets.

"All right, so no money, no land, and none of your stable stock. Fair enough," she said as she ran her hands through her hair.

"Very well. Your wager, m'lady?" He tipped his glass back and finished his drink, never taking his eyes off her.

She sat very still.

Connor saw the change in her as all merriment had left her face. "I win, you take me home to Ireland and we find what has become of Arlen O'Brian."

Not expecting this surprise, he drew back. Arlen O'Brian was a name Connor had not thought of in years— five years, to be exact, when he had passed the information that Reagan had given him to Henry.

"Reagan, it is dangerous business you ask."

"I understood it was dangerous business when I placed a king's bounty on his head," she snapped back, then took a

142

calming breath. "Connor, please, I need to know if the fates have been good to me and he's dead, or if he's still alive."

Connor countered. "How can he be a threat when he would have no way of knowing you have returned?"

"My being here can't be kept quiet forever, Connor. If he's alive, he could theoretically be a threat to me and those I love. Think of the children."

Connor could see that she was serious and deeply concerned, so he deduced a trip to Ireland would be in his near future.

"I need to know, Connor. Some days it eats me alive to think that I may be bringing danger into your home and to those I care about."

*She should not have had to ask me for this,* Connor thought. It was his duty as her provider and protector. He should have realized that she would have been concerned about those who were important to her. In that respect, they were alike.

"Reagan, this is not just my home, but your home as well. Nic, Rafe, and I are here to protect you, but I can see your point, so fair enough. But listen to me, Rea—I will go, but I will not take you back to Ireland. I will not have you anywhere close to him."

"But Ireland is my home, English."

Reagan felt deeply that Ireland being her home was no longer entirely true. Featherstone had come to mean a great deal to her; Connor had come to mean even more to her. That self-confession was liberating to her mind and heart.

"I won't take you as long as I'm unsure of the danger to you. However, I promise I will go and make sure he is never again a threat to you. Once he is eliminated, I will take you, but not until. That is the best you will get out of me for the moment."

"Thank you, Connor." Reagan took a deep breath, relieved of her fear. She was glad the request was out in the open. She reached across the game table and placed a hand on his arm. It was not often she voluntarily touched him, and when she did, it moved him in ways he would never have thought possible.

"And if I win?" Connor asked, cocking his head to the side, one dark brow raised in question.

Their eyes locked, each taking the measure of the opponent. Gently, she squeezed his forearm. He saw the same look she had given him the day in his study all those weeks ago.

"You'll come to me tonight," she said. Her voice slid over him, making him feel a desire unmatched by anything he had ever felt.

The seconds ticked by as each took the other's measure. She did not waver.

"You must be sure, Reagan. I play for keeps. I shall not let you win from some misguided sense of chivalry." His voice was hard-edged with the tight control he felt slipping.

"I'm banking on it, and I'm not asking you to, but I don't want to play chess," she said as she went to the sideboard and poured herself a drink, something he had never seen her do before tonight.

It was Connor's turn to feel the fingers of discomfort and doubt reach in and twist his gut.

"And what would be my lady's pleasure?" Connor asked but was not sure he wanted to know. She could be unpredictable at times, and he feared this was going to be one of those times.

"Swords," she said. *And seeing you gloriously naked in my bed.* She kept that intensely hot thought to herself as she downed half of her drink and turned around to face him. She leaned her hip casually against the sideboard.

"Nay, absolutely not." Connor slashed the air with his hand, giving finality to his words. "It is dangerous. You're no match for me in size or skill and I could unintentionally hurt you. It would not be a fair fight."

144

"Life's not fair, Connor. Swords or not at all. Those are my terms. Take 'em or leave 'em," she said as she walked back to the table and stood in front of him.

"Reagan, do not do this," Connor asked softly.

Again the silence hung between them, each waiting for the concession both knew would never come.

"Then I take it your answer is no?" Reagan did not know if she felt relief.

"My answer is a resounding no. As much as I am sure we would both thoroughly enjoy the spoils, I shall pass the wager."

She set her glass on the table in front of him. "Very well, then I will bid you good night. As always, I enjoyed our game, English." She stood looking down at him with a guarded expression.

"I will walk you to your room."

Connor stood up, feeling his years. He had just turned down a wager that would have satisfied his growing need for her, as well as placing him at an advantage. He felt sure if he ever got her in his bed and deepened their relationship, he would be able to convince her to stay of her own accord and not have to resort to the contract. However, his sense of honor dictated he pass on this one.

They walked to her quarters in silence. Staying true to their agreement, they would share a kiss in Connor's solar most nights. It was always rich and lingering. His kiss was full of passion and unspoken promises. There were nights they burned for each other. Yet never did they give in past the kiss. He never pushed, and she never asked, even though the evidence of their desire for each other was hard to hide.

The kiss she gave him outside her door was usually fleeting, but not tonight. Slowly, Connor pulled her into his embrace without a single word and held her.

She wondered how being in his arms could feel so right, and yet they be so wrong for each other. Maybe she was mistaken to think they were. She always felt so strong, so feminine, and so complete when she was with him. She sighed heavily as he ran his hands slowly down her back and rested his chin on top of her head.

Connor tightened his hold on her, afraid she was slipping from his grasp. He felt it at times, and the longer she stayed, the more it terrified him to think she would ever leave him. Sometimes he tried to imagine what it would be like to never feel her in his arms like this again: warm, relaxed, and tranquil. The thought was always unacceptable.

"You do not have to wager with me for your peace of mind and certainly not with your body. All you had to do was to ask, princess. I would do anything for you and I would have taken you anywhere. God help me, but it is true. I will take you anywhere. You have but to ask," he whispered against her temple, then kissed her there.

"As you, English."

Her softly spoken words sunk in and the enormity of the statement shook him. Connor dropped his head back and closed his eyes.

"I must be ten kinds of a fool," he said to himself.

He took both of her hands in his, kissed her knuckles, and looked into her eyes, knowing what she offered him. It was everything he desired and could not have.

"Nay, Reagan. Not like this. You want something from me, and I would not take the wager knowing I would have to lose to give it to you. And I will not take what you offered in that same wager but did not win. I want you. God, I do, but not like this." Pulling her to him, Connor felt the tears wetting his shirt. It was the only sign he had hurt her.

He held her and knew the moment she emotionally withdrew from him. As she erected walls to guard her heart and mind, she stiffened in his arms. He felt helpless to stop her from slipping away.

"Good night, English."

As she slipped out of his arms and closed the door, Connor felt he was losing her. She had somehow slipped away from him like the fog after the morning sun rises. He knew the fragile bridge they were building together had just been weakened and was now too dangerous to cross.

# Chapter 22

Making his way back to his solar, Connor cursed himself and his sense of honor.

After an hour of staring into the nonexistent fire, he finally realized that she wanted him, but her pride would not allow her to admit she wanted to give herself freely to him. She had made a wager she knew he couldn't possibly lose, but he hadn't accepted that wager. Yet, she had swallowed her pride to have him stay with her.

"May I join you?" Nic asked, breaking into Connor's thoughts.

Connor had not heard Nic walk in. "Suit yourself," he said. He was cranky and frustrated, both sexually and emotionally.

"Hey, I'm a guest, so don't take whatever is eating at you out on me." Nic held up the decanter. "Drink?"

"Help yourself. I have one," Connor held up the half-full glass of Scotch whisky. It was a fairly new malted barley drink derived from *uisage beatha* by Friar John Con and commissioned by the king in 1494. The bottle he had was one of the fifteen hundred made the next year and had been a gift from Henry. It was indeed *lively water*. And he pulled it out only for very special occasions or those times he needed to feel the burn. Reagan had assured him that it would become very popular if the Scots could begin to mass produce it. He and Nic had already discussed investing in a distillery. Reagan had a share when they did. Just one more wager she had won.

"Did you finish your game with Rea?" Nic asked, watching his friend closely.

"Aye." Connor was in no mood to discuss his *game* with her.

"The two of you are usually down here well past midnight. Who won tonight?" Nic had finished pouring his drink and came to sit in one of the two chairs in front of the fireplace. Both men sat comfortably slouched with their long legs stretched out and crossed at the ankles.

"She is getting very good. She has beaten me every night this week and three nights last. She is becoming a very rich woman at my expense."

Nic laughed, knowing the booty she had collected over the last two months.

"She has a brilliant mind, Nic. And the thing is, it really excites me, you know? Having a woman who challenges me mentally is way more desirable than just a beautiful face. I had no idea how much my life was lacking until that firebrand blew into my world."

"Women, or should I say certain women, certainly do change a man's perspective on things," Nic agreed.

"I am not sure what I will do if I cannot win her fairly and totally," Connor sighed heavily.

"And how do you know you haven't already won her?"

"Oh, trust me, Nic. If it were not for Morgan or Rafe, I think she would leave me in a heartbeat just to prove she was right all along."

"And what does she feel she's right about?" Nic asked while bringing the glass to his lips. He knew, but wanted to see if Connor would confess.

"She feels we are wrong for each other."

"And are you?" Nic continued to gently probe.

"Nay," Connor answered without any hesitation. "In fact, I think we are very right for each other." He acknowledged they could go at it like mortal enemies. Granted, he had never met a woman, or man for that matter, who could make him as mad as she could. "Nevertheless, when the dust settles, I still feel the same and have since the moment I realized on those cliffs at Seabridge I could lose her forever. I want her to be the mother of my children." Connor let his idea sink in for a moment. "I never thought I would say that about any woman. How do I know, Nic? I mean really *know* she is the one for all time?"

"Boggles the mind, doesn't it?" Nic asked, understanding fully what Connor was feeling. "I remember the first time I realized I was in love with Morgan. It was a defining moment. By the way, I have you to thank for that," Nic said, then lifted his glass in a silent toast of appreciation. "Do you remember what you told me the night she lay dying of the fever and blood loss?"

"I said a lot of things that night, Nic," Connor said, trying to remember that fateful night.

"You asked me when had I ever let anything belonging to me go without a fight."

Connor nodded. "Aye." He did remember.

Nic closed his eyes for a moment and remembered the helplessness he felt at watching Morgan so sick that they thought she might die. "I knew if I had to live without her I could, but I would just exist and not really live life. If you love Reagan, fight for her, Connor. She's an amazing woman and worth it."

Connor could not have agreed more. He knew she was amazing, bright, and beautiful. Sometimes when she looked at him, his breath caught in his chest.

"It scares me at times the intensity of my feelings for her."

Nic grunted, nodding in understanding. He felt the same way about Morgan and his children.

They sat in a comfortable silence for a while, neither breaking into the thoughts of the other. However, Nic watched Connor closely and knew something was bothering him.

"You wear the face of a guilty man, my friend. What have you done?" Nic asked.

"She signed a marriage contract with me. I sent it to Henry. As the daughter of an earl, her birth is noble enough. Henry has approved."

He had received the confirmation just that morning, delivered in private by the king's own personal messenger.

"Did she knowingly sign?" Nic asked. He was getting a bad feeling about this. He had deceived Morgan in much the same way, and it had nearly cost him the love of his life.

"At first, when I drafted it, I thought that she did. I asked her to marry me, and she agreed, even stating that we should begin right away to secure an heir. Now, I am not sure if what she did was simply in jest and that she signed it thinking it was the terms of her bargain with me. I feel terrible, but I swear to you, if I have to, I will use it to keep her here."

Connor was uncomfortable with the conversation. He knew he was wrong to continue to deceive her. It had not been his intention when he drafted the document. He actually felt that she was agreeing to his proposal, but the last few weeks had shown him that she was not in this relationship for the long run and that the courtship meant nothing to her. However, he would be damned if he would go back at this point. She was his wife and everything he wanted in his woman.

Connor got up and went to his desk, pulling out the document he had written the morning she had first come back. In retrospect, he realized that she had not read the document that she foolishly signed. She hadn't bothered. She trusted him. He definitely felt guilty about it, even if it wasn't intentional. He understood better than any man how she would react to such a deception and that was not the way he wanted to begin his married life with her.

He had kept a copy of the agreement and sent the original to the king that held their signatures. Legally they were husband and wife. He passed it to Nic, who scanned it quickly.

"Standard wording and no loopholes, I see. So you are just as bound to the agreement as Reagan."

"Well, that is usually the way a marriage works, Nic."

Unhappy and not bothering to hide it, Nic furiously handed the document back to Connor, who folded it and placed it into his breast pocket.

"Have you been with her yet?" Nic asked, his lips tightening with anger.

"No," Connor answered, but knew it was just a matter of time. They were on the brink of losing control. "I wanted to wait until it was official just in case Henry had other thoughts. I could not ruin her in that manner."

"Connor, you had better confess to her before you do. Take it from me, the longer you wait, the harder it will be, and the more damage control you'll have to do where she's concerned."

Connor had decided to have another drink. "Do not lecture me, Nic. I feel bad enough as it is, and I am fully aware of what I stand to lose here."

"Nay, I don't think you do!" Nic felt angry with Connor for the first time in years. The man was a fool if he thought this plan would not backfire in his face. It would not matter to Reagan that Connor had not set out initially to deceive her or that it was simply a miscommunication of his intentions and her acceptance. Standing, Nic faced his friend.

"What Morgan and I have is a rare gift. If you have the slightest chance of that with Reagan, you better not mess it up, Connor. You have no idea what true agony is until you have caused deep pain in the woman you love. You can't imagine how it feels to hear her say she wants to live away from you and you no longer have her in your life. I have lived with that feeling. I pray you never do. Don't go any further with this, Connor. Fight, but fight fair, or do not fight at all."

"Go to bed, Nic. I had a father. I do not need another one."

"Connor, don't be an idiot! Think about it. She's proud and strong willed. I have lived with two very strong-willed females for years. If nothing else, Morgan and Hanna have taught me that I'm wrong if I think I control my household and all who abide in it. I control my wife and daughter only because they allow me to do so without having to use a heavy hand. Reagan is not any different. If she thinks she's not in control, you're in for a very rough ride, my friend. You could lose her if you take the choice out of her hands; a choice she could make in your favor all on her own. I have seen the way she looks at you when she thinks no one else is watching. Just think about what I have said. That's all I'm asking. And don't dare hurt her. Otherwise, you'll have me and Rafe to answer to." With that, Nic left Connor standing alone to ponder his advice.

~*****~

Connor finished off his drink. *Do not hurt her,* Nic had warned. Even if it was the honorable action to take, he had hurt her by his gentle rejection. He had wounded her pride as a woman.

Nic was right. It did gnaw at him that he had caused her tears. This just may have been the first time his honor went against the right thing to do.

Rising, he left his study and found his feet planted in front of her chamber door. Indecision weighed on him. He needed to tell her he was sorry and to give her the choice in regard to the marriage. Divorce was not possible, but there could be other arrangements made. None that he liked, but it was not just about his feelings, not anymore. He needed to tell her what he had done and why. Perhaps they could come to terms. She liked him and he would be a good husband. Perhaps, given the truth, she would consider the match and stay of her own accord.

Reaching out, he tried the door. He did not know what he was going to do one way or the other. If the door were locked, would he wake her? If the door were unlocked, would he enter?

~*****~

The soft click of the latch pulled her up out of a light and fitful sleep. She kept her eyes closed, knowing who was in her room. He was by her bed. Or was it a dream?

"Reagan, love, before you speak, I've come to confess and to beg your forgiveness of my sin. I fear I have done you wrong."

"It's not usually a sin to desire someone," she said, never turning to look at him. "And certainly not a sin if you don't."

"But I do want you, Reagan, never doubt that, but I also want to win you fairly, not by wager or by deception. My sin against you is not one of the flesh, but one of the heart."

"You should not be here, Connor," she whispered, eyes still closed as if asleep.

"I know, love, but I could not stay away." He voice was a rough whisper. "Even if staying away is the honorable thing to do until I can claim you openly, I cannot leave you tonight. But if you want me to go after I say my peace, I will, but I need you to know how I feel."

Reagan knew that if he felt as she did, then there was no going back for either of them. Nevertheless, she had taken a sleeping potion and was not sure that he was even real. It would not be the first night she had burned with desire and prayed her desires would conjure him.

"Are you real, or just another dream haunting my nights and leaving me to burn with desire only to wake to an empty bed? Please, be real. Please, don't disappear... stay."

"Open your eyes, princess. You will see I am very real, and I very much want to stay."

He had come to sit beside her. She wanted to stretch out her hand to touch him, but touching him would make him more than just a ghost, and her heart could not take another rejection from him tonight. She ached for him.

Reaching out, he took her hand, lightly kissing the center of her wrist. Then running his tongue softly up the pad of her thumb, he took it into his mouth and gently sucked. She drew in her breath as it sent tiny shivers shooting through her.

"Let me love you, let me stay. Please, princess. I was wrong to leave you. What we share is so right. If you will have me for life, I want our agreement to stand. I want you with me now and always."

Opening her eyes, she looked into the face of the man she knew she had grown to love deeply and desperately. Her heart was lost to him, and her soul cried out to be with him.

"Stay with me. Sleep next to me. Always," she echoed his words of long ago.

"Aye." One small word, a whispered promise as his mouth claimed hers.

He pulled her toward him and removed her nightgown, then hugged her to his chest. Cupping her face, he kissed her deeply, passionately. Just like everything else between them, there could be no halfway.

Her nipples were sensitive as his shirt rubbed her naked flesh. Moaning, she pressed into him, feeling his shaft straining for release from his black leather riding pants. Reluctantly pulling away from her mouth, he untied his shirt, and as he began to remove it, she drew his hands away, finishing the task herself.

Gently, and with agonizing slowness, she ran her hands up his chest, lifting the fabric, kissing and licking the tanned flesh as she slowly exposed it to her view. She pulled his shirt over his head and found she could not breathe. This was like nothing she had ever hoped to feel. She placed her forehead on his chest in an effort to catch her breath.

"Breathe for me, Connor, for I cannot."

Her desperate plea shot through him, and he knew in that instant he would move heaven and earth to keep her with him. His mouth claimed hers once more, breathing life into her. Bringing her down onto the bed in one fluid motion, he flipped her beneath him. His weight felt heavenly, anchoring her to this earth as she cradled him in her thighs.

"Let me love you," he whispered huskily, his voice heavy with desire.

As he kissed her neck and mouth with butterfly kisses soft and fluttery, she felt herself falling.

"I have waited all my life for you."

That was all the encouragement he needed. Fate had brought them together again. If she had one wish, it would be to make time stand still for this one perfect moment. Slowly, he entered her, never taking his eyes off her beautiful face. He was drawing out the moment, almost as if he, too, wanted time to stand still. There would never be another first. Slowly, he filled her and held her close to his heart, savoring the feel of their bodies joined together. They fit perfectly as if nature had created two incomplete halves begging to be made perfect by becoming whole this night.

They were suspended, each giving and taking in equal measure. Deep and fulfilling emotions flowed through them one to the other, and the universe stilled. Chaos calmed, and dark turned to light. They lay there intertwined, silent, and still. The reverence of the moment was tangible with so many words still unspoken between them.

There would be time enough for those words, but not tonight. He lay there, his cheek to hers feeling the softness of her hair, breathing in the smell of her skin. Connor knew Nic was absolutely right. He could exist without her, just as he had until she had come into his life, but he could not really live without her in his life. He knew he wanted her now and forever.

"Stay with me, princess, tomorrow and always," he asked, looking deeply into eyes that were warm and full of desire.

"Love me tonight, Connor, and let tomorrow take care of itself." Cupping his face and pulling his mouth to hers, she silenced any further words.

And he loved her. And the world stood still for one enchanted moment in time. From this moment forward, they knew they would never be the same, having tasted true nirvana.

# Chapter 23

Reagan felt the bed move as he got up to leave. She didn't open her eyes as he dressed, but felt him silently, softly brush her hair away from her face as he leaned over to kiss her forehead.

"I have meetings that will take me through the late afternoon, but I would very much like to dine with you alone this evening. We have much to discuss, love."

Reagan nodded.

Rising, he went to the door, looked over his shoulder, and then he was gone.

She heard the door softly clicking closed as night was giving way to dawn's gray cool morning. Blissfully relaxed, she rolled over to get a few more moments of sleep before the day would demand her all.

~*****~

Reagan opened her eyes feeling joyfully content for the first time in years. It was then that she noticed a piece of parchment on the floor that must have fallen out of Connor's pocket in the night. Getting out of bed, she picked it up to see if it was something he might immediately need for his meetings.

It beckoned her, piqued her curiosity, then crushed her totally.

"What? It can't be," she whispered, standing naked in body and of heart as she read the documents, not believing her eyes. It was a marriage contract to the Countess of Rockport approved by the king.

Connor was married!

Her first reaction was to go seek him out and demand an explanation, but her humiliation was just too great.

The shame that would be cast upon her by the community would be devastating to her reputation as a woman and just as much to her reputation as a healer.

She reread it, and through silent tears, she did the only thing she could do. She vowed he would never touch her again.

# Chapter 24

June 24, 1499

Reagan dressed with the usual care she did every morning. The ritual was important to her, but never so important as today. She needed something familiar to help keep her world from spinning out of control.

Her shock at Connor's betrayal was burning and soul crushing. She had trusted him, and he had lied to her, blindsided her, and she had never seen it coming. More the fool she could never be.

She had fallen hard for him.

Reagan felt Connor had paid court to her, and he had checkmate on her. It had only been a game to him. Rafe had been right all along, and she should have listened to his counsel. Connor had used her in his sick little power game last night. She had let him into her bed, into her body, and, more critically, into her heart. She no longer could deny she loved him. He came to her bed knowing the king had approved his marriage to the countess, and the proof of that marriage had been on her bedroom floor.

Not only was she a fool for having fallen so effortlessly for him, but she had slept with a married man. She would be forgiven; she was sure. She had no prior knowledge of the marriage. Connor had entered her chamber with the full knowledge that he had a wife.

She was shocked and angry, but she found she was more disappointed in his actions. She really thought he was a man of honor. His actions seemed a polar opposite with what she had come to understand and know of him. Yet the proof was there in writing.

Reagan was not unfamiliar with the contract laws of the time. What Connor had given to his bride was more

161

than just his name. He had given her equality. It was something unheard of for this time in history, so for him to have done this, he must feel deeply for the countess. How could she possibly compete?

She should have felt dirty but did not. If this was all the taste of heaven she would know, then so be it, but she knew she could never allow it to happen again.

Looking in the polished mirror, she saw nothing to betray her broken and bleeding heart. The old nurse from Seabridge had said she possessed the strength of her grandmother. She needed that strength and would find more.

Taking in one last deep breath to shore herself up, she turned to face the day knowing her life would never be the same.

# Chapter 25

Passing Connor's rooms that Nic and Morgan shared, she saw Morgan pacing the floor in obvious discomfort.

"Morgan, it's time. You should have sent someone for me," Reagan said calmly, knowing Morgan was in full-blown labor by the noise she was making. By the look of things, she had been for most of the night.

"I did not want to disturb you and Connor." Morgan grinned, then grimaced as another labor pain overtook her.

Reagan blushed, knowing they had not made love in silence, but they had loved with total abandon several times throughout the night. It had been fun, passionate, mind-blowing sex.

Morgan continued to pace the chamber, holding her very extended belly. "Besides, I remember from the last time it took hours. I am still hours away."

"Does Nic know?" Reagan recovered quickly from her embarrassment and turned her attention back to what was more important than her wounded feelings. Morgan needed her to be focused.

"No. You remember how he was when William was born. I thought to save us some aggravation."

Another gripping contraction seized Morgan, doubling her over.

"Come on. Let us get you to my chambers."

Maneuvering Morgan to the bed, Reagan tried to make her comfortable and prepare her for the birth. Sending a maid to find Rafe, Reagan waited for him to arrive with the bag she had prepared especially for this birth. A knock sounded on the door, and then it swung open.

"May I come in, ladies?" Rafe brought the things Reagan had packed, plus a few he had tossed in for good measure. "How far along is she?" he asked as he placed the bundle on the table she had dragged over to the bed.

"A lot further than she thinks. She's eight centimeters and opening fast. No time for anything to help the pain, I'm afraid. I would say we should have our first arriving within the next quarter hour."

"Quarter hour! Nic is gone, Rafe. You have to find him!" Morgan begged.

Rafe left to do Morgan's bidding. How could he refuse when he knew how much Nic wanted to be here and how excited he was about this birth? Nic loved his children unconditionally, and Rafe knew he was already in love with these babies who had yet to make their way into the world.

Reagan calmly reassured Morgan that Nic would be along shortly.

"These little fellows are in a hurry," Reagan commented, knowing the births were imminent.

"Little fellows?" Morgan was not so dazed with pain to miss the implication.

"Aye, Morgan, you are going to have twin boys with blond hair like Cullen and hazel green eyes. And now I have said too much."

"Boys? How do you know?" Morgan was excited by the news Reagan had given her.

"I saw a portrait in the hospital of you and Nic and the children. You will go through this again at least once more."

"One more time? Boy or girl?"

"Nay, Morgan. I won't tell you. If you have another child that's not the sex of the one I saw, then you'll grieve for the loss knowing he or she wouldn't live to adulthood. To know in advance is to sorrow in advance."

Reagan thought that to know after the fact does not keep the sorrow at bay any less.

"Here he comes. Push hard, push!" Reagan said, knowing any moment the next McKinnon was to be born.

164

The baby boy arrived blond just as she predicted, a little small, which was not unexpected with multiple births.

"Don't worry about his head, it will straighten out," Reagan reassured Morgan, then brought the baby up so she could see him, knowing how important it would be for Morgan to see her child alive.

Reagan cut the cord, wiped the baby off, did the reflex check, and laid him beside Morgan on the bed surrounded by pillows.

Just as Morgan was contracting with the second baby, Nic burst through the doorway with Rafe only steps behind.

"Oh, God, I almost missed this," Nic said as he went to stand next to the bed. He took Morgan's hand and kissed it. "It won't be long now?"

Reagan nodded. Nic helped Morgan as she bore down to bring their child into the world. Reagan pulled the child free with a smile. "Look! He's perfect in every way. Nic you want to cut the cord?"

Nic cut the cord, and said, "I sever you from the life-giving body of your mother. From this point forward, you shall stand on your own, but never shall you be alone. You are a McKinnon."

Reagan cleaned the little boy and did a quick check, then handed him back to Nic. Holding his son, he wondered if he would ever get to the point he did not feel wonder at looking at his children. It was then he saw the bundle on the other side of his beloved duchess.

"Two?" Nic was in shock, his eyes wide and his smile wider. Many believed twins were bad luck, but he felt they were twice the blessing.

Reagan took the baby out of Nic's arms and handed him to Morgan for a brief look. "Aye, they are both beautiful boys: identical, whole, and healthy. Rafe, can you please look them over while I get Morgan comfortable? Make sure to tie the blue ribbon around this little one for second born." Reagan understood that it was critical to

165

identify who was the older boy in case the unthinkable happened with William. The line of succession had to be clear.

Connor had stayed out of the way, keeping Amanda, Hanna, and William occupied through the trauma of their mother's labor. Unlike the tragic birth of four years earlier, the children were old enough to know what was going on. Connor had kept them outside and entertained so they would not hear the pain she was in.

Nic opened the shutter on the window, leaned out, and yelled into the courtyard. "Boys! Two of them!" Then he whooped, and it echoed all around the courtyard.

Connor waved up to him in a salute of understanding as a bit of envy passed over his heart. If she wished it, he and Reagan would have children. He knew that he wanted to share children with her. He wanted to share everything life had to offer with her.

Reagan could not help smiling at Nic hanging out the tiny window. This was a joyous occasion, and much of the apprehension surrounding the birth had passed. Both boys were alive and healthy.

Reagan knew Morgan agonized in silence, fearing these two would not draw their first breath, just as their second son had not. Morgan had confided in her, saying she had felt good with her second pregnancy only to deliver stillborn. She had also told Reagan that the nurse gave her a sedative to help her with the labor. Through the haze she swore she heard a cry; however, the nurse had said the boy had not lived. The midwife told Nic the cord had tangled around the baby's neck during the birth, depriving him of air.

Making matters worse, in the commotion the midwife disappeared with the child's body. They searched high and low, but none knew of her. Morgan had been out of her mind with grief.

However, the joy filling their hearts today helped to dispel the doubt and despair they had felt for years.

Rafe carried the boys into the master chamber, and Nic gently placed his wife on the bed. Catching Reagan's eye as she stood in the doorway, he smiled tenderly at her. "Thank you for taking care of us."

She smiled back. Nic saw the gesture did not reach her eyes. Something was different about Reagan. He was sure it had everything to do with Connor.

Later, he would see if she wanted to talk about it. However, right this minute, he wanted nothing more than to spend a few quiet moments with his wife and children.

"Nic, I will leave you and Morgan alone for now. Call Rafe if you need anything. You are so lucky to have each other. Always take care of this love you share."

Feeling like an intruder, she softly closed the door to the chamber and left the couple to share this special moment and to appreciate the new life born from their love.

~*****~

Walking back to her room, her emotions were raw and tears formed that she could not quite control. She let them flow. Impatiently brushing the tears away from her face, she quickly packed her meager worldly possessions.

Picking up her medicine pack, she left the house and headed for the infirmary. There was no longer any need for her to stay in the stronghold, and somewhere between there and the infirmary she came to a decision. It was just divine providence the babies had come this morning, healthy and whole.

*Now, I have no reason to stay*, she told herself, knowing it was a lie.

Once inside the infirmary, Reagan jotted a quick note to Rafe and left it on his workbench where she knew he would eventually see it.

Standing in the main room surrounded by herbs and pots of medicine, she looked around, mentally saying goodbye to the little house she had come to think of as home. She felt her heart constrict. There were no goodbyes, no one to wish her well or beg her to stay. She was right back where she had been in the years after her parents and husband had died. She was alone and on her own once more.

It was breaking her heart to leave, but mounting Gypsy, she passed under the gates. As she passed under the portcullis and rode past the walls, her sense of security shattered as her heart pulled painfully in her chest. The chains binding it were securely anchored to the very foundation of this place.

Connor had won.

She conceded she would not have been able to leave at the end of the year.

What would she have been to him then?

Would she be his whore, his healer, or his greatest mistake?

So now, she was leaving, but her heart would stay behind with the people of Featherstone and with Connor. He may have won, but she was leaving on her own terms with her pride still somewhat in place.

However, her heart was no longer whole, and she certainly was not the same woman who had arrived here two months ago. She was stronger and wiser, but she wondered if that was really true.

Turning to the east and toward London, she left without a backward glance, knowing if she did look back, her resolve would crumble.

Tears began streaming down her cheeks, and she made no move to stop them. Her soul was bleeding. Battered and dying, her heart was breaking wide open with every step Gypsy took from Featherstone.

She would go to King Henry, and then she was going home to Ireland.

What could Arlen O'Brian possibly do to hurt her any worse than what Connor had already done?

# Chapter 26

Connor rifled through his desk. "Where did I put that bloody thing?" He wondered aloud, and the words echoed through the study.

Nic and Rafe opened the door just as he remembered he had put the letter from Henry in his pocket the night before.

*It must be up in Reagan's room*, he thought with a groan.

He stood in a near panic—he had to find the document. The contents of the letter needed to come from his lips. *I should have told her last night*, he thought, feeling quite panicked.

"I do not have time to talk right now. I need to go retrieve—"

Rafe hit Connor full in the face. "What the hell did you do to her, you bastard?" he demanded, catching him by the front of his shirt. His grip was iron hard from anger and concern.

Connor rubbed the back of his hand across his bloody lip, looking at the evidence that Rafe had solidly connected with his mouth. He barely resisted the urge to return the favor.

"I did nothing she did not agree to. Now, take your hands off me," Connor growled.

"She left sometime this morning, you asshole. You must have done something to drive her away. Tell me, damn you! What did you do to her?" Rafe shouted, angrier than he had ever been in his life. "I swear I will kill you with my bare hands if anything happens to her because of these sick little mind games you seem to be so fond of playing."

171

"It is not a game to me. It is deadly serious what is between me and the lady." Connor glared back.

Nic got in between them before any real violence could erupt. "Back off! Both of you! We are all on the same side here, and this is counterproductive. Every second you stand here arguing, the farther away she is from us." Nic turned to Connor. "She's gone, Connor."

Connor was stunned. "What do you mean *gone*? She was here this morning. I saw her not ten minutes ago going into the stable. She has on that ugly brown frock that she wears for birthing livestock."

"No, that was Millie you saw. Read this note she left for me and see for yourself. By the way, she left this for you." Rafe slapped the envelope, with Connor's name scrawled across the front into Connor's chest with more force than was necessary.

Connor stood in disbelief, his heart hammering in his chest, his mind failing to wrap around the implications of Reagan's words in the note to Rafe.

*Keep the reference books and medicines. I will not be back to get them.*

"She cannot be gone. There must be some mistake. I was just with her last night. I left her sleeping this morning, and we were fine. In fact we were more than fine."

Tearing into the makeshift envelope and digging out its contents, he let the empty envelope drop to the floor. Inside, Connor found two things. Both men recognized them as the marriage contract to the Countess of Rockport, complete with king's blessing and a note from Reagan.

*English,*
*It would seem a preeminent agreement*
*has been approved by your king which*
*supersedes our original agreement with each other.*
*Therefore, all bets, bargains, and deals*
*previously agreed to are off.*

172

*I do not care to renegotiate.*
*However, I will keep the horse as payment*
*for services rendered.*
*R.O.*

"Bloody hell." Connor pinched the bridge of his nose to fight the sinking feeling in his gut. Nic had been right. His feelings assaulted him—panic, dread, fear, guilt, and remorse flashed through him at lightning speed.

"What have I done? Christ, what have I done, Nic?"

"That's right, Connor, tell us so we all know. What exactly have you done?" The honey in Morgan's voice did not mask the anger or accusation hanging in the air.

All three sets of eyes turned to look upon the face of the Seventh Duchess of Seabridge.

# Chapter 27

"I married Reagan."

Connor was almost ashamed of the admission, yet he could not quite bring himself to be. He loved her, wanted her, and believed she was meant to be with him. Last night had proven how right it was. He knew marrying her was a selfish act, but one he felt necessary. And both of them had gained from it.

She brought a lot to the table as the Countess of Rockport. The earldom was rich and prosperous. She would make a good mate for him and a wonderful mother to his children. In turn, she had gained a powerful husband, well favored by the king, more wealth than she could ever imagine, safety, security of a well-fortified stronghold, and a husband who understood her need to heal others.

He had not wronged her. He had elevated her. She now had protection she would otherwise have never had. He was protecting her from all those who would have sought her for her title not caring about how wonderful a woman she was inside and out.

Morgan was livid. "You marry her, bed her, and she runs. How very interesting. Am I to gather you took lessons from Nic on the fine art of deceptively trapping a wife and then bedding her before she knows that you are legally wed?"

"I—"

"Be silent, Connor," Morgan commanded. Even in her weakened state after giving birth, she was still strong enough to walk into the room and face the man who had just destroyed her friend's heart. "Listen to me and listen well. This is what you are going to do. You are going to send out groups of men in every direction to find her. You will not go with any of them. You will instruct them to take her where she wants and for as long as she wants. You will not go after her, you will not demand she return, and you will not, *under any circumstances,* demand your rights as a husband before King Henry."

Stepping closer and towering over her, he replied through thin lips and gritted teeth, "Do not begin to think to dictate to me the terms of the search and return of my wife."

Connor had a great deal of respect for Morgan, but she was not going to run his life in the manner in which she ran Nic's.

Not batting an eye, Morgan faced his ire. "Although, at the moment, I do not think you deserve her, you will do as I say if you are to have a prayer in heaven, or hell for that matter, of ever winning her back. Mark my words, it will be a struggle. You have broken her faith and that," Morgan said, looking at Nic, "is never a good thing."

Rafe was close to violence. He was not normally a violent man, but the underhanded way in which Connor had trapped Reagan crossed the line as far as he was concerned. It did not matter to him that Connor had openly proposed and that Reagan had jokingly accepted. It should have been clearly spelled out, leaving nothing to chance.

"Nic, pick Morgan up and carry her back upstairs. It's too soon for her to be up. She can start moving around in the morning. You stay here with your wife. Marcus and I will go and assist in the search," Rafe said.

Rafe was nearly out the door when he looked back at Connor. "Holden, I advise you to stand clear of my path. When we find her, I won't discourage her, but you can bet I won't encourage her to return. Don't look to me as an ally, and you had better pray nothing happens to her because you do not want me as an enemy, either. I'm a man with nothing to lose. You would do well to remember that."

# Chapter 28

Rafe assisted the party heading west and thought they were making good time. The weather was holding, so there was little to keep them from catching her. Reagan's lead was several hours at best, so he felt sure she would be found if nothing had befallen her.

He had heard the horror stories all his life of the attack on Morgan and Nic along this same road, and how Morgan had very nearly lost her life. He shuddered to think of the terrible things that could happen to a woman traveling alone.

The party reached Seabridge on the evening of the fourth day. It had been over two months since Rafe had been here. David was waiting, having been forewarned by the gatekeeper that a band of riders was approaching bearing the standards of the Duke of Seabridge and Duke of Featherstone.

"Welcome back, Rafe. What brings you?" David asked, surprised at this unannounced visit.

Rafe looked around for Reagan. "Is she here?" he asked, bounding out of his saddle and handing the reins of his horse to the stable boy.

"Is who here?" David drew his brows together.

"Damn! If you have to ask, then she's not."

Rafe and his party had not seen any sign of Reagan along the way. He had finally come to the conclusion she had to have gone in a different direction, but he dared not double back for fear she would arrive by another route.

"Rafe, what's going on? It's Reagan, isn't it? Has she gone missing? Tell me, man!" All the color drained from David's face as the gravity of Reagan being gone began to sink in.

"Missing? No." Rafe shook his head. "Four days ago she walked out of Featherstone. Connor sent out parties in all directions. I felt sure she would come here. However, we saw absolutely no sign of her along the way, no eyewitnesses to her passing, not a single piece of evidence she came this way," Rafe said, stumbling over some of the words. However, David was having no trouble following Rafe's terribly accented dialogue.

"Then we'll return to Featherstone and see what news there is from the other parties. I cannot sit by if she's in trouble." David waved over the master-at-arms.

"We need to stay here in case she does show up. There's nothing we can do except wait for news from Nic. He said he would send a messenger every day. The first should arrive tomorrow."

David hesitated. "Very well, tomorrow. That's all I am giving you. Then we ride."

# Chapter 29

As Rafe's party had headed steadily westward, another party caught up with Reagan as she headed east. A messenger was dispatched back to Featherstone, giving them the news the Lady Reagan was safe and being escorted to London. Morgan and Nic both breathed a sigh of relief.

Connor immediately sent a messenger to London with a packet containing one communication to the king and a note to a trusted friend Ian Scott. A letter to Reagan contained his apology and his admission of his love for her. He then locked himself away in his study, rarely leaving for the next full week.

Nic knew the signs. Connor was getting business in order, so he could be gone for a while. However, Nic did not know if his friend was going to London or elsewhere. Connor had not confided in him, and Nic knew better than to ask. Everyone, including himself, had stayed away from Connor as much as possible. The man had been gruff, ill tempered, and withdrawn since Reagan had left him. Nic knew he was anxious to go after her but had taken Morgan's advice, leaving Reagan alone, at least thus far.

Nic doubted Connor would last much longer and was surprised at the restraint he had shown up to this point. Connor was not known for his patience.

Nic was not sure he could have been as restrained had he been in Connor's place and Morgan was the one who had left. He prayed he never had to find out. Nevertheless, she had been angry with him because he had known about the marriage, but it would take more than that for his love to leave him. Still, the cold shoulder she had given him was enough. Morgan was just beginning to speak to him again.

Connor was getting his affairs in order with meeting after meeting with stewards, masons, stable masters, the harvest foreman, his housekeeper, and finally his priest.

Connor leaned his elbows on the highly polished desk. Pressing his fingertips together, he looked at the man across from him. Father Francis had been his spiritual advisor for as long as he could remember, serving him and the people of Featherstone for nearly forty years.

"Father, I would ask for God's forgiveness, but somehow I think it would be hypocritical. I love her, and I am not sorry in the least. I am positive I could have handled things a bit differently, but I would not change the end result."

"Maybe, Connor, it is not God from whom you need to ask forgiveness? Have you considered that, my son?"

"Aye, I have, but what is done is done, and I have it from a good source I need to leave her alone for a while." He leaned back heavily in his chair with an exasperated sigh.

Father Francis smiled to himself. "What does your heart say?"

The question was spoken in the same calm voice Connor had remembered since childhood. The only time Connor ever remembered Father Francis being anything except his ever-present calm self was the morning he had been summoned to Morgan's deathbed. She had been close to dying, unconscious from fever and blood loss, and dressed in men's clothing.

When Nic had asked the father to marry them, he balked, citing the church did not ordain such debauchery, thinking she was a boy. He regained his composure only after Connor had threatened to replace him. Well, that and the fact Nic had produced the necessary documents signed by none other than the king himself.

"What does my heart tell me? Run to her as fast as I can," Connor answered honestly.

"Then might I suggest you do so, and when you do, ask forgiveness, and then let her go if that's still her desire."

"No. Absolutely not."

It was spoken with such authority that the father believed without a doubt that Connor meant it.

Connor thought that would not happen today or ever. She was his wife, and she had to come to terms with the situation. As her husband, he was her protector and he would not allow his wife to be out there vulnerable and alone.

Thoughts of Reagan fending off others' advances made him uneasy until he thought perhaps she would welcome them. He was instantly filled with a rage so acute it burned. After the night they had shared, he was sure they were meant to be together. No man would ever come between them. No man would touch her and live.

"Listen to me, my son. You know I speak true. As it stands, she's lost to you either way. Give her the choice. Let her follow her heart, not the laws of man."

"So, I am to go to her, say my peace, and then walk away, just like that?" Connor asked, snapping his fingers and trying to keep his voice to a normal volume, yet he was having little success.

"Aye, just like that. God gave his only son as a sacrifice to us as sinners. You have only to sacrifice your heart. It may well be the price of your deception, Connor."

"My heart is of no consequence, but turning my back on my lady is a high price, and one I am not prepared to concede. She is a woman and needs my protection. Besides, we do not know what danger she will face if Arlen O'Brian is still alive. We must look at him as a threat to her until we can learn if he lives or not."

"Then you must find your answers, Connor. If O'Brian lives, you must eliminate him." The father was deadly serious in his advice to the younger man.

"Strong words coming from a priest."

"And it comes from a man who cares for you and who understands the need to protect his own. You may find it hard to believe, but I have not always been a man of the cloth, Connor. If we know O'Brian would harm your lady, then I think God understands, and if He does not, then we will burn together for the action. I would not allow you to burn alone for it."

"And what if I should find O'Brian has gone and met his Almighty maker? What then?" Connor asked, already knowing what the priest would say.

"If he's dead, then you must allow her to make her choice and prepare for the outcome, for I know you, young man, and you will not give up easily. I have seen you born, grow, and develop into a fine and honorable man. However, Connor, I have to say this may prove to be your greatest mistake. This deception is a grave sin against Lady Reagan. You must give her space or surely lose her for all time."

"Somehow, I knew you would say that," he said and sighed.

"Remember, Connor, pride goes before a fall. Just think on what we have talked about. God will guide you when you need it. Just make sure to listen to that guidance when He does."

# Chapter 30

The King's Outer Chambers
London
July 6, 1499

Reagan had been in London for eight days, and thus far the king had not granted her an audience. He was holding council and was not to be bothered, his chamberlain had told her.

Each day after she requested an audience, she waited for hours only to be turned away. She was not going anywhere; she was prepared to stay as long as it took. Where else did she have to go? For whatever reason, the king had put her up in nice quarters made complete with a small staff to meet her needs.

Late in the afternoon of the eighth day, she had been waiting as she had the previous seven when the door to the outer chamber swung open, and a gentleman she had not seen before came out meandering his way to where she sat patiently waiting. He looked at her as if she were a blight, a thing to avoid and despise.

"Madame, His Majesty will see you now. He has granted you five minutes of his time. I suggest you not waste it. This way, please."

Reagan concluded the gentleman did not like her—the dislike radiating off him like heat waves from a fire. Yet she knew she had never met him. However, before she could ponder the issue further, she found herself in the presence of Henry VII, king of England.

"Kneel, you stupid woman!" The hiss came from the man who had escorted her in. Standing in the royal court, she did not know exactly what to do. He was not her king, yet he was a person of importance. He deserved respect for the sheer reason he was someone's king.

Henry's voice was pleasant, deep, and smooth. "So… It has come to my attention you have waited for the last eight days to speak to me. Thus, can I gather your business is of some importance?"

"I would hope, Your Majesty, anyone taking up the time of a king would only come for business that is important." Reagan kept her head high.

"One would think, yes. However, you might be surprised," Henry replied, thinking of all the hours of his life that he would never get back from dealing with issues he never should have heard.

"Then, again," she said, as if reading his thoughts, "I might not be so surprised that there are those who would waste your time. It's all a matter of perspective as to what is important and to whom. Is that not correct, Your Majesty?"

She heard the gasps from the court, but Henry gave her a small half grin in answer. That gave her courage to continue.

"I have come about a matter that's of some years past but may still be an issue. I have come about a little problem in Ireland." She hoped it would be enough to jog his memory. There were too many ears in the room.

Henry looked at her for a split second, then snapped his fingers, barking his command, "Clear the room!"

Immediately the onlookers filed out, leaving only the man who had brought her into the room and the scribe who was there to take the notes of every meeting.

"You two go." Henry addressed the two remaining men.

Her unknown enemy had stepped forward, noticeably uncomfortable with the command. "But, Your Majesty, I will not leave you alone with this woman. We do not know her. She could mean you harm. I beg you, sire, do not be pulled in by a pretty face. You're not Edward!"

Henry was furious. "Nay, I am not Edward and you insult me, Lord Weston, if you think I am so easily swayed by beauty even if it is unique. Go! Leave us before I lose my good cheer for you and send you to the north of Scotland to do my bidding."

Reagan didn't miss the look this Lord Weston gave her as he grudgingly left the room. Chills scampered down her spine; he was now an enemy.

Henry addressed her once the room cleared. "So, you are Lady Reagan."

Henry was leaning forward, measuring her while resting his bejeweled hand loosely on the arm of his massive throne. She felt him sizing her up. She could see why he was well loved by his people—he was an honorable man. The respect he received from his subjects was given because of the man he was, not because he was king.

*Although it probably doesn't hurt to be king,* she thought.

Henry sat back in his chair, crossing his left calf over his right thigh. He balled his fist up under his chin, and she watched as his index finger lightly tapped his lips.

"What do you feel you can bring to me, Reagan O'Riley?"

"I'm returning to Ireland, sir. I propose I help to flush Arlen O'Brian out if he's still a problem for you."

Henry raised a dark brow. "He most likely would love to string you up, madam. After all, you did place a king's bounty on his head because of the information you provided to me five years ago."

"I was useful to you before, and I could help to draw him out now if that's something you wish done."

She was standing there as fearless as any warrior he had ever seen. Yet Henry knew she was shaking inside. He was a master at reading people, and he could readily see she was neither in awe of him or his power, nor was she nervous in his presence. She was terrified at the prospect of placing herself into the arms of her enemy. She would be like a lamb led to the slaughter, and she intrigued him with her mantle of determination to place herself in harm's way as bait.

Furthermore, she was absolutely correct that the information she had shared had proven useful in rounding up several treasonous Englishman who were now his permanent guests in the White Tower of London. It had also served to place a large enough bounty on the head of the Irish ringleader to drive him well underground.

Henry knew there was only so much honor among thieves where money was concerned, and eventually someone would confess O'Brian's whereabouts. Nevertheless, in the meantime, the outlaw and thief was raising hell in Ireland at his expense.

"And what does Lord Holden say to this, Lady Reagan?" Henry had to know if Connor was aware of the plan that his bride had just placed into motion.

Reagan huffed. Why did every man think that every woman needed a man to think for her?

"Holden? He has nothing to say in anything I do, Your Majesty. He's English. I'm Irish. No disrespect intended, but as far as I can tell, no Englishman has the right to command me. Least of all would be that particular Englishman."

Henry smiled down at her and laughed softly. *Oh yes, Connor has outdone himself this time,* Henry thought. Connor had saddled himself with an Irishwoman who was as willful as she was intelligent and beautiful. His guess was the latter two qualities would only go so far with Connor to tolerate her willfulness.

*So,* he thought, *she is not admitting her marriage to my loyal and trusted knight.* Henry thought he would play along to see where this would go. It had been days since he

186

had been amused, and she amused him. Truth be told, he was relieved to see there was at least one person in his kingdom who did not feel the need to kiss his royal arse. She was honest and respectful. He would accept that for now.

*Come to think of it, Nic and Connor have never felt the need to cater to me either*, Henry mused. Those two had forever been just a bit irreverent.

Again, he smiled at the thought of them. They had been like younger brothers to him, and both were brave, honorable, and loyal to him to the death. Henry could not ask for better at his back.

And Connor had finally met his match, fallen in love, and married her. He could see why Connor had begged his indulgence not to marry until he could have this Irish beauty. Henry was satisfied in his curiosity about the woman who could so captivate Connor to the point he would risk a king's anger.

"So, you owe no fealty to anything English, yet you are willing to help me. Why?"

"By flushing O'Brian out and having your men destroy him, you are removing a threat to me and those I love. As long as he lives, I have no peace of mind. So, I have come to you out of a very selfish motive. I want you to protect those who are important to me."

"Ah, so you want my help in return for placing yourself as bait."

"Yes."

"Which would also place you in my debt. Most would find it uncomfortable to be in the king's debt." Henry continued to note her reactions to him and the circumstances she found herself in. He could tell she had given the issue a great deal of consideration and was not entering this bargain lightly.

"Well, I beg to differ, Your Majesty. I do not see either of us indebted to the other. I would prefer to think of it as a partnership, both breaking even in the end. You get your traitor, and I get my life in Ireland back."

"All right, I will concede the point to you. However, it would require me giving up resources."

Henry was thinking about it. Reagan saw as much.

"Everything comes with a price, Your Majesty. The questions would seem to be whether or not you are willing to pay the price and is the prize worth the cost?"

She should have asked herself the same question before letting Connor into her heart and into her bed. The price was proving to be very high indeed.

"It seems you drive a hard bargain, Lady Reagan, but you have yourself a deal. I shall send my men in to eliminate O'Brian. In turn, you shall be the one to draw the slimy bastard out if need be."

Her arrival was providential as far as Henry was concerned. O'Brian had indeed been blessedly quiet these last four or five years, but suddenly, he had resurfaced and was engaging in his activities with more gall and nerve than before.

"Pack your things, Lady Reagan. You leave tomorrow for Ireland. I shall send you with an armed escort."

"Nay, but I thank you. I shall take only two men-at-arms, dressed as peasants. O'Brian is not an unintelligent man, Your Majesty, nor is he without his sources. He would smell a trap if I'm seen in the presence of the king's armed guards."

"And your plan?"

"There's an inn on the southern shore of Ireland called The Green Horse. At least I'm hoping it's still there. A woman named Essie O'Foster was the patron. Send a single man. It would alert O'Brian if too many arrive at once, sending him underground, which is exactly what we do not want to happen."

She was going to leave instructions with Essie where the soldiers could safely meet with her to devise the plan to ferret him out. She told the king to have his man ask for pudding pie and a mug of milk. The response would be that they do not have any, but knew of a place that did.

"Essie will then give your man written instructions where he can find me."

"It would seem you have given this a great deal of thought," Henry said.

"I have had eight days, sir, with nothing to do save think."

That was not exactly true. She had spent the last twelve days since leaving Featherstone thinking only of Connor.

She missed him terribly. She ached at night for the love they had shared. She was not so blind as not to see how right and special it was. She had tasted heaven, finding her other perfect half, only to realize he belonged to another. Yet it did not stop her heart from longing. It never would.

Henry agreed it was a sound plan and would send in his best men. "You shall have your peace of mind, Reagan, even if you do not hold fealty to me or to Connor. Now, go and have your rest until tomorrow. I shall send the two men you have requested, and they will be in the stable in the morning just before first light."

"Thank you, sir. I shall send you word once I leave for Ireland." She gave him a deep curtsy, which did not go unnoticed by the king.

She went back to her chambers, grateful her trip had not been in vain. Perhaps with some prayer and luck, she could go back to Ireland and put the last year out of her mind and pretend it never happened.

While at it, perhaps she could also convince the earth to rotate backwards.

# Chapter 31

"How did you find her, sire?" Connor asked. He sat across from his king in the private chambers. They had been served a supper of veal with wine, cheese, and fresh strawberries.

Henry took a strawberry and popped it in his mouth. A moment later he spoke. "She is, indeed, beautiful, smart, and very determined to go home." Henry could feel Connor's impatience as he sipped his wine.

"She is more than welcome to come home. There's nothing keeping her from Featherstone."

Connor was surprised at Henry's comment. Surely, she did not feel she was unwelcome, or he would be so angry about her leaving he would not let her come home. There was no reason for her not to willingly come back.

"Connor, she did not even acknowledge you as husband. Care to share with your sire what is going on between you?"

Connor took a long draw of his wine. "Excellent vintage, my lord."

Henry snapped. "Do not think to change the subject on me, Connor. Your king is *not* amused."

Sighing, Connor ventured only to partially answer the question he had asked himself often of late. What exactly was between them? If someone had asked him the morning after they had been together, he would have answered them very differently than today.

"What is between the lady and me is complicated, Henry." Connor did not wish to air his laundry to the king, so he did not comment further.

Henry smiled. He fully understood Connor's plight. "Well, a woman who is intelligent and beautiful like my Elizebeth and your Reagan will do that to a man's life. I

191

fear it has always been so and will always be. It is the price we pay for the privilege of having such amazing women grace our lives."

"So it would seem. What are my orders?" Connor asked, then poured them more wine.

"For the love of Christ, Connor, can we not enjoy the dinner first before talking about what I need you to do for me?"

Henry had indeed called him here to give him orders, but he was also looking forward to a dinner with one of his favorites. He had always enjoyed Connor's quick mind. It was just too bad Nic was not here as well, but the news of the healthy young twins was good news indeed. More loyal subjects to the Tudor crown.

"As you wish," Connor said in a flat tone, trying to hide his edginess. He wanted to go to Reagan. She was within his reach, yet his king had demanded his attendance this evening. It was almost all he could do not to defy him, which surprised Connor a bit. He loved Henry and had always wanted to serve him well. He had never been torn in his duty to his king until now.

"You are going to be a lousy dinner companion tonight?" Henry looked at Connor, not expecting an answer. "Very well," Henry said with an exasperated sigh. "You are going to Ireland. You are going to track down and kill Arlen O'Brian. You shall do this for me as your king, but more importantly, you shall do this for your bride."

Connor was taken aback to hear this from Henry. It was just too coincidental Henry would call him to do his bidding now after five years.

"We know O'Brian lives?" Connor shifted into high alert.

If O'Brian was alive, then his woman was not safe. Adrenaline streamed through his body at the thought of taking O'Brian permanently out of the picture and being able to give Reagan that which had been important enough to bargain for.

"Unfortunately, yes, he lives," Henry said, then finished off his meal. He told Connor how he had been wreaking havoc in the English settlements and garrisons within The Pale. Connor grimaced at the deeds the outlaw had done.

"He is a menace and must be dealt with, Connor, and swiftly. I do not care what you do to find him, just find him. His men raped and murdered five women and three young girls, then butchered the old men. His deeds are becoming more violent, and his activity is increasing with no resistance to stop him. Neither Englishmen nor Irishmen are safe from this man. Removing him is your mission, and I cannot make that any plainer."

Connor's mind was racing. He was eager to do his king's bidding, and arresting or killing O'Brian would mean giving Reagan one of the things she wanted most: the knowledge that O'Brian was dead and no longer a threat to them. Once that was done, he would turn his full attention to making things right between them. He knew Reagan would never stay at Featherstone, for obvious reasons. Seabridge was too close to Ireland and David for his comfort.

"My lord, you know I will do your bidding without question, but may I ask your indulgence to keep my wife here until my return?"

Henry shook his head. "Nay, I have other arrangements for her. She is serving me in a special capacity. One reason I called you to me tonight was to give you your orders, but that is not the only reason. She came to me and made me an offer I could not refuse."

"And that would be?" Connor had a sinking feeling gnawing the pit of his stomach.

"She has offered herself as enticement to draw O'Brian out. Now, you will go to protect her."

Connor was livid. He was angry with Reagan for making such a foolish offer and placing herself in harm's way. He was also angry at Henry for allowing her to do so. She was a woman, for Christ's sake, but more importantly, she was his woman.

"You would send a defenseless woman into the den of a rapist and murderer? What were you thinking?" Connor asked.

"Watch yourself, Connor. You will not question me," Henry warned. Even he had his limits where Nic and Connor were concerned.

"Henry, she cannot possibly know what she is doing. There is no way she would have done this if she knew how far the man has gone down hell's path. I beg you, do not allow this. She is my wife. Let us send a decoy. Let me do this without her. I cannot do your bidding with that kind of distraction hanging between my prey and me. It could get us both killed."

"How am I to stop her, Connor? You could not. Am I to lock her up and throw away the key until we find and kill O'Brian?"

"If need be, yes. It would be for her own good." Connor was thinking he should do that very thing with his bride if it meant keeping her safe on English soil.

"It could take years to pull him out of hiding without an incentive if he goes underground again. Her offer is the thing we need, Connor. From a military standpoint, you know I am right. He will not be able to resist the opportunity to take his revenge on the one person who took his golden egg and forced him to live like an animal in hiding all these years." Henry could see that Connor was not happy. "Connor, do not think I like this anymore than you, but we have to leverage any advantage we have, and right now, Reagan is the best leverage we have to draw upon."

"But, sir—"

Henry held up his hand and silenced him. "Understand me, Connor. I am not unsympathetic to your plight as a man and as a husband. I would never wish my Elizabeth to be placed in such a position. However, I must first be king before I am a man. You must be a soldier before you are a husband."

Groaning and running his hand down his jaw, Connor, as a military man, knew Henry was right, but as a husband and lover, his mind and heart were screaming that there had to be another way. But if she was determined to leave him behind in England and place herself in harm's way, then he would damn well be sure she was protected. Henry had laid out the plan Reagan had suggested. Again, Connor was amazed at her intelligence and bravery.

"I will be one of the men she meets in the morning. I will be near her the whole time," Connor said as he paced the small chamber like a caged animal on a very short chain.

Henry was watching him pace, and it reminded him of a dark panther. "For you and Nic to go was my thought. However, the more I think about it, I do not think that would be the wisest course of action for two reasons."

Connor stopped his pacing and faced his king. "First, Nic's face is well known to O'Brian from the time Nic spent in his custody. I get that. What is the second?" Connor asked.

"Second, it would likely cause Reagan to slip away from you long before she gets to Ireland. She left you behind for reasons I really do not care to understand. Leave her in the hands of my men for now. I am not going to waste my breath and tell you not to worry. I like her, Connor. She is exceptional for a woman, and I shall see to her safety until you can personally oversee her protection."

"Who do you have in mind?"

"She will have the very best, and I think you should approve of my choices."

Connor stopped his pacing, and thought of the men he felt were competent enough to look to his wife's well-being. That list was pretty damn short.

"I will send her to Seabridge with Law and Larkin DeCourcy. We can trust them. I want you, on the other hand, to follow a different path to Ireland, but one that will lead you to her, nonetheless."

Henry knew Connor well enough that he could see he was already devising a plan to destroy the threat to his woman. Connor would do his bidding. Not that Connor had ever failed before, but he had a personal interest in seeing the job done quickly and with the cold and ruthless precision that Henry had seen Connor execute his commands in years past. There was little doubt in Henry's mine that O'Brian would no longer be a threat to the crown or his subjects and had all but dismissed O'Brian as any further threat.

Connor did not like the situation one bit. He did not like his wife being left to the protection of others. That protection was his duty and his privilege alone, and if he could not guard her, then he knew those who would.

"Sire, I would request I be allowed to call my own band of men together. I approve of your choice of Law and Larkin. I do trust them. They are good men, but I would like men from my group. I would request I also be given permission to leave immediately. If I am to secure her protection, then that protection needs to be in place before she ever leaves London."

Connor was impatient and eager to get the wheels turning on the plan to remove this very real threat to the woman he loved.

"Oh, for heaven's sake, she is in the west wing. Cyrus will take you to her. He is just outside. Go." Henry smiled and waved him on. He knew he would not have to tell Connor twice.

# Chapter 32

Reagan tucked the last of her things into her bag. She was going home to her beloved Ireland. *Why does the prospect not excite me more?* she wondered.

She loved Ireland for its beauty, its people, and the enchantment, yet she was also miserable. She was leaving a lot behind. England was not home to her, but Featherstone was. However, she could never go back because to do so would mean she would see Connor again. Seeing him would tear her to pieces.

She ran her hand over the bag Connor had made for her after she placed her medicines inside. Thinking back, she realized how honorable a man he usually was. He was good to his people, good to his family, and he had been good to her. He could make her angry, make her laugh, frustrate her, and twist her gut, but she knew he felt deeply for her. Nobody could fake the feelings they shared in that chamber, lost in each other's arms. The depths of emotion had surprised both of them. That one fact alone made it harder to leave.

Could she live without him? More importantly, if she stayed, could she live with him in shame? This was not the twentieth century where such things did not result in becoming an outcast. She would be forced to live in the shadows on the fringe of acceptable society. She would not be allowed to live with him and share his day-to-day life. It would be only a tiny echo of what life would be like with him if they were free to share their love in the light of day.

*No,* she thought, *it's better to never have him than have a life that was a mere shadow of what it should be.* It would leave them both unfulfilled. It would not be fair to his wife and his legitimate children. It certainly would not be fair to the children they might produce out of this forbidden affair.

She would leave and never look back. Fearing if she did look back, it would break down her resolve to leave. Besides, it served no purpose. How many times had she dispensed such good advice?

She loved him. There was no sense in trying to deny it, certainly not to herself. Somewhere along the way, she had let her guard down, and he had charged in, mowing down any defenses she had against the assault he had waged to her heart. She had to leave. It was the only way to begin healing.

She pulled out the letter Connor had written to her. It had arrived four days earlier. She had not read it. She was still looking for the courage.

Holding it, she was afraid to open it, knowing it would wound her, no matter the message it contained.

If he had begged her to return, she probably would and live with him, however she could have him and however he would take her. She would swallow her pride, beg for God's forgiveness, and become the other woman in his marriage.

It would devastate her if his last words were angry and accusatory. As far as he knew, she left without a backward glance. He would have no way of knowing it had ripped her apart to leave Featherstone.

She studied his handwriting. It spoke of a man who was confident and outgoing, maybe a bit impulsive, but no doubt decisive.

"Oh, English, how could I have let it get this far?"

She placed the letter in the window, leaning her forehead on the casing. The dampness from outside crept into her skin, and she prayed it would cover her heart, sealing it inside a tomb of ice, forever quenching the flame she carried for her English knight. She would leave tomorrow.

Standing at the window, she felt her heart constrict, her insides tightening with fear of the unknown. She knew she was throwing herself into danger, into a den of wolves. However, nothing else mattered except going home, and if it meant facing O'Brian, then so be it.

She heard the outer door open behind her. She did not turn around.

"Please leave the tray on the table," she said as she tried to keep the tears out of her voice. She really did not care if the king's servants knew she was upset. After tonight, she would be forever gone. There would never be another cause for this Irish peasant to darken the doors of the English high court.

Connor's heart wrenched when he saw how vulnerable, hurting, and beautiful she was. He walked silently to her and put his arms around her, turning her to face him.

Her shock registered in her expression.

"Be easy, princess." He held her close to him even though she slightly resisted his embrace.

"Let me go!" She struggled in vain to free herself.

"Never." Connor held her tighter.

"How could you do that to me! You're contemptible." She sighed as he began to kiss her face. Her body and heart were at odds with her mind and logic. She was in quicksand and sinking fast.

"You're beautiful," he countered in a soft voice, not rising to the ire and not relenting in his tender assault on her senses.

"I hate… you." She knew she didn't mean it.

So did he, and he knew he was wearing down her resolve.

"I love you," Connor confessed the words she longed to hear. He kissed her mouth and moved to her neck. He breathed her in, feeling alive for the first time in days.

"I… despise… you…" she said, melting in his arms. This was where she wanted to spend the rest of her life. Her arms had wrapped around his neck of their own accord.

"I adore you." Connor knew he was winning this battle.

Her body could not help but respond with all the love she felt for him. She could not say no this man. Her body and heart would not allow it.

"I… hate… you…" she said, her voice faltering.

He had pulled away from her just enough to look deeply into her eyes. "Nay, princess, you do not," he said, holding her gently, and then leaned in for another kiss.

"Oh, please, God, forgive me," she whispered as Connor's lips met hers.

Connor kissed her, wanting to possess her body and soul. Scooping her up into his arms, she did not fight; she could not fight. There was no fight left in her as his long stride crossed the room into the private chamber. He used his booted foot to slam the door behind them, shutting out the rest of the outside world. Slowly and with agonizing deliberateness, he let her slide down the full length of his body, never taking his eyes off of her. Tenderly placing her feet on the floor by the bed, he began to undress her. Reagan would not think about tomorrow and what it would mean for her or for them. She was leaving him behind forever.

*How can you leave him?* her heart cried out.

How could she let him go when she so desperately needed him in her life and she so completely loved him? She knew she should turn him away before it was too late. Yet she knew they were already past the point of no return and had been the moment he had taken her into his arms. Her sin was already great, and if she burned for it, then let her burn, but she would have this night fate had given her.

"You should go before it's too late."

200

"Oh, princess, it is way past that point. And tell me you do not want this as much as I do." Connor whispered while he kissed her neck lightly, nipping at the sensitive skin beneath her ear.

"Aye, I want this, but—"

He silenced her with a kiss that left her breathless.

"But what, princess?" He let out a husky laugh as she desperately tried to catch her breath and pull her thoughts back together.

"You're just an evil man, Connor," Reagan said in a sigh as she leaned into him.

"And you, my lady, have on too many clothes to suit me."

Laughing, they quickly undressed and found each other. Hands, mouths, arms, legs, breaths intertwining, their bodies and souls mingling, becoming one. Desperate for each other, their hearts were beating in one accord as they touched as if for the first time, exploring and memorizing each other. The feel of their skin, the taste of their lips, the sound of their sighs filled the room.

"Oh, God, Reagan, you are so beautiful. I could look at you like this lying beneath me forever. I love—"

She placed her finger over his lips. It hurt too much to hear the words. "Shh, do not say it. Just show me."

Connor wanted desperately to make it right between them. She was his wife, but more importantly, she was his friend and the other half of his soul. He was no longer a whole man without her in his world. The days she had been away from him had proven that true.

"God help me, princess, but what I feel for you takes my breath, and I know I have no right to love you. I do not deserve you." He leaned on an elbow and gently brushed the hair away from her face, then kissed her softly.

She knew he was right. Neither deserved or had the right to love the other, but she would worry about her sin tomorrow, not tonight.

"Connor, sometimes fate brings us gifts. This night is a gift. Neither of us deserves it, but for once in my life, I'm going to be selfish. I will worry about redemption tomorrow," she said, sliding her fingers through his long and silky hair as it cascaded over them.

"Before this night is over, I swear you will no longer have any doubt about what we have together is right."

He was branding her, marking her as his as his lips moved over her body. "No other will ever come close to what I can give you, Reagan. I will be the man to give you everything your heart desires. I am the only man you will ever want."

She knew he already was.

"Just love me tonight; that's all I want. No promises, no lies, English. Just this," she whispered as her hand trailed up his chest. "Just this," she said, pulling his lips to her mouth, and he began to move inside her.

# Chapter 33

Reagan could not sleep. They were lying in bed, and Connor's arm was protectively draped around her waist. She spooned up against him, pressing against his warm skin. He felt so good lying next to her.

*Stay with me. Sleep next to me,* he had asked her all those months ago.

They had made love through the night, sleeping occasionally, but never letting go of each other. Neither could put into words the emotions running between them. They knew each other's mind and body. Coming together was so natural and comfortable in a way only longtime lovers could feel—each instinctively knowing what the other needed, what was pleasing, and what they wanted.

It was almost frightening, the intensity of the physical act itself, and coupled with the intense emotion, their connection was like two chemicals that caused a grand explosion.

She was sore and felt abused in a way only hard and desperate lovemaking could leave a woman. She had never been left as satisfied, still starving for more.

"Care to share your thoughts with me, beautiful?" Kissing her neck, Connor knew she was awake and had been for a while. He had left her to her thoughts long enough and wanted to see if she would share with him where she was going. He hoped she would trust him.

After last night, he felt their relationship had deepened. He felt the bond growing stronger and tying them together. He knew she loved him even if she had not said the actual words. There was no way she could give herself over to him with as much abandon as she had and not feel the same as he did.

Reagan was not the kind of woman to love causally. He had told her over and over he loved her, how he wanted her, and just how beautiful she was. He had also told her he wanted her to be his always and forever.

"You are awake," she said, looking back over her shoulder and thinking he was right. He had ruined her for every other man. He was magnificent and all the man she ever wanted, and no other would ever take his place. She was too far gone for that.

"Umm," he said, kissing the curve of her neck and biting her teasingly. It sent little chills of desire shooting through her. "I want you again, Reagan. You are like a drug to me."

"Then by all means let me satisfy that need," she said with her eyes closed in ecstasy as she ran her fingers through his hair, pressing his head to her neck.

"Is that doctor's orders?" he asked, flipping her beneath him.

"Absolutely."

~*****~

After making love to her again, Connor held her, yet a thought chilled him to the bone. They had not taken any precautionary measures.

"Christ, what were we thinking?"

"Thinking about what?" she asked, puzzled.

He hadn't been thinking at all. That was the problem. "We did not take precautionary measures to prevent you from being with child," he said. He should have pulled out at the very least. The thought had never entered his mind. "You could already be carrying my heir."

She was leaving in just a few hours to strike out on a journey surrounded by danger, but with his baby at risk, he would never allow her to leave. That was final and Henry could just go to hell.

She tried to put his mind at rest. "Nay, Connor. You are worrying over nothing. I have a birth control implant." She showed it to him and explained how it functioned. She had gotten the dermal implant several years ago. Now she was grateful she had.

"Is it permanent?"

"No. It should be good for another year. We do not have to worry about an unwanted pregnancy."

"I said nothing about unwanted, Reagan. I was thinking more of the timing with things being so unsettled." Then he had another thought. "Do you not want to share a child with me?" Connor was puzzled and hurt at the thought of her not wanting his baby.

She sensed his hurt.

*How dare he*, she thought. He should be glad to not be siring a bastard. He should be asking his wife to give him children, not his lover, especially when she so desperately wanted his children more than life itself. She wanted all of him. She wanted everything, yet she could have nothing. The grim reality of the morning came crashing in for her.

"That's not fair, Connor. Don't dare ask me that, not now."

Annoyed, she pushed him off and got out of bed and began to gather her clothes from where they had landed the night before.

Connor watched as she picked up her things. Her body was enticingly full and tempting. He saw the love bites he had left on her soft and creamy flesh, and he loved the way her bare breasts swayed as she moved around the room. He loved the roundness of her hips and derrière as she bent over, and to his eyes she was a feast on which to dine.

"It is still early. Come back to bed, princess. I did not mean to upset you. It is a legitimate question even if the timing is a bit off. Come back to me. I want more of you," he teased, then reached out for her as she passed.

She sidestepped his advances.

205

He did not understand why it had perturbed her, but he knew her well enough not to press the issue at the moment.

She stopped picking up the clothing and stood with her back to him like an alabaster statue. It would not have done for him to see the longing on her face.

"There's no time. I have an errand this morning for the king, and I'm already running late."

She began to clean herself and dress, leaving Connor behind in the bedroom.

"What kind of errand, princess? It is an honor to have the king ask a favor. It places him in your debt," he called from the sleeping area as he sat on the side of the bed, pulling on his boots. He got up and walked into the main room as he was belting on his sword.

"Oh, my God," she whispered as she turned to look at him.

He saw the look on her face, and he loved it. She loved him. No matter how hard she may try to fight it, he knew she was already his. He felt victorious. He had her heart. The rest would come, given time.

*Oh, God, help me,* she thought as he stood there, not realizing she had spoken the plea out loud. She would take this mental picture with her. His hair long and loose, long legs spread wide, and his fists on his hips. He was so beautiful with his wild warrior looks. She knew she was totally in love with him, totally beyond redemption, and the intensity of her love frightened her.

"The king has asked and I have agreed. I'm going to Ireland, Connor." It came out in a rush before her resolve dissolved to nothingness. Fully dressed with pack in hand, she stood in the open doorway as the moments suspended in time.

*Please, Connor, stop me!* her heart begged him.

Connor was incensed at her indifference. She knew the danger she was placing herself into, yet she was acting as if there was not a thing wrong with her going. He wanted her angry; he wanted her fighting. Of all times, he did not want her passive. She needed her spirit and fire to protect her. Connor felt she was vulnerable if she was not on full alert and ready for a fight. He had to make her see the folly.

"If that is what you think you need to do, then by all means, Reagan, just be my guest. Go." He gestured to the door. "Go place yourself in the line of fire. Go place yourself into the den of a murderer and rapist. Shall I send a messenger to O'Brian, giving him warning of your impending arrival, so he can put a knife to that pretty throat of yours two minutes after you are back on Irish soil? Is that what you want?" he bellowed.

"Of course that isn't what I want!" she snapped.

"Well, then tell me what you do want to accomplish with this madness?"

"I just want to feel safe again. I want… It doesn't matter what I want. Not anymore. Maybe it never has."

They were where they had been so often in their relationship, at a stalemate. Taking a different approach, he came toward her, stopping just short of being too close to her.

He raised his hand to stroke her hair away from her face. "You would leave me after last night? You would leave me again?"

She leaned her cheek into his palm, closing her eyes. She was only a breath away from begging him to come with her. She stepped backward, away from his gentle touch.

"Especially after last night, English."

She opened the door, and walked out without turning around. "Goodbye, Connor." She began to pull the door closed behind her.

"Reagan, wait."

Her heart pounded with joy, only to be crushed with his next words.

"Here. If you are leaving, at least take these."

His face was unreadable as he handed her a dagger and a pouch of coins.

*Oh, God, he is letting me leave.* Just like that, he would let her walk away. She had hoped, just for a moment, he would ask her to stay. She thought after last night there would be no greater emotion. She loved him. Yet this hurt went in and through, piercing her to the quick, as if she had been shot through the heart.

She had been a fool! She looked down at his hands and remembered how those hands had felt on her body and how his touch had made her feel so alive, so cherished, and so deeply loved. It was a touch she could never feel again.

"I will take your dagger, English, but not the gold. I already feel like a whore. Do not make me feel like a paid one."

Never meeting his eyes, Connor saw the single tear slide down her face as she left him standing in her empty chamber. Anger roiled inside him. He knew he had hurt her. Deep down he understood that she wanted him to ask her to stay. He could not.

Damn Henry and damn O'Brian.

Watching her leave was the hardest thing he had ever done because he knew he had deceived her again. If there had ever been any doubt, it was laid to rest.

O'Brian was a dead man.

# Chapter 34

Royal Stables of Henry's Court
July 7, 1499

Gypsy was saddled and ready to go by the time Reagan arrived at the stables. The king had been a man of his word, and she had two armed guards dressed as peasants to escort her. However, if anyone looked closely, there would be no doubt these two were anything but humble farmers. Hopefully, no one was watching them that closely.

"Good day, Lady Reagan. Connor and the king send their regards," Law spoke softly as he helped her mount her horse.

Reagan gave him a simple nod of her head. And with that, they were off.

~*****~

Eleven days later, the party of exhausted travelers was granted entrance into Seabridge. Little did Reagan know, Connor had sent a messenger who had arrived days earlier with news of her impending arrival.

David was waiting to help her off her mount. "Reagan, it is good to see you. Come in and relax. I am sure your journey from London was a tiring one."

Exhausted from the trip and lack of sleep, she momentarily rested against him. David leaned in to kiss her, and she turned her cheek.

"Thank you, David. It's good to see you, too."

Reagan was sick at heart. The parting she and Connor had in London had left her feeling numb, but there was no going back. He had dismissed her with a dagger and a bag of coins. She understood her part in it. It was not all his fault.

"Hello, friend," Rafe said softly as he stood behind her.

"Rafe! Oh, Rafe!" Reagan turned and dislodged herself from David and threw her arms around Rafe's neck while battling back the tears. "I'm glad you are here."

Relieved to see her friend, Reagan wiped tears of exhaustion and joy from her face. His very presence eased her suffering.

"Are you trying to get home?" she whispered.

"Me? Trying to get home by myself, not hardly. No, I came here looking for you. However, now that I think about it, trying to get home isn't a bad idea with one exception. I don't know exactly where I'd end up. Better to dance with the devil you know than the one you don't," Rafe said. He believed, in this instance, it was an understatement.

He gently seized her arm and led her toward the stronghold. The men who were escorting her faded into the background. Rafe gave them a subtle wave. They were ghosts and probably Connor's men. Rafe recognized the tactic, and knew he would not see them while Reagan was here. They were on to Ireland.

"I can see your point, Rafe. But sometimes the dance even with the devil you know can be too much to bear, and the unknown is far more desirable. You knew I was arriving today?"

"Connor sent word ahead."

"Oh…" she said. Of course he would think about her safety. "That was thoughtful of him. And Rafe"—she placed a pleading hand on his arm and felt her eyes grow misty— "I do not want to talk about him or anything associated with him, please. I need time, not questions."

Laying his hand over hers, he smiled with understanding. "You take whatever time you need, Rea. I'm not going to pry or encourage you one way or the other."

Rafe looked at David. "And neither is he. Are you, David?" Rafe gave David a look, leaving him with little doubt.

David felt chagrined, even though he knew Rafe was right. Reagan needed space because she was hurting. "Nay, I will not push, but I am here if you want to talk."

All she really wanted was a bath and some warm food. "May I impose?" Reagan wanted to be alone.

"Your bath is ready per Connor's instructions. Delilah will be your lady's maid. She's expecting you," David informed her.

*Damn Connor Holden's sorry-ass hide,* Rafe thought.

Connor needed to make it right with this woman, and if he didn't, then he would personally see to it Connor lived in complete and utter agony for a very long time. Death was too good for Connor Holden. By God, he needed to hurt. At least Rea had the good sense to come to Seabridge before going to Ireland. Furthermore, Connor had the sense to ask Rafe to go with her when the time came for her to leave.

~*****~

David's thoughts were paralleling Rafe's with one exception. He was going to give her physical comfort even if Rafe was not. If she needed arms to hold her and a shoulder to lean on, it was damn well going to be his. He was not about to leave her to suffer alone.

David loved her. This he knew and had known it for years, but he had no idea how deeply he was in love until he saw her riding back through the gates, her face downcast, and her spirit crushed. He vowed to help her heal.

211

# Chapter 35

Reagan was struck by the richness of the castle. It was apparent Morgan had indeed inherited a fortune. No wonder her uncle had fought to the death to possess such wealth. The two times she had spent here had been brief and full of anxiety, so she never had time to absorb her surroundings until now.

Seabridge's Great Hall was cavernous with its gilded archways. She noted that there were no rushes on hard-packed dirt or rough stone floors. The polished Italian marble floors were graced by the spoils of the Crusades in the form of incredibly soft Persian carpets that had only improved beautifully with age. Immense beams of highly polished rosewood soared thirty feet above to join with the massive trussed ceiling.

Usually reserved for churches due to the extreme cost and rarity, the stained-glass works of art adorned the windows, bathing the hall with a rainbow of color. Each frame told a part of a larger story of knights on crusade. The walls were painted a soft rose, and the nooks, all along the walls, bore antiquities of various Egyptian and Roman busts and statues. The sconces and chandeliers numbered in the hundreds, each lit with torches soaked in fresh oil and expensive beeswax candles, which left little soot or smoke.

The elegant tapestries covering the walls, created by Byzantine Empire artists, were priceless in their depiction of the mythological hunts of the unicorn and other mystical creatures.

Catching her eye the most was the massive twin swords and shield hanging above the colossal fireplace; their blades were a full five feet long and the hilts were encrusted with gems and diamonds worth a king's ransom. Embedded in the shield were gold medallions, and the center was graced by a ruby of three hundred carats, worth millions on the twentieth-century market.

Those were truly things of beauty even if they were instruments of death.

Reagan thought many of life's temptations were just like this. They were beautiful to look at but deadly if a person came in contact with them.

Rafe silently crossed the space between them, stood behind her, and placed his hands on her shoulders. "Hard to believe, isn't it? There's so much wealth here. Yet Morgan won't step foot on Seabridge soil."

He gently squeezed her as she leaned back against him. She reached up and touched his hand. He was her friend, and she was glad he was here.

"Morgan may return given time or the proper incentive," she said, looking back over her shoulder at him. In so many ways, he reminded her of Nic, not just in looks, but his disposition, too.

"Perhaps, but some issues are never worked through or gotten over, no matter the time that passes." It was a rhetorical statement, and one for which Rafe did not expect a response. "Plenty of time later to ponder the philosophical, Reagan. For now, let's go get you comfortable."

Reagan thought perhaps he was right. Some things were never gotten over. She prayed Connor Holden was not one of those things.

# Chapter 36

Featherstone Castle
July 26, 1499

Connor had made his way back to Featherstone from London just as soon as he was sure Reagan was surrounded by his troops. He commissioned a trustworthy band to leave at the same time she did to ensure a large assemblage for added safety.

The trustworthy men, handpicked by Ian Scott, a lighthearted fellow who used his charm to the fullest, would protect her. Ian had served under Connor in Shadow Operations for years until he had inherited his title. Then he left Henry's service to do his duty by his wife. It would seem he had. He was the father of four.

Connor was in his debt. Ian had jumped at the chance to aid Connor in guarding his lovely lady. Ian, although enjoying his marriage and parenthood, longed for the good old days of intrigue and being the king's spy by his own admission.

Connor collected his arms and men, making ready to leave for Ireland. His hope was that the delay tactics he and Rafe had devised would slow Reagan in leaving to allow him and his men to get to Ireland and ready themselves before her arrival. He had a good idea where she was going, so it was just a matter of securing his troops and heading west.

He would stop by Seabridge before sailing on to Ireland. The arrangements were already made for a secret meeting with Rafe, and he would check on Reagan while he was there. As hard as it was going to be, she could never know he was at Seabridge. She was a smart woman and would easily figure out his plan.

Connor knew it was going to be agonizing for him to be close to her but not be able to hold her and be with her. He had been truthful when he told her she was like a drug to him. She was in his blood and in his soul, and their separation tore at his insides.

"Connor," Nic said as he walked into Featherstone's armory. "I have a stake in Reagan going to Ireland. I have a score to settle with O'Brian, and it's long overdue. Over six years to be exact."

"Nic, Morgan is not ready for you to leave her. The twins are still small. Besides, what makes you think she will allow you to leave?" He did not want to be critical, but Nic had told him that night in his solar that he called the shots only because Morgan let him. "Need I remind you of what happened the last time you tried to leave her behind?" Connor threw that in for good measure.

Nic winced. The last time he had tried to force a separation on Morgan, she had foiled any attempts at keeping her safe. She had let his children go off to York with David while she had hidden away until it was too late to make her go back.

Thinking about her disobedience still made Nic angry, so he chose never to think on it. Nonetheless, he was grateful she had defied him. If she had not been up on the cliffs of Seabridge that fateful day, both he and Cullen would be dead, and her life would most likely be gone as well at the hands of her traitorous uncle. It had been five years, and in all that time, they had not slept a single night apart.

His imprisonment in O'Brian's hellhole all those years ago had a marked impact on her sense of security as far as his safety was concerned. She would become anxious if he was out of her sight for very long periods of time.

Even during the day, she would seek him out, and often all she needed was to see him. Other times, she had to have the physical contact to ease her fear. Both knew this deep-seated fear was unfounded and unnatural, but neither knew how to dispel it, so they had learned to live with it. Nic had become used to their routine and did not give it much thought.

Until now.

She would not like it. He did not care for the idea of leaving her behind with his newborn babies, knowing the emotional trauma it would cause her, but this confrontation was long overdue. Connor was not the only one with a score to settle.

O'Brian had slaughtered his men six years earlier, leaving several for dead who desperately needed medical attention. O'Brian had taken three others as prisoners besides Nic, and Nic was never able to ransom them.

"Well, I don't like it either, but I have a score to settle with him. I still don't know the fate of my men, and I swore I would be back. Now I can fulfill my vow."

"Well, let me know before you tell her. I do not want to be anywhere around," Connor quipped as he strapped on the ten-inch dagger.

"Gone soft, Connor?" Nic grinned trying to make light of the conversation, but he knew Connor was right. Morgan was not going to be happy, and when she wasn't happy, everyone else around knew it, too.

She was a breathtaking woman and a wonderful mother and most often easy to please, but he knew this was going to be a battle of wills like he had not faced with her in years.

"Nic, you can call it what you want, but she is not going to sit back and let you go. The babies are even smaller this time, but who is to say she would not leave them. I am not saying she is a bad mother. She is a wonderful mother, but her fear for you is deep and unfathomable. If you go and she stays, how miserable will she become because of it?"

217

Six years earlier, Nic was so angry with her that he had refused to go to her or to let her see him for two days. It was for her own good to keep him from inadvertently hurting her physically. He remembered how she was after those two days. It was bad enough Reagan had asked for Connor's help. He had never put her through that again.

"Nic, I appreciate your desire for revenge, but I need you here. Let me handle this." Nic needed to be at Featherstone in case things went wrong. Nic was his heir, and his strong hand should be here to manage all his holdings.

Connor began to tell him of his plan and how he had hopes of Rafe convincing Reagan to stay at Seabridge and let him handle the matter of O'Brian. But, of course, she wouldn't listen, so he decided to have her guarded like a hawk. Rafe would go with her when and if the time ever arrived. Connor felt that if he could not be there, then the other man in this world who cared for her besides he and Nic would be there.

As he and Henry had planned, the king spread innuendo at court that Connor had fallen from his favor. Before Connor left, Henry publicly banished him from England, stating he suspected but had no proof that Connor had committed treason. He appeared to be fleeing England in disgrace.

He was to go to Ireland as a man without a country, bitter and enraged at his king for stripping him of all his wealth and titles. Nic was now the Duke of Featherstone and was also installed as the Marquis of Devonshire and Earl of Rockport.

"Oh, and by the way, do not get too comfortable in the roles, Nic. I plan on coming back."

"You had better come back. My being the Duke of Seabridge is enough for me."

Connor told him about a document in his strongbox. Henry had signed the document stating this was all a charade to get O'Brian. Henry had it drawn up and witnessed by his queen and two other trusted men in case anything happened to Henry before all could be cleared up. They did not want anything to go wrong and Connor end up being stripped of his lands based on a mission of which only a select few would have knowledge.

"Above everything else, Nic, I need you here to protect Reagan should something happen to me," Connor said.

Nic studied his friend. "So, let me get this clear in my mind. Your hope is to have O'Brian take you in based on the fact you are so disgraced and disgruntled? Is that not just a little bit weak? After all, he will likely see through it."

"It is the best we have, Nic." Connor could see Nic's point.

"If I were a betting man, I would say he does not trust easily. How are you going to get him to let you in?"

He and Henry had devised a brilliant plan. Henry was nothing if not a flawless military tactician. Their plan was quite simple. Connor was to have a renegade band of his own. There were to be several skirmishes strategically staged to build his credibility as an outlaw after which he was going to approach O'Brian with an offer he could not refuse. He would offer to band together as an even stronger group and expand the range of their territory.

If that failed to pull O'Brian out and allow for infiltration, then and only then, would Reagan be brought into the action.

He had hoped to find a decoy who looked enough like her to fool O'Brian from a distance but had failed in such regard. Her coloring was unusual for England, and her natural, wholesome beauty was an even rarer find.

She was not a classical beauty, but she held his interest and drew him to her like steel to a magnet. He had been with some of the kingdom's most beautiful women, whose faces could launch a thousand ships, faces that could have matched Helen of Troy, but they were not Reagan. She, alone, moved him as none other ever had or ever could.

"Does Rafe know the plan?" Nic asked as they walked back to the stable in final preparation to leave.

"Aye, he knows. I saw no reason not to take him into confidence. If he is to help protect and control her, I felt it best."

"You trust him?" Nic asked, raising his eyebrows in question.

"Aye, explicitly," Connor answered without hesitation.

His decision to include Rafe surprised Nic. He trusted Rafe, but after the way the two men had gone at each other, this was unexpected.

Sending word ahead to Rafe by way of Ian, Connor trusted the man despite the fact Rafe hated him personally. He had no delusions about why Rafe had agreed to help him. He knew he cared deeply for Reagan, and their bond of friendship was strong. She alone was the reason the McKinnon would aid him. It was for her sake and had absolutely nothing to do with king or country. He was a man with nothing to lose except her.

David Hale, on the other hand, was an unknown element. He was not so sure David would not be in it for gain. David was a good man, but Connor himself was living proof that good men will do questionable things when love for a woman was involved. Hale wanted Reagan. It was that simple and Connor knew it. How far David was willing to go to gain her was the risk he was running by having her anywhere around David.

Under any other circumstance, he would trust David without hesitation, but this time he was uneasy at the prospect of having Hale in Ireland. Unfortunately, he saw no way around it if David was set on coming, so he would just have to take the chance he would not prove to be the weakest link or turn on them as a Judas.

Connor felt sure David was not going to stand idly by if Reagan was at risk, even if the risks were calculated, controlled, and with her consent. Somehow Connor had to make David understand she was his wife, and he was not going to let danger anywhere near her, not when he still had breath in his body. He just had to convince the man to keep his cool, no matter the actions being taken.

Connor's gut clenched at the thought of Reagan being anywhere around O'Brian. Having no illusions about the outlaw, Connor knew O'Brian would quickly kill Reagan or worst—torture her and then kill her slowly—for what she had done to him. Could he play the hardened and newly turned criminal if she was anywhere around him? God, he hoped he never had to find out.

"You need to stay behind, Nic. There are too many things that can go wrong, and I need someone here to help unravel the mess should things go bad. Besides, O'Brian would never buy you wanting to be his new best friend, not after the scars left on your body from his whips."

"I could hang back and be there should you need me," Nic said, trying one last approach to convince Connor to allow him to come.

"Nay, Ian and his men are going to shadow us."

Both had a gut feeling that even though Ian may claim to be out of the game, it was just about as far from the truth as it got. They both believed he had been in the game all along and was still one of the best in the business of the king's intelligence and national security.

Nic sighed. Connor and Reagan were better served with him here, so he would stay. "Verray well, then I'll wish you Godspeed. Try to slip us word when you can safely do so. If we don't hear from you by All Hollows' Eve, I'm coming after you."

# Chapter 37

Seabridge Castle
Midnight
July 31, 1499

Elusive as a dream upon waking, Connor became part of the night. Using the veil of darkness as a shroud, he slipped into the role he had been trained to be—a phantom in the night.

His mission usually entailed covertly sliding in, acquiring the target, and getting back out completely unseen. It was a trait both he and Nic had perfected through the years. Silent as a specter, Connor stealthily passed the night watchmen, making a mental note to have Rafe fortify the position and post more men about. If he could get past, so could others trained like him. He eased his way through the outer bailey and to the place he had agreed to meet Rafe.

"You're late," Rafe whispered.

Connor was surprised Rafe had sensed him. There was no way he could see him. It was apparent he was not the only one with the ability to blend into the shadows.

"Shoot me later for it," Connor answered indifferently.

"Don't tempt me, Connor. What do you want me to do?" Rafe asked, barely able to keep his tongue civil. He was still livid with Connor, but Rafe knew now was not the time or the place to settle a personal score. Reagan's safety was at stake, and his feelings would just have to wait.

"Good, I like a man who gets straight to the point. But first, how is she? Anything I need to know?" Connor asked, feeling edgy. He was glancing around on full alert.

"She's fine, reserved, but fine. You've cut her deeply, Holden, and it will take her time to come to terms.

Fortunately, for you, she's a practical woman." Rafe was not so sure that he would ever come to terms with the way Connor had handled the situation. However it was not about him. It was about Reagan.

"I think she will see the upside soon enough."

Connor's tone was confident, almost cocky to Rafe's ear.

"Pfffft! You're an asshole, Holden, and don't deserve her, and if it weren't for her, I wouldn't piss on you if you were on fire." Rafe's gaze burned with an intensity Connor could feel.

"At least I know where I stand with you, and furthermore, I do not have to justify my actions to you. If you will recall, she walked out on me not once, but twice. She is my wife, Rafe, a relationship I have no intention of denying or changing."

Granted, he probably could have done things differently, but he had not, and he was the first to admit his wrong in the misunderstanding. "And, when we get down to the basics, this is none of your affair, Rafe. So, let us move past it, shall we?"

"Possibly." Rafe was not about to let him off so easily.

"The main thing now is to see she is protected. Agreed?" Connor had to get Rafe off the fence where he was concerned.

"On that one point, yes, we agree."

"Good. First order is to increase the guard. I slipped past them easily. So could others."

Galled, Connor did not like to leave her protection in the hands of other lesser men. However, there was nothing he could do at the present. The situation dictated the terms, and the longer she was here, the greater his chances of catching their man before she even had a chance to set foot on Irish soil.

"She means the world to me, Rafe, so do not let me down. I need you to keep her here as long as possible. Once

O'Brian is no longer a threat, I swear as God as my witness, I will make it right between us. Whatever the countess wishes, I vow I will do."

"Good, and just so we are crystal clear, if you don't make it right, Holden, I will personally see to it you regret the day you ever touched her."

Connor was the first to look away and moved on from a topic they both knew was volatile.

"Is Hale a problem?" Connor asked for confirmation of his suspicions.

"Yes, I'm keeping a close eye on him," Rafe acknowledged. "Ultimately, it's your call, and you know the man better than I do, but I don't think we should bring him in on this. At least not yet."

Rafe did not get warm feelings from David, and he felt David needed to stay behind should he and Reagan depart for Ireland.

"Agreed. He's an unknown in this." Connor looked around nervously. If Hale were worth his salt as a military man, this meeting would be discovered, and all their carefully laid plans would be blown to hell.

Connor knew Rafe well enough to know he would keep David in the dark and as far away from Reagan as he could.

"Can you arrange to keep Hale here if you personally end up in Ireland?" Connor asked.

Rafe shrugged. He really did not know. "Possibly. To be honest, I'm not sure. He feels strongly about the issues affecting Rea."

"He's Nic's man now. I could get Nic to devise reasons for him to go to London. However, he may feel strongly enough about going to Ireland with Reagan that even Nic may not be able to control his actions."

"That's a distinct possibility," Rafe said.

"If that turns out to be the case, then I am leaving it up to you to see that he does not, or at the very least, keep him out of my way."

That set Rafe's teeth on edge. He wasn't Connor's errand boy. "I'm not babysitting him to keep him off your ass, Connor. He's your problem, not mine. I'll run as much interference as I can to keep him away from Reagan, because she's vulnerable and he senses it. He wants her, Connor. I won't have him trying to corner her or pressure her for something she doesn't have the willpower to withstand, because she's emotionally weak. But I won't do your dirty work. If you want him out of the way, you do it yourself."

"All right, if it comes down to that. I do not trust him with her. I trust you, Rafe, but no one else. No one, and I mean no one, is to touch my woman. If he touches her, I will kill him."

Rafe knew during this time frame in history Holden would be well within his rights to run a man through for inappropriate behavior towards his wife, but personally, he did not care one way or the other about either of them, but he did care about Reagan.

"I have your back as long as it's to her benefit, and getting rid of O'Brian is definitely to her benefit. So, you can trust that I'll do what you ask of me when it comes to her. I'll do what I can to stall her, but you know as well as I, once she has her mind set, that will be the end of it."

"Fair enough."

The two men finished laying out the plan. With that done, Connor was eager to look in on Reagan. He knew he could not talk to her, but he just could not leave without seeing her either.

~\*\*\*\*\*~

Connor eased into her room like mist with the same stealth he had used to pass the night watchmen. She was a light sleeper and was often awake for long stretches of time. That much he knew from all the months she had lived under his protection. But tonight luck was with him.

As he came to her side of the bed, he looked down at his sleeping bride. She was his and his alone, and he was proud of her for many reasons. Tendrils of her hair had spilled out of her ponytail as they often did and were framing her face. Lightly, he brushed them back, and a fierce protectiveness washed over him. He could not allow her to go into danger and silently swore to eliminate O'Brian for her peace of mind. He swore to always remove any threat coming her way. He would make it right between them if he just got the chance, but that chance would not happen until O'Brian was dead.

"Good night, beautiful." Leaning down, he kissed her forehead.

"Connor," she sighed his name in her sleep as she shifted positions.

"Go back to sleep. I am just a dream." Quickly, he slipped back into the shadows of her bedroom, blending into the night.

"Stay with me." Her eyes fluttered open, and in her drowsy state, she would have sworn he was just there. With a soft cry, she knew it was only a dream, and throwing the covers off of her heated skin, she drifted back to sleep as he watched her relax, aching to touch her.

*Stay with me.* Her plea echoed in his mind and pulled at his heart.

"God, princess, if only I could."

Soundlessly, he faded back into the steamy summer night and was gone.

# Chapter 38

Seabridge
August 1, 1499

"What do you mean Connor has given you direction not to let me leave until you are sure I'm not pregnant?"

Reagan was livid. She placed her hands on her hips and faced Rafe in the room she had set up as a temporary infirmary.

"Reagan, it's not that big of a deal," Rafe argued. "This situation has waited five years. A few more weeks won't matter."

"I'm not pregnant and I'm not waiting. And why are you taking his side?" Reagan said as she stopped her pacing, feeling a little betrayed by her friend.

"I'm not taking sides, Rea. I just happen to agree with him. If you're carrying Connor's child, you have no business going to Ireland and placing an innocent unborn child in danger. I don't give a damn how hurt you are at the moment. You will not run away and take his child with you."

"I'm not running away, Rafe." She tried to correct him. Maybe she was but it was her choice.

"Yes, you are and he has rights, and I know you, Reagan. You wouldn't be so callous to deny him those rights."

"And I can't believe he told you we slept together. So, am I to suffer an examination? Would he have me embarrassed further? It's bad enough you know the possibility is there." Reagan felt her skin heat with a blush.

"I hold you in the highest regard. That will never change."

229

He wanted her to believe there was no need to feel shame in what had happened between her and Connor. She might not have realized they were married the first time they were together, but Connor wouldn't have taken advantage of her if they had not been married. Rafe understood her discomfort in feeling Connor had shared something personal that should have stayed that way. However, he was her doctor, and he felt it best there not be a repeat of what Morgan did in not telling Cullen she was carrying Nic's child while they spent weeks chasing rumors and lies all over Ireland looking for Nic.

"Connor didn't want to take a chance with you or his child. He didn't ask for an examination but told me he wants proof."

"And you waited until now to tell me this?" She had already had a cycle since they left London. "It will be another three weeks at this point."

"Then we wait."

He had just installed delay tactic number one.

# Chapter 39

Seabridge Castle
September 5, 1499

Reagan was having no difficulty filling her days. It always seemed no matter where she went the sick were there and needed her help.

Rafe had helped her to establish a makeshift hospital, and surgery was performed with great success on a gentleman with a hernia. The fact she and Rafe had brand-new precision surgical instruments accounted for a great part of the success. She had thanked Rafe for the instruments, but he denied having them made for her. He had said it was Connor who had the tools commissioned months before while they were still at Featherstone. Rafe had just provided the designs, and the silversmith had done the rest.

General ailments and complaints were dealt with, and Rafe was more than happy to take charge of any emergencies. Emergency medicine had never been her strong suit, and Rafe had taught her so much as they worked side by side.

The weeks had gone by quickly, and Rafe was assured without doubt—she was not carrying Connor's child. The sick and needy just kept coming, and it was not in her to turn them away.

If her days were full, her nights were excruciatingly empty, punctuated by her loneliness for Connor. She missed him terribly. So much so, she would swear he was near. Some of her dreams had been almost too vivid with the feel of his kiss on her skin after she awakened.

Her heart cried, and her disappointment grew with each day. As far as she knew, he had made no attempt to see her or write to her, but what had she really expected? She had been the one to walk away, and she was a fool to think he would come to her. But that was what she was waiting for him to do.

She was hoping he would stop her, for she knew once she left England, any hope was truly lost. However, with each passing day, her certainty he would not arrive only increased and the more she knew she had to leave. Fate would show her when the time was right. Soon, she would leave, but staying a few more days could not hurt.

And the sick just kept coming.

# Chapter 40

Connor met three times in secret with Ian and Rafe. Each time, Connor brought updates for the king and asked Rafe to deliver those in secret. Rafe told him there was no child for him to be concerned over, and Connor was disappointed. He knew, without a child, there was nothing to tie Reagan to him except a marriage she had seen fit to deny.

However, he was also relieved. At the rate the engagements were going, he very well might not live to see any child of his born, much less grown. They were bloody and fierce, but it was one small consolation and relief to know she was content to stay in England for now. He knew his chances to take care of O'Brian increased without her involvement, and the longer she stayed on English soil, the better. That being the case, Connor prayed his luck would hold, and fate would be kind. He was having his doubts. At one point, he had told Nic that if he thought Fate was a witch, then just wait until he met her sister Destiny. Well, Connor had met both Fate and Destiny, and he was finding that their other sister Luck was making Fate and Destiny look like angels.

# Chapter 41

As the weeks passed, if Reagan was with David, Rafe rarely let her out of his sight. Tonight was no exception. He was only a few feet away, reading a reference manual on poisonous plants.

Reagan found it odd as she began to notice Rafe's behavior pattern, and she had the distinct impression he was trying to protect her, but for the life of her, she did not know from what. Surely, it could not be from David. But what else could it be? David was attentive, and as always, she enjoyed his company.

Lately, however, she was becoming uncomfortable with the increased physical contact between them. Even though it seemed innocent enough—a brush of his arm here, a well-placed kiss on the cheek there—it made her feel uncomfortable. The contact was nothing anyone could say was inappropriate. Still, she knew she needed to say something sooner rather than later, and she pondered how to broach the subject during a boring game of draughts in the solar.

David looked up from the board. "Rafe, I have heard some disturbing news, and I'm wondering if it is true. Have you heard that Connor has been stripped of all his wealth and titles because the king suspects him of treason? Seems he has fled in disgrace with a sizable bounty on his head. Reagan, it's your move."

Reagan was stunned. She wanted to talk to David about the uncomfortable contact between them, but this news was so much more important.

Rafe faced them. He went deadly still, his expression guarded. He and Connor had agreed not to tell Hale the truth. That decision may have just proved to be a miscalculation on their part.

Reagan whipped around to look at Rafe. "Is this true? Tell me what you know."

"Reagan, I'm sure David has it wrong." He was not going to commit to anything.

"Rafe, I can tell by your face you know something." Reagan was sitting wide-eyed, looking toward Rafe for answers. She couldn't believe he would have held back this kind of news from her. Even though she and Connor were over and done romantically, Rafe knew she still cared about Connor's well-being.

Rafe looked at David, resisting the urge to kill the man. "Hale, that wasn't necessary. Your words don't serve any purpose except to raise her anxiety level," he said, calmly. Calm was not how he really felt.

David saw it differently. "Rafe, she has a right to know the kind of man he has become. She is pining over a traitor, for Christ's sake! He is a wanted man and would find his head on the block if anyone got their hands on him. It is exactly what he deserves if he has become an outlaw."

"David, how can you say such things about Connor?" She turned to Rafe once more. "Rafe? What is going on?" She looked back and forth between the two men. "Please, will one of you just tell me something? Please," she pleaded.

Sighing, Rafe scratched his head and debated exactly what to do. David had called this hand much sooner than he and Connor were prepared to deal with it, but deal he must. Tight-lipped and still angry, he figured he might as well tell her the truth, at least the truth as the world knew it.

"I wanted to spare you, but since good old Dave over there has seen fit to let the cows out of the barn, then I see no reason to shut the barn door now. Connor's a wanted man as far as England is concerned, Reagan. Henry has banished him, and Nic is holding his titles."

Rafe hated lying to her, but he saw no alternative, thanks to David's untimely maneuver. Reagan was visibly upset. Rafe expected nothing less.

"Connor, an outlaw? Nay, I don't believe that!"

She could not believe Connor had betrayed his king and his country. She could not reconcile the man she knew with the outlaw David was saying he had become. She would grant that he could be many things but treasonous just did not fit him—the man she loved. There had to be some mistake. Henry loved Connor and would never believe the lies, and neither did she.

Then it dawned on her. If Connor had a price on his head, then he was hiding, which was why he had not come to her. Surely there was something she could do to help.

"Rafe, we have to help him. Where is he? You know, don't you?"

Before Rafe could silence him, David supplied the answer.

"He has fled to Ireland."

"Shut up, Hale. Just shut your stupid mouth." Rafe was furious. He knew instinctively this was the catalyst to stir Reagan to action, and sure enough, she was going toward the door.

"Rafe, we must go. He may need us."

"Damn you, David. Now, you have gone and done it. Reagan, sit down. We are not going anywhere. I have my orders, and they include keeping you safely here at Seabridge. Leaving tonight is not in the cards."

"Not in the cards? *Not in the cards?*" she repeated, her voice raised by an octave. "Well, I'm dealing us a new hand," she shot back.

"We can't go off half-cocked." Rafe glared at David. He blamed the man fully for this unfolding disaster.

"Well, we certainly cannot sit by if he needs our help. We have to go."

237

Her insides were churning at the thought of Connor on the run. It did not matter if he had been stripped of his titles, it did not matter he was married, and it sure as hell didn't matter he was now considered an outlaw.

She knew him, heart and soul. What David had just told her was a lie, a falsehood.

*No way in hell can it be true*, she thought.

Connor needed their help, and she would go to him. She could help him clear his name. She and Rafe could go places he couldn't.

David was angry that Reagan was not reacting as he felt she should. She should have been shocked and scandalized. She could not possibly be thinking to help Connor, but that was exactly where she was heading. He was a criminal, and the second she aided him, she would be an accessory to his crimes. Henry would execute her just as easily as a man if she were caught helping him.

"I will not allow you to help him, Reagan. And, even if I find it as difficult to believe as you do, it does not matter what our personal feelings are in this situation. If Henry has declared Connor an enemy of the crown and an outlaw, then he deserves what he gets."

"David, you know Connor as well as we do. There has to be some mistake. We have to get word to Nic that we are willing to help. He can help keep our actions secret until we can get Connor cleared. I know he would. Rafe?"

Rafe had never seen her like this. Gone were her usual practical nature and ever-present calm. She was as white as a blanket of newly fallen snow and looked as if she was close to passing out because she was hyperventilating. Going to her, he led her to the chair and pushed her back down to the cushions.

"Here, sit down and put your head between your knees before you faint. Just breathe slowly, Reagan. Hale, for once, go make yourself useful and pour her a drink. Make it a strong one." Rafe went down on one knee. "Reagan, honey, listen to me. Connor is going to be fine. Besides, he wouldn't want you this upset, so just try to relax and we can work something out."

David handed him the requested drink, and he pressed it into her hand. "Here, drink this. It will settle your nerves. David, I want to talk to you. Outside, now."

Stepping into the hallway, Rafe immediately turned on David. "I don't know what you thought to accomplish by that behavior just now, but all you have done is made my job doubly hard. How long do you think we will be able to keep her here now? If you hadn't opened your mouth, we could have possibly kept her here through winter. After tonight, you can bet she will be gone with or without us at the first opportunity."

"She needs to let him go, Rafe, and as long as he is sterling in her eyes, that will never happen. She needs to know what her life will be like if she chooses to stay with him. It was for her own good."

"Oh, don't you try to play the saint here. You want her, and you thought to undermine Connor for your own gain. Well, I would be careful if I were in your shoes, David. Connor is already a wanted man, so why not add assault or murder to the trumped-up charges? If she ends up leaving because of this and she's hurt, you and I both know he'll kill you and not bat an eye. I'm not sure I wouldn't just stand by and let it happen."

# Chapter 42

Ireland
October 4, 1499

Connor had been in Ireland several months, and he hated the country. Until now his plan was seemingly fruitless, which only made him despise his situation more. He was no closer to flushing out O'Brian than the day he had first set foot there. He had spent the last weeks staging raid after raid in an effort to make his cover look authentic.

He was beginning to look the part of the renegade outlaw with each passing day. He had begun to think, look, and behave like an outlaw. It was becoming even more dangerous for him as his reputation was spreading, and as of a week ago, there were bounties on his head from both the Irish and the English.

*So much for straddling the fence*, he thought.

There were days he did not recognize himself because he had become so immersed in the role that only those rare contacts with Rafe and Ian kept him from truly going over the edge. The bits of news of home were his lifelines. However, thoughts of his love for Reagan were a luxury he did not allow himself and could not afford. He needed a hard edge, and that edge was dulled by the love of a good woman. His need for that sharp edge did not stop him from thinking about her in times just like this. He had received an urgent letter from Rafe. Ian had risked much to deliver it, and after opening that brief but urgent correspondence, he could understand why.

Connor was definitely unhappy.

Rafe had spelled out the events of the evening Hale had seen fit to share his downfall with Reagan. He would kill the man for this. It tore at him to know she thought of him as a traitor. Her opinion of him mattered, and until now he had not cared about what others thought of him. He was a good man and honorable, and his actions were his own. Only God had the right to judge him, but it did matter to him what she thought. It mattered a great deal.

Damn David for trying to undermine his attempts to keep her safe. Did the fool not realize she was a woman of action, and now that she knew he was in Ireland, she would be set on leaving?

She was intelligent and undoubtedly would soon figure out why he was here. It would be just like her to want to follow through with her plan to help flush out O'Brian, and thus free him to put aside this charade. She was having a hard time believing he had turned into a traitor, Rafe had said and had confirmed his fears that she was insistent on leaving.

Rafe had delayed her yet again, but the stall tactic would only last so long. They should be in Ireland by month's end. Connor knew he had to make sure she did not come for his sake. He had to keep her away from O'Brian. The things he had learned about the man only increased his fear for her welfare. O'Brian had crossed the line from outlaw to dangerous viper miles past, and the world would be a much better place without him in it.

Connor had redoubled his focus on erasing the threat to his woman. Once the threat of O'Brian was gone, then and only then, could he turn his attentions back to her. The challenge of winning back her trust, and thereby her heart, would just have to wait. Until O'Brian was eliminated, he could not let himself be distracted, and her presence would be distraction in its greatest form.

# Chapter 43

Seabridge Castle

Seated at her worktable, Reagan thought the evening was exceptionally chilly, but she could not tear herself away from her work long enough to stoke the fire. She was updating her reference books and properly storing her herbs.

She was hurrying to finish.

Knowing Rafe was due back at any moment from looking in on his patients, she was not alarmed when she didn't hear the door open, but felt the draft on her feet.

"You are back earlier than I expected," she said, never looking up.

One hand clamped over her mouth before she had a chance to scream as the other arm snaked around her waist, just under her breast, pulling her hard against a rock-solid chest.

"Easy, princess, it's me," Connor whispered into her ear. "I am sorry if I frightened you. I am going to uncover your mouth now."

She nodded her head as adrenaline slammed through her veins.

Connor released his hold on her, and quickly she turned, slapping him twice on the arm.

"You scared the life out of me!"

"Then start locking your damn door!" he snapped back.

She paused and then it registered—Connor was here!

"Oh, Connor!" she cried, throwing her arms around his neck, forgetting she had sworn to harden her heart to him. But seeing him had softened her resolve until it slipped completely away. He looked leaner, deadlier, and very much like the renegade he was, but he was still Connor underneath it all.

He folded her into his embrace, securing her head with his hand as he fisted his fingers into her hair. She felt like she was home again.

Now, her fear was for an entirely different reason. He was a wanted man and not just by her. This made her desperately afraid for him.

Fearful of discovery, she whispered frantically, "And just what exactly do you think you're doing here?"

Connor saw emotions run rampant across her face. He was afraid she was going to ask him to leave.

"Do not turn me out, Reagan, please." He hugged her closer.

He needed to see her and to hold her. Not realizing until just this very moment how close to the edge he had come, he needed her to pull him back away from the precipice on which he was teetering and save him from falling into this deadly abyss.

"It's not safe. What if they catch you?" she said, looking back at the unlocked door.

Now, understanding her fears, he covered her mouth with his, silencing any further cries of protest. His kiss was demanding and sensually invasive as his tongue sought the warmth of her mouth.

Months of pent-up frustration, dread, and need for her fueled his passion. He was possessive as he reaffirmed his brand on her. He knew what he was doing and so did she, and her body answered his call. Moaning as his mouth sought hers again and again, her logical mind shut down as passion swept them away in a firestorm so intense it threatened to consume them both.

The clothing separating them seemed too much, and fingers untied laces and buttons went flying. She wrapped her bare legs around his hips, and he carried her into her room, his mouth never leaving hers. Within moments, they were in her bed. Skin touched skin, mouth on mouth, feeling, touching, needing to drink deeply from each other.

"Easy, love. We have all night," he said, slowing the fevered pitch of their pace. It was exquisite torture. He did not know when he would see her again after tonight, and he was damn well going to enjoy the time he did have.

Rolling off of her, he brought her to his side. Propping up on his elbow, he looked deeply into her eyes as he leisurely trailed his fingertips from her gently rounded hip to the flesh of her breast.

Instinctively, her body arched, granting him access. Snaking his arm around her waist, he pulled her closer and found the sensitive place at the base of her throat. He felt her pulse beating wildly as he sucked the throbbing vein, nipping the tender skin. He had her under siege and was fully breaking down any barriers she might think to erect.

Her passions were alive, and he knew she would welcome him in her bed and into her body. He gloried in the responsiveness of her body to his, knowing fully she could not resist him any more than he could her.

He might dominate her, but she drove him just as wild. Their love was explosive and volatile and was never in question when they were together like this. It was the aftermath Connor knew he had to control, but that was hours away. He had her tonight, and she was going to be his in every sense of the word. He wasn't leaving until he had fully branded her as his for all time.

Gentling his touch, he began to rediscover her, and he found himself falling in love with her all over again. Leaving no part of her untouched with his exploration, he was staking his claim to every inch of flesh he touched.

"You are mine," he reaffirmed as something shifted inside him, and the possessive male surfaced from deep within him.

It was primal, feral, and dangerous. She was his and his alone, and no one was going to hurt her. He would die first before ever letting that happen.

Rolling her on her back, he pulled her arms above her head, trapping her there. She felt helpless as he dominated her sexually, yet she felt safe knowing he would never hurt her, no matter how aroused he became.

He was strong, yet his touch was amazingly tender. His strong hands squeezed her just before the point of pain, but never did he bruise her fair and delicate skin, biting her but never crossing the line. Running his tongue along the line of her inner arms, he nipped and teased her skin, bringing every nerve ending alive as he continued the sensual assault on her body.

He was memorizing her, how she tasted, how she felt. He wanted to take this night back with him. It would keep him sane, and it would carry him through the coming months as fate and the sea separated them.

Letting her hands go, he ran his fingertips down the sensitive skin of her inner arms. Framing her face, he kissed her forehead as he had each time he had come to see her as a phantom of the night.

Then realization began to dawn for her as he moved his lips to her cheeks, brushing kisses over smooth creamy skin, edging his way to her mouth.

"You've come to me before tonight, haven't you?" She knew. She had felt his presence, and instinctively her body had recognized her lover even in sleep.

"Aye, Reagan, I had to see you. I need you." She was all that had kept him sane.

"I can't deny you, and I won't deny myself." She desperately needed to feel her body joined with his. Her spirit needed to feel him deep inside her. He felt her shift on the bed to better accommodate him.

"Connor, please."

"Please what, princess?" He was torturing her, making her beg as he gently ran his hand up her leg, touching her in all the places he knew set her on fire. She was on fire for him and him alone.

"Please…"

"Tell me."

"You're going to make me beg? Please…" Her plea was not unmatched by his own desires.

Up on his knees, he pulled her feet to his chest, grabbed her ankles, and spread her wide, angling her hips to grant him access to the deepest part of her core. When he plunged in, she arched her back giving him her all.

"Is this what you want, Reagan? Tell me." He continued to play with her.

"Aye, oh aye. Oh, God, I have missed this," she said, sighing as he began to fill her inch by glorious inch.

Her comment instantly incensed him. *She does not miss me*, he thought. She missed him having sex with her. Was he a dammed stud to service her? He prayed to God that was not all he was to her.

"Look at me, Reagan!" he spat out angrily. "I want you to look at me. If all you want from me is sex, then that's exactly what you will get."

~*****~

Lying in each other's arms, Reagan was stroking his chest, enjoying the feel of his strong arms enfolding her. She could feel his withdrawal. He was distant.

"Talk to me, Connor. What is bothering you?"

"Nay, not now, Reagan," he said, pulling her a little tighter to him, kissing her temple.

Little did she know he was racking himself with guilt over the way he had just treated her. He felt that it had been only a couple of rungs up the ladder from rape, and he loathed himself for it. He had been rough with her when he

247

should have been tender. It had been months since he had been with her, and he had treated common whores better than he had her.

Reagan, on the other hand, felt calm, complete, and safe. This was right and good, and where she longed to stay. She was never going to be able to deny him as long as he held this spell over her. She should loathe her weakness for him. She didn't. She was an independent woman, who was making her own way, and she was uneasy with his dominance over her. She had no thought past the moment and had no regrets.

She was his woman. Her fate was now forever sealed. There was no denying it to herself or to Connor. It was time she told him: she was here to help him. It was her right, if not as his wife, then as his lover and friend.

Pushing up, she cupped the side of his cheek, pulling his face toward hers. She tenderly kissed the side of his mouth, gently lingering there, savoring the feel of his lips on hers. With reluctance, she pulled away, laying her head once more on his strong shoulder.

"I love you, English, and I have missed you terribly," she admitted softly. "I kept telling myself I would get over you and could walk away. I'm not even going to fool myself any longer. I can't. I can't walk away. Yet I can't live like this either. I won't love you in the shadows."

Kissing her temple and letting out a moan of regret, Connor was moved. Her soft and heartfelt confession was driven deeply like a dagger into his soul, wrenching his gut. He felt even greater remorse for his conduct now that he knew he had misjudged her.

"I am truly remorseful I was so rough with you, princess. Please, please forgive me," he begged, his kiss lingering on her temple.

"Connor, there's nothing to forgive. I grant you, it was a little over the edge, even for us, but I wanted it like that just as much as you did."

Connor did not miss the blush gracing her beautiful face.

"Still, I should never have manhandled you. It was inexcusable. I could have hurt you, and I swear I will never do that again. I love you, Reagan. Never doubt that. I want you always to be with me, and I promise I am going to make this right, but not right now. Soon, I promise we will love, fight, and laugh in the full light of day and never have to be in the shadows. I will always be there to protect you and love you. But for now, I need you to stay here. Please, love. I need to know you are safe. I need time to get O'Brian. I need time, and I need you here where I do not have to worry so much about your safety."

"Connor, please let me help you. I can help you. You know I can. Even Henry agrees." She pushed off his chest, brushing the hair away from her face and tucking it behind her ear. She sat cross-legged beside him on the bed.

He ran a fingertip softly down her collarbone to the swell of her breast. "I know you are brave, but let us not act foolishly here. I will not have you place yourself into harm's way, not for my sake and certainly not for Henry's. Let me deal with this my way, princess. If O'Brian got his hands on you, I would be at a distinct disadvantage, and I do not need any distractions. And you, my beautiful lady, are definitely a distraction." He pulled her to him and kissed her soundly.

"But, Connor," she said, hardly having enough breath left after that kiss to say his name.

"No buts, my love. I will beg you on bended knee if I have to, but stay here where Rafe and David can keep you safe for me. The thought of O'Brian getting his hands on you makes me physically ill. You have no idea of the deeds he has done. The man has gone way over the edge, and if you distract me, you could get me killed. This is a deadly and dangerous game I am playing, Reagan."

Even if it was all true, he knew he was playing dirty with her by playing on her guilt and her responsibility for his safety. He desperately wanted to take her into his confidence, longing to tell her of his true mission and share that he was on the king's business. He wanted her to know he was acting with Henry's full knowledge and blessing to be doing what he was doing. He wanted and needed to soothe her fears and to confirm her suspicion that he was not a traitor and the rumors about his activities were nothing more than a cover for him to be in Ireland.

He needed to infiltrate O'Brian's camp, and the only way to do that was by gaining his confidence as a fellow outlaw. It was just one more deception on his part that wedged between them.

However, his fear was that if he did bring her into his confidence, she would be all the more determined to assist him in his duty to the king. He was teetering in his decision as he watched her eyes turn smoky.

"They say you're an outlaw. What you do to me could be considered a crime. Did you know that, English?" she asked and ran her hands over his strongly muscled chest. Then she kissed his right nipple, running her tongue around it, all the while watching him watching her.

He grabbed her by the hair and pulled her mouth to his. *Maybe I'll tell her later*, he told himself. *Maybe.*

Releasing her mouth, he grabbed her by the hips. Lifting her effortlessly onto his chest, he let her straddle him. Reaching up, he framed her face and brought her down to kiss her on the forehead and then held her tightly against him.

"Oh God, Reagan, if you only knew. Sometimes, I am hanging on by a thread. I have you, and that's the only thing keeping me from becoming the man they say I am, the man I am swiftly becoming. Now, let me kiss that lovely mouth of yours."

She pushed off his chest. "Connor, do Rafe and David know you're here?"

He stopped in midway to her mouth, sighed, and dropped his head back on the pillow.

"Rafe, yes. I trust him with you and to have my back. Hale? No. I do not trust him, Reagan. He wants something from me that I will never let him have, not under any circumstances. He thinks himself in love with you, not that I blame him, but you are mine, and only mine. I will kill him, Rea, if he touches you. I will kill any man who lays hands on you."

She believed him. He was on the edge of becoming the very thing he was tracking down to kill. He looked dark, deadly, and predatory. He was gripping her upper arms, unaware his anger had fueled his already massive strength. He released her instantly when he felt her wince.

"Oh, God, I am so sorry. I did not mean... Oh, princess, I would never hurt you." He could see the faint bruising beginning to rise on the creamy flesh of her arms. "I would never hurt you," he vowed, then kissed her skin that would be bruised.

"I know, I know. Love me, again, English. Love me again," she whispered against his mouth as she slid down onto him.

"Who am I to say nay to my lady's pleasure?"

# Chapter 44

Reagan awoke slowly, feeling wonderfully sated. The night with Connor had been so sensual, full of passion and with desires fulfilled. She leisurely stretched out like a cat, and would have purred had she been physically capable. Then realization slammed into her dreamy thoughts, and she opened her eyes.

She was alone in the bed where they had loved.

The bed was cold with only a note where he had slept beside her. Numb, she reached over to his pillow where the note lightly rested in the indention left from where he had laid his head.

> *Princess,*
> *The ring belonged to my mother.*
> *Stay here, please.*
> *Rafe will watch over you.*
> *Know I love you,*
> *Connor*

She looked down at the middle finger of her left hand and saw the purple sparkle of the amethyst surrounded by perfectly matched pearls and set in a braided silver and gold band. The ring was beautiful. Yet he was gone again. Just like that, he had left her without so much as a goodbye kiss. She guessed he didn't want to risk her tears and pleas to stay. Maybe, he'd been right to let her sleep.

She had no right to ask him to risk his life to stay with her in daylight. Their love was only for the shadows, like a dirty little secret, and something of which to be ashamed. She was beginning to feel like she was his very own personal plaything, and she was damned to fall in his arms every time he touched her.

Throwing the covers back, she was hit by the cool morning air of autumn.

He had asked her to stay safely tucked away here in England and had just assumed his word would be followed without question. Well, she had made a promise to the king, and it was her time to fulfill it. Connor had come to her as she had hoped, and he had made promises of a future together. She hadn't asked promises of him, but he had given those promises freely and in earnest.

He wanted her. And she wanted him, but he had no right to make those promises, and she had no rights to him or his future. His future was not hers to take when it already belonged to another.

His passions may belong to her, but not his life, not his children, or the title of duchess. Those belonged to the faceless Countess of Rockport.

Reagan knew her time with Connor was over. Sooner or later, the countess would come to claim her rightful place at his side as his wife and mother of his children. Once Connor cleared his name, the countess would come. If she knew she had a man like Connor at the end of the rainbow, Reagan would claim that particularly tasty pot of gold. The countess had to know the prize she had in Connor. His reputation preceded him. Even if it didn't, one look at him would be enough.

Reagan's mind churned with questions. She knew she would get no answers today, but one thing she did know was Connor was using valuable time chasing after an elusive outlaw on her behalf when he should have been here making a life for himself and his bride.

She couldn't share his future with him, but she would help him gain his true identity and life back. She was going to Ireland. She was ready and nothing was going to stop her. Her uncle Fergus was already standing ready, and had Connor come to her tonight instead of last, he would have found her bed empty.

She had sent word to her uncle the morning after David had told her about Connor and asked him to come get her with all haste. She had told him she was in desperate need of returning to Ireland to help save a friend, which was true. She had to help save Connor.

His summons arrived late yesterday to let her know he was there and was ready to take her back across the sea at such point that she could slip away. She would be gone before Rafe could stop her, and he would try if he knew. So she was making sure he didn't know until it was just too late.

After last night she was sure Connor was behind every delay they had faced, for the sole purpose of keeping her here. That meant Rafe was in on it, too.

"Damn it, Rafe," she cursed him under her breath. "You too?"

Even though she appreciated the gesture, she was taking back control of her life.

# Chapter 45

Later that evening as they were all dining, Reagan announced that she would be leaving early the next morning to look in on a woman she was treating. Her plans were to spend the next night away in case the woman had further complications. Marcus had joined her from Featherstone over a month past, so she quickly asked for him to go with her, thinking to cut short any objections Rafe might have.

Rafe hesitantly allowed it only after she solemnly promised to go nowhere else and to take Marcus with her.

She knew Marcus would not allow her to go to her uncle, and as bad as she hated the necessity, she slipped everyone sleeping potions at various points in the evening. It was her only hope of slipping away unnoticed.

Reagan waited enough time for Rafe to fall asleep and sought Marcus out. "Marcus? If you have time, I need you to come help me for just a little while."

"Of course. It's too early to retire."

Leading the way back to the infirmary, she calmly chatted about the day and all the things she needed to do to wrap it up. She knew she was unusually talkative, but her nerves were strung as tight as a drum, and she knew it was just a byproduct. Marcus, however, did not seem to notice anything out of the ordinary. *Thank goodness,* she thought.

"I could use a drink. Please, share one with me, Marcus," she said and handed her helper a drink. He took it gladly, not one bit suspicious that she was drugging him. "I find once the day winds down if I come back here it helps to ease my mind about loose ends. If I go back to the castle, I just wonder if I did or did not do something."

"I understand, m'lady. I often do the same thing myself," he said, then stifled a yawn.

"Well, what I need tonight is to be sure I have all the stores in the proper place down in the storage cellar. Would you be so kind as to assist me? There should be two crates of emergency rations and water back there in the corner. It would be enough for a person to live comfortably for a week or more if necessary. There are also reading materials, blankets, pillows, and candles."

"Sounds like you are preparing for a small siege," he said as they made their way into the cellar.

"Well, not exactly. It's just one can never tell when they might accidentally lock themselves in here."

Marcus had sat down on a stack of crates. "I understa—" he said, slumping over before finishing his thought.

"Oh, Marcus, I'm sorry to have to do this to you. Please, forgive me," she offered, pleading with the unconscious young man and feeling guilty for her actions, no matter how mandatory.

Pulling him gently over to the corner, she placed a pillow under his head. There were enough blankets to keep him comfortable for the night. None would be hurt from this, except for their male pride.

Locking Marcus inside, she made her way back to Rafe's room and found him passed out in his chair. She left him a note saying she and Marcus had gotten an early start, and she would see him day after tomorrow. That should buy her enough time to get to the ship and be gone before the alarm sounded.

Waiting for the right moment when she knew the guard was changing, Reagan used the momentary distraction to make her way to the secret gate she and Rafe had entered all those months ago. She had been preparing for this night for a while and had only two days ago oiled the rusty hinges of the hidden gate. Now, it opened soundlessly as she slipped out into the night with only a single backward glance and feelings of extreme guilt at her own treachery.

"Uncle? Are you there?" She knew she had not been followed, so she felt it safe to call out to her uncle Fergus.

"Aye, lass, I'm here. Hurry up there, now. We'll miss the tide if ye tarry overlong," the burly Irishman answered, then took her pack from her.

Getting into the rowboat, they pushed off, and with the four men Fergus had brought along, they made good time getting back out to his ship anchored inside a cove about half a mile from the estate.

The seas were choppy, the going treacherous for the tiny vessel, but the seasoned sailors managed to get the boat and six passengers back safely aboard.

With years of practice behind the crew, the ship was ready to sail and underway in no time. The wind caught the massive sails with a mighty pop, making her jump.

Watching, she stood at the back rail, knowing she was closing one more chapter of her life. She was now waiting for the next to reveal itself.

Under the full harvest moon, Seabridge was soon nothing more than a dark rock on the distant horizon. Then, with one more dip of the bow into the mighty ocean, Seabridge was gone from sight.

End Part 1
Unfinished Business
##########

**Preview**
Shades of Grace
Book 3 (Parts 1 and 2)
The McKinnon Legends
A Time Travel Series

Hitting the power button on his computer, Cullen waited for the system to boot up; his mind drifted to Morgan as it often did. It had been six years since he had seen her. Yet the sadness of losing her was still fresh. After all, she was the one woman he wanted and could never have. Not because she was his brother's wife, even though she had been, but because he had left her in 1494.

She had been dead now for over four and a half centuries.

Lately, he wondered if he would ever be able to move past her memory and the love he felt for her. He was not sure he even wanted to.

He typed in the instant messaging address. The address had been provided in the cover letter from the genealogical service he had hired to find the lineage of his nephew Decklyn. Looking at the screen, he hesitated over the enter button, having the strangest feeling his life was about to make another shift. Shrugging off the feeling, he typed and hit send.

Grace saw the signals on her system. Her client had just logged on. The strangest feeling washed over her and sent a shiver up her spine. She had felt this feeling of anticipation from the moment she had received his request for her services.

"All right. Here we go," Grace said, taking a deep breath while cracking her knuckles. She began to type:

*Good evening, Mr. McKinnon. I'm sure you are a busy man, so let's just get straight to the point. Do you have questions about the contract I sent to you?*

"Ahh, Scout, this one is all business I see. That's good. I like that trait in a man," Cullen said while scratching his golden retriever behind the ear. "And you're right. I'm a very busy man," he talked to himself as he typed his reply.

*No questions. All looks to be in order. I have signed and sent the contract to the Parcel Store in Dallas as instructed. It went against my grain to pay the deposit in cash. I will expect a receipt.*

Grace grimaced, "Ouch, that stings. Just call me a thief, why don't you?"

She looked down at the newspaper article she had come across in the society pages. It contained a photo of Cullen leaning against a red sports car he had won in a charity raffle. The goatee he sported was several shades darker than his sandy blond hair. His six-foot-six frame was encased in a pair of black jeans. The black cowboy hat, black sunglasses, and white tank top made him look like temptation in the flesh.

"Easy on the eyes, too, but I'd bet hell on a girl's heart," she said, turning her attention back to the screen.

She had seen this reaction to the cash deposit before in other clients and knew she needed to tread lightly. Three thousand dollars was a lot of money, and it would have been fine to send it back, but she wanted this job for other reasons that she could not quite pinpoint.

*You will find your trust in us will not be ill-placed, Mr. McKinnon. I received the deposit today, and a receipt for $3,000 from Stallings and York should be in your e-mail box. We use them as a cash clearinghouse for recording* *purposes. Most of our clients approve of an e-receipt. If this is not satisfactory, we can make other arrangements.*

"Hmm, all right. Let's just check that out, shall we, boy?" Cullen said to Scout as he opened his e-mail box. The receipt was there. Stallings and York was reputable and not known for dealing with fly-by-night businesses. This made Cullen feel a little less leery about doing business with Amazing Grace Genealogy Services.

*E-receipt is fine for now.*

Grace had a funny feeling about this case. It was intriguing, and she had been holding her breath on his reply. It was not a problem to refund his money, but she really wanted to find this man's ancestor. She had already been doing some research and found the McKinnon family line was strong. The stories she had dug up were the stuff of legends.

*I have found this to be a very interesting case, Mr. McKinnon. I appreciate the opportunity to research your family. Normally, I stay in the background but have decided to take this case on personally.*

"Hey, Scout, we're getting personal service here. Either he's finding our quest for Decklyn interesting or he really needs a life. What do you think, boy?" Cullen asked while patting Scout on the head.

*Very good, Mr.???*

Cullen waited for the reply as the cursor continued to blink. He was hoping to get a better feel for exactly whom he was dealing with. The information he had currently at hand was very sketchy. He hoped, at the very least, for a name. Working for the US Marshal Service had made him just a little suspicious of anything out of the ordinary, and so far, this business deal was more than just a little unorthodox. He would not have used this company except for the fact one of the ladies in the San Antonio office where he worked had been using Amazing Grace for three years with great success. Never once had the money just disappeared even though they always required cash payments.

Unknown to Cullen, Grace was not in Dallas, but sitting just across town watching her own cursor blink and debating using her real name. It had been so long since she had used her name that lately she was beginning to feel like she no longer existed, not necessarily a bad thing given her circumstances.

However, anonymity was the only thing that had kept her alive the past three years, and now was not the time to get sloppy. She would continue to use the cover she had put into place three years ago. It left everyone with the impression she was a man serving her purposes well.

*You still there?* Cullen typed.

*Yeah, I'm still here... Just call me Martin.*

*Nice to meet you, Martin.*

*Now we have the introductions out of the way, let's get on with it, shall we?* ☺

"How sweet," Cullen said with a small laugh. "Look, Scout, a smiley face. I thought only chicks did that. Guess, I was wrong."

*This is your ball game, Martin, so lead the way.*

Grace felt excited about this case.

*It should be a very interesting ride, Mr. McKinnon...
So buckle up. Often, I discover things while on the journey
into a person's past that at times surprises and shocks
them.*

Cullen snorted at the monitor. "You are going to shock
me after what I've been through? I seriously doubt it. But
all right, I'm game," Cullen said pursing his lips to repress
a smile and continued to talk to the monitor. "Hey, Martin,
bet you never came across time travel while digging
through all those moldy records of yours. Or maybe he
has," Cullen said while looking at Lady, his other golden
retriever. "I know I would never fess up, girl. Toss me into
the loony bin for sure." Lady barked once in response.
Cullen typed.

*Believe me, Martin, from where I sit, there isn't a lot
that could faze me at this point, but I'm willing to let you
wow me.*

Cullen took a long draw from his beer and waited on
the reply. He was feeling edgy and restless and really could
not pinpoint why.

*My job is not to impress my clients, Mr. McKinnon, but
to deliver. Sixty days for delivery or you get your money
back less actual expenses, of course.*

"Of course, tic, tic, tic," Cullen said as the grandfather
clock in his study struck the quarter hour.

*Then let the quest begin.*

*Then let the quest begin.*

Both logged off as the thunder began to roll. It was going to be a very dark night indeed.

#######

# Other Series By Ranay James

Series by Ranay James available in e-book format at all major retailers through the following website:

## WWW.booklaunch.io/ranayjames

*The McKinnon Legends* A Time Travel Series

*The McKinnon American Men* A Romantic Suspense Series

*Vampires Of Nirvana* is a ten part series that with each book will leave you begging for more. If you love the McKinnons, then you are going to love the royal family of Nirvana.

## Print Editions Available:

Vampires of Nirvana:Book 1- Never Kiss Me Goodbye
Vampires of Nirvana: Book 2 - Point of No Return
The McKinnon The Beginning: Book One Part 1
The McKinnon The Beginning: Book One Part 2
Unfinished Business: Book Two Part 1
Unfinished Business: Book Two Part 2

## Large Print Editions:
The McKinnon The Beginning: Book One Part 1
Vampires of Nirvana Book 1 - Never Kiss Me Goodbye

## Print Coming 2016

**Vampires of Nirvana:**
Vampires of Nirvana Book 2 - Point of No Return (Large Print Edition)

**The McKinnon Legends-A Time Travel Series:**
Shades of Grace: Book Three Part 1
Shades of Grace Book Three Part 2
Of Purest Blood: Book Four Part 1
Of Purest Blood: Book Four Part 2
The Missing One: Book Five

## Audiobook Editions:

**Audiobook Bundles available at Audiobooks.com and Audible.com**
The McKinnon The Beginning: Book 1 Parts 1 and 2
Unfinished Business: Book Two Parts 1 and 2
The McKinnon Legends Books One and Two: Part 1 and 2

**Individual Audiobooks:**
The McKinnon The Beginning Book One Part 1
The McKinnon The Beginning Book One Part 2
Unfinished Business Book Two Part 1
Unfinished Business Book Two Part 2

# Contact the Author

Please visit Ranay James on Facebook:
http://www.facebook.com/pages/Ranay-James/441095109282762

Join The James Gang Newsletter
http://ow.ly/tTIqH

Twitter
https://twitter.com/ranayjames

Email Me
info@ranayjames.com

Google+
http://goo.gl/KcsKNx

# About The Author

Ranay James moved to a small farm in East Texas along with her husband and two dogs after walking away from the fast-paced corporate life in 2012.

Ranay graduated from college majoring in accounting and finance with a minor in business management and law. This is very concrete subject matter as a major. Becoming a romance writer seems a most unlikely path for a woman who spent most of her career managing people and operational practices within the corporate environment.

It all began in 2004 on New Year's Day. Having made a list of things that she wanted to accomplish for the year, she added some items to that list that would push her skill set, and take her out of her comfort zone. Learning to speak Spanish and write a novel were the two items that she felt would stretch her abilities the most, having no prior training in either. Later that day, Ranay sat down at her computer. Looking at that blank Word document, she simply wrote the first thing that came into her mind.

"What were you thinking?" she wrote, having remembered the line from a dream she had in a hotel room in Houston, Texas in 2002. Several chapters in, Ranay found her voice as the story began to form. It poured out from a place that she never knew existed. Ranay began to write that day in 2004 and simply never stopped.

With twelve published works to her name, and nine more completed awaiting publication, Ranay has found a new passion—the love of storytelling and sharing her characters with the world.

www.ingramcontent.com/pod-product-compliance
Lightning Source LLC
Chambersburg PA
CBHW031301170626
46807CB00001B/254